PISTILS

BOOK 2

KATE MCNEIL
BRITT GOODWIN

TWINTYPE BOOKS LLC

*To our families, our friends, and our fans, thank you.
We dedicate this to you.*

VIVIAN

"You have a new case, dearie."

The corners of my mouth curled up reluctantly. No matter how many times I'd heard those words come from Gran's sweet little mouth, it always cracked me up. She may have looked every inch the elderly southern lady of leisure, but Gran hadn't retired, not by a long shot.

"What is it?"

"Possible cheating husband, wife is the client," she rattled off, barely looking at the sheet covered with hand-scrawled notes before her. "Lots of money involved, plus a prenup. Big names. Absolute discretion, of course."

"Of course," I echoed her. "Anyone we'd recognize?"

Gran fluttered a blue-veined hand in the air, sharp eyes peering over her spectacles. "Jackson and Lisa Piedmont."

"The Piedmonts?" I repeated, lifting my eyebrows. Everyone in Savannah knew who the Piedmont family was; they were the next generation of old money, charity balls, and society pages. Oh, and the fact that Randall Piedmont, Jackson's father, was a United States senator for the state of Georgia. *Damn.* Parker and I had worked for plenty of high-profile and wealthy clients since starting our two-woman private investigation business, but a senator's daughter-in-law was something else entirely. "Lisa wants us? Don't they have enough money to, oh I don't know, hire some ex-military contracting firm or something?"

"Lisa wants you," Gran stated firmly. "She's convinced Jackson is having an affair, but wants proof before she takes any action. And apparently one of her friends told her about you." She shoved a handful of papers at me. "Here are the details, her contact information, and what I was able to pull off the internet about both of them. I told her you two would meet with her this afternoon, and she's expecting you at three-thirty sharp."

Having been summarily dismissed from Gran's office, I took a deep breath and headed up to the front of our florist shop. Pistils. There were very few people who knew about or appreciated the humor in our choice of name for our cover business, and the customers who only came in for flowers and balloons certainly had no idea. The shop itself was the epitome of cheer and color, and enormous front windows let in plenty of daylight, showing off the rainbow of floral displays to their best advantage. The hardwood floor gleamed, and the soft off-white walls were the perfect backdrop. It had been a flower shop before we'd bought it, but we had transformed it into something else entirely, and it was one of our two greatest accomplishments.

Parker was right where I expected her to be, humming happily to a tune on the iPod we had plugged in behind the counter, the pink tips on her blonde hair bobbing as she bounced to the music. In front of her was a gorgeous vase filled with roses. Arranging flowers was a knack she'd apparently inherited from Gran, a very fortunate thing since plants and I didn't exactly get along. Parker usually relegated me to writing out the note cards and making deliveries, and for good reason.

I sighed softly at seeing my best friend in such an obviously good mood. I was always reluctant to tell Parker that we had another cheating case, even though they made up seventy-five percent of our business. Along with crooked employees and attempted hitman-hirings, they were our bread-and-butter. But I always did dread it, since I knew that every single cheating case reminded her of the past, even if just a little.

Parker was the ultimate romantic at heart, and in the very best way possible. The sweet, outgoing kind girl she'd been in high school had grown into an empathetic woman who still believed in happily-ever-afters, the romance of grand gestures, and that it was perfectly acceptable and expected to hold out for commitment until your soul mate came along. That someone had almost knocked all of that out of her was still enough to make me see red.

It was, in the long run, the reason we'd gone into private investigation.

Three years ago, Parker's gut had told her that Shane, an asshole I'd never liked, might be stepping out on her. I'd just returned from Langley and, not being in the most charitable state of mind toward anyone, let alone him, suggested we nose around. Just to put her mind at ease, of course. After all, they'd been together for five and a half years.

We'd found out two things. One, Shane was a two-timing snake who was so used to cheating on my best friend, he'd gotten slightly careless in covering it up. Two, we discovered that we were remarkably good at finding things. Like, scary good.

I guess it shouldn't have been surprising, with my years of working as a CIA case officer and Parker's unerringly good gut instincts. Since moving to Savannah over two years ago, ostensibly to buy out a struggling flower shop, we'd slowly built up quite a respectable business. We were discreet, efficient and, above all, good. P&V, Inc. wasn't in the Yellow Pages, however. Oh no. You had to know someone who knew us. Socialites, locally based celebrities, athletes, and members of ladies' clubs… they would discreetly slip their friends a Pistils business card while clueing them in on the magic words: "Ask for Parker or Vivian to call you back." Our clientele was overwhelmingly female, but we'd had our fair share of men seeking help too. Our results built respect.

Now, since Pistils was operating in the black, and P&V, Inc. was able to charge more-than-decent non-refundable rates, all three of us were doing just fine. Gran had her own cottage close to all the social activities she enjoyed, while Parker and I shared a comfortable apartment east of downtown. We were in a good place all the way around, there was no denying it.

"Hey you." I slid onto one of the stools we kept behind the counter. "New case. Gran already set us up an appointment and everything."

"She's the best thing we brought with us from Charleston." Parker grinned and reached back to turn down the volume on the music. "Details?"

I made my voice as neutral as possible; this was just business, after all. "Possible cheating, big money, big names. Wife is the client."

I saw a shadow pass across my best friend's eyes, but it was gone in a moment as she slipped into PI mode. "Who is it?"

"Jackson and Lisa Piedmont."

Parker whistled softly. "That'll be a touchy one. Lisa thinks he's fooling around? Couldn't she just have the Secret Service tail him or something?"

"Senators and their families don't normally have Secret

Service privileges," I said absently, glancing over Gran's notes again. "We have an appointment with her at three-thirty, at their place. According to Gran, we're supposedly there to discuss floral arrangements for his parents' fiftieth wedding anniversary. Which *is* legitimate, we picked up that gig too. It's at the Grantham House in a few weeks."

"That's cutting it pretty tight, we'll need to sit down and plan as soon as we have details. Three-thirty, huh? I can have these done by then if you'll help me clean up." Her blue eyes slipped back over to the roses. "Let's get to it."

PRECISELY TWO MINUTES BEFORE OUR SCHEDULED appointment, Parker and I pulled up to the Piedmonts' home in a Pistils delivery van. It wasn't quite a historic district mansion like Jackson's parents', but he and Lisa lived in an expensive gated community just west of downtown, where sprawling green lawns and carefully manicured flower beds were de rigueur.

"I still don't get it," Parker had muttered, as we pulled away from the guard shack after being checked against the approved visitors list. "I mean, we're good, but why us?"

I'd shrugged. I was still surprised myself that a member of what was arguably Savannah's most wealthy and prominent old families had singled us out for a case of this magnitude. A Piedmont divorce would be huge news, and there was always a chance we would be called to testify in court. This was the kind of thing you'd want the biggest, best, and most expensive private investigators on. But hell, you never knew, and I wasn't one to wonder... too much. "Maybe she's more comfortable with two young women. Maybe whoever referred us really sang our praises. Who knows?"

"Good point." Parker swung the van into the long driveway of the gorgeous home. "Shall we?"

Both of us were wearing all white, except for the Pistils logo on the front of our perfectly starched, expensive polos. We looked fresh as daisies, pretty as buttercups. I left my .45 under the seat. I never went anywhere without it; it was a risky business we were in after all. It didn't exactly match my work uniform, though.

Lisa Piedmont herself answered the glorious doorbell. We both recognized her immediately from grainy society news photos as well as the pictures Gran had printed off the internet. Of course those hadn't included black splotches of mascara under her eyes and the tears that had streaked her foundation. Even through that, you could tell that she was an attractive woman, in her own way. Long blonde hair with expensive highlights, a slim toned body, and a smooth tan. If she'd had any work done, the plastic surgeon had done an excellent job making it look natural. She gave us a wobbly smile, and we followed her inside.

"I just don't know what to do!" she burst out after we were settled in the front room, or the parlor, or whatever it was the rich called it. "I know he's having an affair, I just know it! But I don't know what to do!" Then she completely broke down into sobs.

Parker and I exchanged a glance. We'd dealt with plenty of hysterical wives in our short career, and established that she was much more empathetic and able to comfort women than I'd ever be able to. I could play the role if I needed to, but were it up to me, I'd take the route of slapping her and telling her to pull herself together. I had very little patience for histrionics.

My best friend moved over to the couch next to the wailing Lisa and put her arm around her shoulders. "Mrs. Piedmont, listen, I know you're upset. But I need you to take a few deep breaths and then answer a question or two, okay? Can you do that for us?"

Lisa's blotchy face quivered. "I'll try."

"Okay, that's all we ask. First off, is there anyone in the house besides us right now? Anyone you don't want over-hearing this conversation?"

She shook her head, blonde hair now sticking to her wet cheeks. "I sent the housekeeper out on a bunch of errands."

Of course you did, I thought, before mentally chastising myself. Making assumptions or judgments about the client was not appropriate or professional.

"All right then," Parker soothed, and once again I found myself in awe of her. She really was the nicest person I knew. "Why don't you start from the beginning, and we'll work from there?"

Lisa drew in a deep shaking breath. "It's just, I don't know, a gut feeling? He's so distant, I don't think he really even likes me anymore. And we haven't, um, we haven't had sex in forever, so..."

Parker patted her shoulder. "We understand. Keep going."

"Just...all those things you read about in magazines, how to know if your man is cheating on you? Jack fits all of those!" Lisa looked ready to break down again. "I really thought we were happy, but I guess he was happier with someone else."

"What kinds of things?" Parker encouraged.

"He works all the time. I know he's busy, he's an architect with his own firm. But now he spends all his time there, sometimes he even sleeps at the office! When he is here, he's distant. We don't talk. He doesn't seem to care about me or my interests at all anymore. We don't do anything together. And as I mentioned, our love life is completely non-existent now."

"About how long ago did this start?"

"Oh, a few months ago, maybe?"

My turn. "It sounds like a solid place for us to start from, Mrs. Piedmont, we just need you to tell us exactly what you want." Parker was definitely the better people-person, but I tended to be the hard-ass when it came to having them spell out what they were hiring us for and then committing to it. We weren't there as therapists, after all.

Lisa blotted her red face with a tissue. "I just need to know. I want proof. I can't live *not* knowing one way or the other." Her face crumpled again. "I just need to see it with my own eyes."

Parker and I exchanged glances once more; Lisa was still being too vague. We needed to know exactly what was expected of us, and how far she wanted us to go. "Mrs. Piedmont, we can follow your husband, check up on his activities, and document them accordingly. But we always ask up front, just so we know what we're getting into… if we find admissible evidence that he's cheating, will you want us to testify in court, should you choose to divorce him?"

Her pink lips quivered. "I hate to think of it, but if he's cheating on me, I just can't stay with him. I can't. I love him, but I couldn't get past something like that. So yes, anything you find, if it comes to that, I'll need that to back me up."

I lifted my eyebrows at Parker, and she shrugged. There was no reason for us not to take the case. And once again, I got to be the hard-ass, a role I'd played so many times before. "We'll take your case, Mrs. Piedmont. Let's go through our contract and take it from there."

PARKER AND I WERE BOTH SUNK IN OUR OWN THOUGHTS AS WE left the Piedmont residence. Lisa had signed the contract and immediately written a personal check without a single reservation about our terms or rates. We had our mark. And yet...

"What did you think?" I finally broke the silence.

Parker pursed her lips. "I want to believe her. I can't help but think she's just going for guilt, though... like if she caught him cheating, she might be furious or devastated, but she might not necessarily divorce him. Hell, it would be diamonds and St. Lucia every year if she rode him hard enough about it."

This was why Parker and I worked so perfectly together, our gut instincts were usually right on. "I wonder which one she loves more, Jackson or his money? Or both equally?"

"I could see it either way," Parker said thoughtfully. "I mean, she was obviously upset. Who wouldn't be? But having him by the balls and getting all the goodies and being able to privately keep him in check...I just can't shake that it might be the angle she's playing."

"Except she flat out said she would want a divorce." I rubbed my forehead. "Unless she plans on having a sudden change of heart, even if we get pictures of him with his pants around his ankles."

"Good point."

"We've got our work cut out for us, then. I'll get to work on tracking Jackson, you want to find out what he's been up to over the past few months?"

Parker flashed me her trademark cheerful smile. "I'm on it."

PARKER

T hree Years Ago...

VIVIAN AND I SAT IN FRONT OF MY LAPTOP, STARING AT THE screen thoughtfully as I tapped my nails against the plastic. I knew without a shadow of a doubt that I wanted to do this, to mortify and shame him like he'd done me. The crux of the matter was that I'd never done anything so underhanded.

"That miserable excuse of a human being deserves this, Parker. Don't forget that for a single second."

I let Vivian's words, spoken with so much conviction, seep into my pores and give me the bravery I needed to go through with this. She was going through her own personal turmoil considering her career had just ended with the CIA. She wouldn't give me any other details, but I knew it couldn't have been a good situation. I was just selfishly happy that she was home, because I needed my best friend more than anything. Taking a deep breath, I replayed the last two weeks of my life that had brought me to this very moment.

It all began with a coincidental insult slung at me by a disgruntled woman who was taking my self-defense class. "Just because she can kick ass, she thinks she's a pink Powerpuff Girl now. Well, at least the annoying high-pitched voice is accurate."

Familiar words. Eerily familiar.

Words spoken by my boyfriend Shane the night I came home with hot pink tips on my long, blonde hair. I loved them. They made me feel empowered and real. He mocked me. "Just because you know how to beat some ass, you think you're a pink Powerpuff girl now? What was her name anyway, Blossom?"

Their words ate at me, my mind constantly trying to conjure up a way to convince me this was nothing more than a coincidence. But honestly, a Powerpuff Girl? Blossom didn't even have pink hair...

By the time my obsession with finding the truth about the man I had adored for five and a half years became more than I could handle, Vivian was already on her way back to Charleston. She bounded through my front door, throwing her things in the nearest chair and hugging me tight. "You want answers, P? Well... let's find them."

For as much as my heart was breaking, it exhilarated me to no end being able to investigate like that with my best friend. I'd learned so much that night, and it was fascinating to see the skill and precision Vivian had acquired in her years with the CIA. From hacking Shane's computer and email passwords with ease, to knowing just what to search for in order to discover what he was hiding, I felt like her student, and I was more than eager to learn.

I knew I'd had it in me all along but researching to find the truth, to right a wrong, to truly stand up for myself... as painful as the whole situation was, it made me realize my true calling.

Investigating brought me back to life, even when the only life I'd ever known was falling apart around me.

When one Facebook comment led to a Tumblr account, and a link led to a Twitter account, and that Twitter account led to another link to a WordPress blog, we'd finally found the source of *my coincidental situation. All modesty aside, it had nothing to do with luck. Viv and I were unstoppable when we were on a mission.*

"STUPID SHIT MY GIRLFRIEND DOES"

That was the name of his blog. Tears rolled down my cheeks and Vivian slammed her fist against the desktop so hard our wine glasses went flying as we read excerpts of my life with Shane. We cowered at pictures of me sleeping with drool on my chin, my face in a green cleansing mask. And it just kept on going. Me with a giant zit, rat's nest hair, and then I stumbled upon the many heartless lists he made for fun.

*"**Girls I'd rather nail than Parker**"*

*"**Shane's awesome list of things he'd rather do than listen to his girlfriend speak**"*

*"**Shane's top ten lies to feed your woman to get what you want**"*

Then of course there was the section where his pig-headed, disgusting followers could submit questions.

The majority of them asked things that made me sick, and Shane's equally disturbing replies had me questioning how I had existed with this man for almost six years when he was quite obviously a stranger to me.

Some of his followers were demanding to know how he could do this to a seemingly sweet and very attractive girl. "Because I can," was his answer.

Why don't you just break up with her? *"When I find a woman hot enough to ditch her for, I will. There's no point leaving when I have a built-in housecleaner, clothes washer, dish doer, and a piece of ass when I need it."*

As my best friend held me tight, I'd found the proof I needed. A short blurb that provided the evidence to us, clear as day.

"STUPID SHIT MY GIRLFRIEND DOES, EXAMPLE **103955**... I'VE **Completely Lost Count**"

So she comes home last night, totally forgetting to pick up the dry cleaning I'd reminded her about that morning, and her hair is pink. Fucking pink. Who does she think she is, a punk? A rebellious teenager? She's almost thirty and looks absolutely ridiculous. I mean, just because she teaches people how to kick ass and she's tiny as hell, she thinks she's a Powerpuff Girl now? That pink one... Blossom. Her high-pitched voice annoyed me to no end which, ironically enough, goes the same for Parker. At least that part is accurate.

So maybe she is that pathetic little Powerpuff Girl, thinking she's hot shit because she has pink hair. But is it a cry for help? A mid-life crisis? Like the forty-year-old dude with a red Corvette, is she just trying to be young again? Whatever... I need to get laid, and the next person riding me will not have pink goddamn hair, of that I can assure you. Peace out!

THERE IT WAS, IN BLACK AND WHITE. VIVIAN WANTED TO KILL HIM, and considering her background and current temperament, I wasn't quite sure she only meant figuratively. But as the tears ran silently down my cheeks, an eerie calm settled over me. One word, heavy and determined, sat on the tip of my tongue. "Revenge. I want revenge, Vivian."

So, as I sat there with my finger hovering over the mouse, seconds away from posting every one of his dirty little secrets, I let my hesitation fly out the window. I was a damn good person, and this was something I owed to myself, that he owed me after years of slander and cheating and lying straight to my face.

I stared at the computer, ready to share one final post on his blog.

We'd changed all his passwords to something so complex, there was no way in hell he'd ever be getting into it again.

I hit Enter.
Nothing had ever felt so sweet.

"Stupid Shit I Do, By Parker"

1. The laundry of a pathetic cheating bastard who never appreciated how good he had it. Click here and here to see every skid-marked pair of underwear he owns.

2. Fake hundreds upon hundreds of orgasms, letting Shane Montgomery think his manhood was something to write home about. Click here, here, and here to see numerous examples of said manhood, erect and embarrassingly small. Honestly, a baby carrot would have provided me more pleasure.

3. Find incriminating photos on my boyfriend's computer, his hand buried beneath Lilith Stanton's immaculate dress, tongue shoved in her mouth at last year's Christmas party. Who knew he was so talented at taking selfies? Click here to see Shane and the boss's wife rounding second base and on the fast track to third. Oops, I think I emailed these to Mr. James Stanton, president and CEO of the company Shane works for. His wife does look lovely in chiffon.

4. Link every contact in his address book to this little blog, chronicling my idiocy and showcasing just how much of an awesome, big macho man he is. Click here to see Shane cramming his large frame into one of my baby doll lingerie dresses and heels, posing otherwise naked for the camera.

5. The dumbest thing I have ever done is give over five years of my life to a man that has appreciated none of it. I was an idiot for putting his needs before mine, for letting him crush and stifle every beautiful, unique thing about me. And finally, I'm beyond stupid for letting him think I'm anything other than a strong, amazing woman. If you're curi-

ous, here is an accurate picture of me, ink peeking out beneath my sleeveless shirt, pink tips bright and fierce as my hair lays long and wavy down my back. If you're wondering why my smile is so wide and the fire in my eyes so bright, it's probably because revenge is just that sweet.

WOULD A REAL MAN DO THIS TO A WOMAN? SHANE Montgomery is a pathetic excuse for a human being, but after all this, I can't really be mad at him.

His ignorance has set me free…

…and I'm more than ready to fly.

Sincerely,

The girl who does stupid shit

PRESENT DAY…

I AWOKE WITH A START, MY HEAD JERKING UP FROM THE COUCH cushion with a random piece of paper stuck to my face. This certainly wasn't the first time I'd fallen asleep while investigating our potential bad guy, but waking up to memories of a past that seemed like forever ago wasn't exactly my idea of a good time.

I couldn't understand why thoughts of Shane pummeled me every time we began a new cheating investigation. Cases like these made up the majority of our business, but it never failed to bring forth memories I simply wanted to forget.

It wasn't like I missed Shane, not by a long shot. Truth be told, I was in denial for the last few years of my relationship with him, ignoring the reality of what we were because I just didn't want to acknowledge it. Our first two years together were, for lack of a better and less whimsical word, magic. We were head over heels in love, he treated me like a princess, and even when tragedy struck, I was blessed with his love and constant support to get me through the loss of my mother to ovarian cancer. With Vivian out on assignment and no chance of coming home, it was nearly unbearable to experience that kind of devastation without her. If I hadn't had Shane to get me through that time, I don't know how I would have survived.

I could count on one hand how many times my best friend and boyfriend had met one another, and still they couldn't see eye to eye. Thankfully, they at least pretended to tolerate each other for my sake, because at the time I'd thought that I needed them both equally. I should have listened to Vivian's reservations about Shane, but he practically worshipped the ground I walked on and made me feel so safe. Even after the magic had somehow become lost in our relationship after a handful of years, we still worked well as a team. Maybe I was in a relationship that I knew was ho-hum to both of us, but I was under the pretense that growing up meant sacrificing that puppy dog love.

It turned out that ho-hum to Shane meant three years of cheating and then later publicly humiliating the woman who had stood by his side through thick and thin. So even though he no longer meant anything to me, it was obvious why cheating cases still left a bit of an ache in my bruised and battered heart.

After Señor Douchebag was out of my life and revenge was gratifyingly handed to him, I vowed to always listen to myself, my uncanny intuition, and most of all my raw gut instinct that I had suppressed during my time with Shane.

The real problem was that I was guarding my heart so closely now, afraid I'd be blindsided again by someone I let myself trust. I hadn't had a real date in years, even though I'd occasionally found someone to help scratch the itch, but the fear of getting hurt again was the only thing keeping me from opening up completely to another person.

This case certainly wasn't helping matters.

Lisa Piedmont put on quite a show during our first meeting at her lavish home two days ago. While I'd *wanted* to believe her theatrical performance, my instincts were telling me that something wasn't right. Whether she had an ulterior motive or there was a piece of the story that she'd left out, I knew there was something that had yet to be discovered. Unfortunately for me she was not the mark, and instead I was being paid to learn more about Jackson Piedmont.

It was easy enough to find information on his professional life, like his company profile and a few gala pictures featuring him smiling widely and shaking hands with other obviously well-to-do gentlemen. But after researching him relentlessly for the past forty-eight hours, I was hitting every dead end imaginable regarding his personal life.

Dude didn't even have Facebook for crying out loud.

I sighed, running a hand through my hair. As good as I knew I was at getting to the bottom of things, I needed my other half in order to really function properly, especially with my mind conjuring up unpleasant memories from the past. When Vivian and I got together, we were absolutely unstoppable.

I heard the key in the door and I closed my laptop. "Speak of the devil."

Vivian glanced around and gave me a judgmental look. "You were speaking to yourself about me? Creepy, P."

I laughed, shaking my head. "Never mind. This computer is frying my brain. Chinese?"

"We should probably make it takeout," she sighed, nodding toward the door. "And you better un-fry your brain, because we have a lot of work to do."

Yep, as usual, it was going to be a late night.

I'D DECIDED TO TAG ALONG ON OUR TAKEOUT RUN SO VIV AND I could go over the timeline for the case. In the past we had come up with some majorly good ideas while driving and talking, but at that moment I was too hungry to even think. I was waiting in the parking lot for Viv to come out with our food so we could book it back home and get to work, when my ringing phone broke the silence of the car. I smiled as I checked the caller ID and saw Gran's face on the screen.

"Hello, is this Parker Chase, Private Investigator Extraordinaire? I have a hot case for you, dear. I can't seem to find my glasses."

I couldn't help but laugh. We wouldn't have been able to leave Charleston if Gran hadn't agreed to come along. Even though I'd been more than ready to leave town and start fresh, my Gran was the light of my life, and we were the last two family members remaining in our hometown. It didn't take much convincing. After telling her our grand plan and insisting we'd need her help for our cover business, she was downright excited to come along. My Gran had run her own florist shop, Black-Eyed Susans, for over forty years, so she was more than happy to help us with the ins and outs of the business.

She was even more excited to help us "nail the cheating bastards of the world to the wall."

"Gran, did you really call me to help you find your glasses?" I chuckled.

"No, honey. I did lose them, but I'm sure they're around here somewhere. I was really wondering if my girls have found anything on the Piedmont case yet."

"Not a thing," I sighed despondently. "Looks like it's going to be a late one. We're actually just grabbing some takeout now, and then it'll be time to put our game faces on."

"I'll open up the shop tomorrow. I figured you'd both be busy with such a high-profile case hanging in the balance."

"I don't know what we'd do without you, Gran."

She laughed softly. "Oh honey, doing this with you girls has been the highlight of my very long life. I should be the one thanking you. Now don't stay up all night trying to crack this case. Everything will be brought to light when the time is right."

"Did you write that little poem yourself?" I teased.

Gran scoffed. "Of course I did. One of these days Hallmark is going to pick up the card slogans I've been emailing them and your inheritance will be even sweeter!"

Just then I saw Vivian throw open the front door of Mr. Chang's, peer into the windows next door, and then dart in my direction. Something was definitely up. "They're fools if they don't take note of your creative genius, Gran, there's no doubt about that. We're about ready to head home, talk to you tomorrow?"

We exchanged I-love-yous, and I disconnected the call just as Vivian threw open the driver's side door, tossing a brown bag of food in my lap and giving me a maniacal look. A jolt of exhilaration shot through me. "Well, what is it?" I asked impatiently.

She grinned widely and gestured toward the adjoining restaurant. "I think we just hit the lottery."

3

VIVIAN

"I can't believe this case could possibly be this easy," Parker chuckled. "Hand me one of those spring rolls, would you?"

"I can't believe my luck." I passed her the little bag with our cooling dinner in it. I'd spent exactly thirty-eight seconds earlier that afternoon planting a tracking device onto Jackson Piedmont's car, so as I waited in line for our takeout, I recognized it easily in the parking lot outside. A quick peek in the windows of the restaurant next door when I came out confirmed that it was Jackson, clearly visible sitting in the front, with a redheaded woman who was most certainly not Lisa Piedmont.

"It has to be said, if she's the mistress, she must be either an amazing conversationalist or a wildcat in bed."

I snickered. Jackson's dinner date was by no means ugly, but she was quite a bit older than him, and had that rode-hard-and-put-away-wet look to her. "If they head to a hotel after this, we can officially classify this as our easiest case to date. Did you find anything interesting on our unhappy couple?"

Parker shook her head and bit into her spring roll. "Not a thing. They're all smiles and cheery in the society pictures I found, and there's not a whisper of scandal in the gossip columns. She doesn't have a job, but everything else seems to indicate she's the picture-perfect stay-at-home wife and he's the successful architect."

"She said the problems started a few months ago, so either they're really good at hiding it, or her dates are off. Uh oh, here we go."

The waiter approached the table and handed Jackson a black folio. He glanced at it and then tucked in a few bills before standing and extending his hand to help the redhead up from her chair.

"No credit card trail," Parker murmured.

"Nope."

I snapped a few more pictures as the two emerged from the restaurant, exchanged goodbyes, and then went to separate cars.

"Bummer, a nice goodbye kiss would have made for a lovely exhibit at the divorce hearing." I lowered the camera and blew out my cheeks in frustration. "Who should we follow?"

Parker considered it. "You've already got him tagged, but we can just trace her by her license plate. Let's find out who she is before we waste too much time on her. She could be one of his coworkers for all we know."

"Good call." I snapped a couple of pictures of the redhead's car as she pulled away, making sure the license plate was clear and visible. Parker took the camera from me as I started my car, but Jackson didn't seem to be in a hurry to leave. He pulled out his cell phone, and I cursed. "I knew I should have bugged his car when I had the chance. But with all those security cameras in the parking lot, I didn't want to risk doing it there. Slapping the tracker on was bad enough."

That was one good thing I could say about my years with the CIA... Charlie Baumgartner was my favorite of a few shady contacts that could get me the more advanced technology that we needed to do our job. You definitely couldn't buy it from the vanilla side of the internet or at a strip mall store.

Some of the methods Parker and I employed weren't exactly on the legal side, which technically could have cost us our license or resulted in jail time if we were caught. I suffered absolutely no crisis of conscience over it, being that the government had paid me to bribe foreign assets into committing treason for seven years. I told Parker from the beginning that if there was anything she was uncomfortable doing, she could refuse with no hard feelings, but it never seemed to bother her either. Sometimes using shady methods gave us a lead we could follow up on legally and testify to in court. So listening in on Jackson Piedmont's private phone calls wouldn't have bothered me a bit, I was just annoyed we couldn't do it at the moment.

Jackson appeared to be agitated as his phone conversation progressed. "I wonder if he's talking to Lisa?" Parker mused.

"Could be." I couldn't help but chuckle as Jackson abruptly ended the call and threw his phone onto the passenger seat, his lips clearly forming an obscenity. "Well, if it was her, he may not be going home right away."

He did drive straight home, though, with us trailing him at a safe distance. He pulled up to his gated community, and we kept going. "Well, let's go get some work done, shall we?"

"Rhiannon Simons, 1265 Lyndhurst Lane," I read out

loud to Parker. Getting the redhead's information from her license plate had been child's play.

"On it," my best friend replied from her own computer, and for the next hour we were absorbed in tracking down every snippet of information about the mysterious Ms. Simons. This was when Parker and I did our best work, bouncing ideas and suggestions off each other.

"So she's a divorced insurance fraud investigator with a clean record," I said finally, after we agreed to call it a night and plopped down on the couch. "But Jackson's an architect. Why the hell would she be investigating an architectural firm? Or why would they need her?"

Parker shrugged. "Maybe she really is the girlfriend."

"Maybe, but I'm just not getting that feeling. There didn't seem to be much chemistry there. Familiarity, definitely. But no goodnight kiss or anything?"

"They were in public," Parker pointed out. "Maybe he's just smarter and more discreet than ninety-nine percent of those cheating assholes. We sure haven't found any hard evidence yet… but then again, we're just getting started."

As we'd arranged with Lisa, later that week I pecked Jackson's cell number into our shop phone. He answered almost immediately. "This is Jack Piedmont."

I made a mental note that he must go by Jack all the time, Lisa had called him that too. "Hi Mr. Piedmont! This is Vivian calling from Pistils Flower Shop, to schedule an appointment for your floral consultation!"

"Umm…" He definitely sounded confused. "I'm sorry, but I think you have the wrong number. I don't need a… a what? Floral consultation?"

"Ohhh, I'm so sorry!" I used my most contrite voice. "I

assumed your wife, Lisa, told you. She wanted you to be in charge of the floral arrangements for your parents' fiftieth wedding anniversary party!"

If Jack had sounded confused before, he was downright baffled now. "Lisa wants me to be in charge of *that?*"

"Yes, she said that she's swamped with planning the final details, and completely forgot about the flowers. Luckily we were able to squeeze you in, and she said you'd know better what your parents' tastes are anyway."

"And she assumed I'd have time to do something like that?" Irritation was creeping into his voice now. "I'm sorry Miss, umm..."

"Just Vivian."

"Vivian. I don't mean to be rude to you, I really don't, but I'm a very busy man. I honestly don't have time to sit around figuring out which flowers my parents would like. I don't have a clue what they'd like, actually."

"If you like, I could just bring you some pictures of arrangements for similar parties we've done," I said encouragingly. I had to meet this guy in person, if only to get a read on him and his feelings about his wife. Getting close enough to wirelessly transmit bugging software onto his cell phone would be a bonus too.

He sighed. "I can't believe she did this... actually, yes I do. All right, Vivian, can you maybe e-mail them to me?"

"We prefer to meet with you in person," I said woefully. "And you'll need to sign the invoice. But I promise not to take up any more than half an hour of your time, how's that?"

"I give up," he muttered. "I have a hole in my schedule this afternoon at 3:15, and that's the best I can do."

"That's perfect for me!" I enthused. "Thirty minutes, or maybe even less."

Jack did not share my enthusiasm. "All right, let me give you my work address."

I already had all his information, of course, but I pretended to scratch it down anyway. "Sounds good, I'll see you then!"

"Goodbye, Vivian."

"That's the perkiest I've heard you sound in a while," Parker giggled. "You sounded like me."

"I take my lessons from the best. Sweet, I'll definitely bug his office then."

Parker handed me a glossy binder. "Here's some anniversary stuff. He'll probably just pick the first ones, but steer him toward the third theme. I'd like to do that one again."

"Will do. So, what are you up to this afternoon?" Gran ran the shop for us when we were thick in the middle of a case.

"I think I'll just get some things done around here, actually. We had a few orders come in through the website a little bit ago. I'm also going to set up a meeting with Lisa for tomorrow to show her those pictures, to see if she recognizes this Rhiannon chick. If she does and can confirm she's no one to worry about, we can cross her off our to-do list."

"Okay, I'll just see you back at home then."

"Sounds good!"

JACK'S ARCHITECTURAL FIRM WAS ENSCONCED IN A GORGEOUS old Savannah house, but the interior was strictly modern. I gave my name to the receptionist, and she immediately escorted me into his office. He must have really wanted to get it over with.

I knew Jack Piedmont was a good-looking guy, but up close, he was even more so. His green eyes went straight to mine and held my gaze as he shook my hand. Just the tiniest touch of gray threaded through the dark brown hair at his temples, and his handshake was warm and firm.

Quit checking out the mark, Vivian...

"Mr. Piedmont, thank you for seeing me, I'm so sorry that this was sprung on you like this."

"Please, call me Jack. And I should be apologizing to you." He gestured politely to a chair and waited for me to sit before he went back around his desk. "I'm sorry I was so rude to you earlier, that was inexcusable on my part. It's just that my wife tends to drop these things on me last-minute without considering that I might not be able to accommodate her."

"Well, I won't take up a second more of your time than necessary." I smiled and handed him the binder.

He looked at the Pistils logo on the front and laughed. "Oh, I get it now. On the phone earlier, I assumed you meant *Pistols*, and I've been wondering all afternoon why in the world a flower shop would be named after a gun."

I laughed too. Good thing he didn't know it was an intentional double entendre, a joke between Parker and me. We both had handguns with concealed carry permits, not to mention the sniper rifle and the semi-automatic 9mm carbine I had locked safely away in my closet at home. Parker's Kel-Tec had custom pink grips, something I still teased her about, while my .45 Bersa was strictly business-black. Some might have called us over-cautious or downright paranoid, we considered it being prepared and protected in our field.

"Well, some people still don't get it, you know, pistils, stamens, all that. I'm impressed that you do."

"I paid attention in science class." He flashed a grin at me before flipping open the binder. "Honestly Vivian... I'm a guy. I know nothing about floral arrangements, much less ones for parties. Can you help me out here? The party isn't going to be over-the-top since my mom has put the kibosh on it being a political back-slapping extravaganza." He paused and his cheeks flushed slightly. "I'm guessing you know who my dad is?"

"Of course, Jack. And we can make it as elegant or as simple as you think your parents would prefer." I guided him to the third theme, as Parker had requested. "This is one of my favorites. They'll look gorgeous in the Grantham House; we've worked there before and we're familiar with it."

He flipped through the photos, paying more attention than I'd expected him to. "You do nice work. These look better than the flowers at my wedding."

Thank God for Parker and Gran. "We don't do too many weddings, only if they're pretty small. There are only three of us running the business, so we can't take on too much at once."

"I know the feeling, we're a small business too. Me, my partner, and three associates." He kept paging through the binder.

Just then, the alarm I'd pre-set on my phone went off, making it sound as though I had an incoming call. "Oh, I'm so sorry! Let me just mute that."

"No problem," he murmured.

I jabbed the mute button on the phone in my purse, grabbed the tiny bug and then quickly stuck it to the underside of his desk. It would wirelessly record and transmit the sounds in his office to my computer until either Parker or I retrieved it, after the case was over.

I straightened back up just as Jack shut the binder. "I like the ones you suggested, let's go with those. I take it Lisa hasn't paid you either?"

"No, but if you'll sign the invoice, we'll bill you." I handed the paper over to him, and he signed it neatly at the bottom.

"If you knew my wife…" he said, half to himself.

"She seemed very stressed when we met with her on Monday," I said sympathetically.

His eyebrows went up. "You met with her, and she couldn't do this then?"

"She really wanted you to be part of the planning, I think."

"That's… odd." His brow furrowed. "She usually wants me to keep my nose out of any kind of party she's planning."

I shrugged, hoping he didn't suspect anything. "Maybe because it's your parents? This was your token job?"

That got another laugh out of him. "Well, Vivian from Pistils Flower Shop, do you have a card on you? I really like what I just saw, and you do much better work than the florist we currently use for our clients. You'll be getting some business from us."

"Oh, thank you, we appreciate it!" I handed him one of my business cards and he looked at it immediately.

"Vivian Carmichael."

"My best friend teases me that I have a soap opera name. It's a bit of a mouthful."

"It's a very nice name." He tucked the card in his pocket and stood. "I'll walk you out." He put a polite hand on my back, warm through my Pistils polo. Then he opened the door for me, every inch the gentleman.

Good-looking and good manners to boot. It really made me hope that this guy wasn't a cheating asshole.

4

PARKER

It took me all of two seconds to realize that Gran was up to no good as soon as I returned from my delivery. When I'd gotten a call earlier that morning from a man asking to have one of our most expensive arrangements delivered to his girlfriend's workplace on her birthday, my heart swelled. Maybe romance wasn't dead after all.

But then I walked into her office and discovered her in a hardcore make-out session with a man who most certainly wasn't her boyfriend.

Yep. Romance was as dead as a doornail.

"How did the delivery go?"

I sighed. "Don't ask, Gran. Trust me. Why do you look like the cat that ate the canary?"

"Oh no reason," she sang, putting the finishing touches on a tiger lily arrangement before adding it to the display in front of her. "There was just a charming young man who stopped in about a half hour ago. That boy was slicker than a can of grease, but sincere about it. He was very sweet."

I chuckled. "Are you looking for a boy-toy or something?"

She shook her head, smiling wryly. "No ma'am. Actually, he stopped in here asking for you."

"*Me?*" I squeaked, bewildered. Viv and I didn't really hit the Savannah club scene, and the only men I knew were the ones we shot with at the range. While quite a few of them were smoking hot, I sort of made it a point not to hook up with our shooting buddies.

"Oh yes, he seemed a little nervous, too. I assured him you'd be back in an hour or so." She looked at me pointedly over a newly started arrangement. "Maybe you should stick around, sweet pea."

My heart rate accelerated, and I wasn't even sure why. I mean, of course I hadn't dated in quite a while, but I didn't even know this man, or what he wanted. Why did I automatically think he was a possible love interest? Maybe I was being served a court order? Perhaps I'd won the Publisher's Clearinghouse Sweepstakes? Whatever the reason, I wouldn't be wasting another thought on it. We had a case to solve.

"No can do, Gran. I've got a meeting with Lisa Piedmont in thirty minutes. Yesterday Viv visited Jackson at his office to plant a bug and gather some intel, and today it's my turn to touch base with Lisa. We might have a solid lead and I don't want to waste any time."

"Fine," she huffed. "Have it your way. Just remember, all work and no play makes Parker a spinster with twenty cats."

I rolled my eyes, kissing her on the cheek. "Save that little line for your greeting cards."

I ARRIVED AT THE PIEDMONTS' FIVE MINUTES EARLY, AND before I could even ring the doorbell, Lisa had the door thrown open with a frantic look on her face.

"Well, what did you find?" she demanded hastily.

I smiled brightly, holding out a hand that she reluctantly took. "It's great to see you again, Mrs. Piedmont! Why don't we have a seat, I just have a few questions, there's no reason for alarm."

She took a calming breath and nodded, leading me through her pristine foyer and into an all-white sitting room to the left of a grand staircase. "I didn't mean to be so rude," she murmured sheepishly, gesturing for me to sit next to her on the sofa. "I've been such a wreck ever since I hired the two of you to check up on Jack. I'm terrified of what you'll find. I've convinced myself it'll be the absolute worst, and if it reflects badly on his parents…"

I patted her hand and set my black portfolio on the glass coffee table in front of us. "There's no reason to make premature assumptions at this point, Mrs. Piedmont. We just need to take this investigation one step at a time until Vivian and I get the answers you deserve. So, has anything changed in your situation since we last talked?"

She shook her head, sniffling as her eyes filled up with tears. "Not really. Jack's still sleeping in the guest room. Instead of working on our problems, he just wants to run away from them. He's as distant as he's ever been."

I nodded sympathetically, pulling out a manila folder from my file. "Mrs. Piedmont, two nights ago we managed to find your husband at a local seafood restaurant. He was with someone and I'd like to show you a picture to see if you recognize her, all right?"

This brought forth a brand-new round of wails, and I just barely held back my eye-roll. I had more compassion than the average person, but this was just getting exhausting. "Ready?"

I pulled out a crystal-clear picture of Rhiannon Simons.

Lisa brought a hand to her mouth, a muted shriek echoing throughout the room. "He's cheating on me... with *her*?"

"Now remember, Mrs. Piedmont, we have absolutely no proof that this woman has had any improper conduct with your husband. She could be a colleague or an acquaintance, and to be frank she doesn't fit the typical mistress profile. For right now I just need to know if she's someone you recognize."

"No," she sniffled, dabbing at her eyes delicately with a handkerchief. "I've never seen that woman in my life."

"Have you ever heard your husband speak of someone named Rhiannon Simons?"

She shook her head again. "No, the name doesn't sound familiar."

I nodded, tucking the pictures back inside my portfolio and turning to face our client. "Mrs. Piedmont, I'm going to ask that you don't jump to conclusions during this process. There could be a multitude of dead ends before we find anything on your husband... if we find anything. I need you to trust me, as well as Vivian. We are professionals. We know what we're doing, and we most certainly won't lead you astray."

She smiled apologetically. "Thank you so much for everything you and your partner have done. I know I'm not easy to deal with, especially when I'm so emotional. I just want answers. I need answers, Parker."

"We'll do the best we can, Mrs. Piedmont. I can promise you that."

Just then the doorbell sounded, and the housekeeper let in a group of very well-dressed thirty-something women. "Li-Li," one of them chimed, completely ignoring my presence as she lowered her sunglasses. "Are you ready for some retail therapy, darling?"

I took that as my cue, bidding Lisa a good day and exiting

toward our delivery van. I opened the back doors, making a show of securing some flowers I had in the back and purposely stalling as the ladies piled into a shiny black sedan and pulled from the driveway. Lisa had clearly recovered from her emotional woes, laughing with her girlfriends as if she didn't have a care in the world.

Huh.

I waved and smiled brightly as they pulled out of the driveway, closing the back doors of the van. I was about to climb inside and leave as well when I saw movement out of the corner of my eye. Instinctively I ducked to the side of the van and peeked out from around it just in time to see a familiar looking silver car speed off after Lisa Piedmont, bright red hair flying in the breeze.

Rhiannon Simons.

Rhiannon Simons was following right behind Lisa Piedmont. "Holy shit," I muttered, jumping into the van and immediately calling Vivian.

She forwent a hello, instead teasing me about the mystery man asking for me at the shop. Apparently news traveled fast. "So, my dear sweet friend, who is this charming young man that flirted with Gran while asking about you, hmm?"

"Viv! Not now! I'm at the Piedmonts', Lisa just left with her friends, and I saw Rhiannon Simons go speeding off behind her. I'm not sure what this means!"

Vivian took a deep breath. "Okay, I guess that would take precedence over your potential love interest. Did Lisa say she recognized Rhiannon in the pictures?"

"No! She said she's never seen her or heard her name. Do I follow them, Viv? I probably have time to catch up, but our Pistils van isn't exactly discreet. How do I explain myself if Lisa sees me? And even if I did follow, I'm not sure what it would accomplish, you know?"

Vivian was quiet for a moment, contemplating my next

step. "No," she said finally. "We can't risk our client seeing you tail her. All that will do is break our line of trust. Besides, we have Rhiannon's home address. We can follow her whenever we want. There's no point in taking that big of a chance on being exposed."

I nodded, sighing in relief. "You're right, definitely. So why the hell would Rhiannon be following Lisa? Maybe she is a jealous girlfriend after all?"

"Or maybe there's an element to this whole thing that we don't understand just yet..." Vivian trailed off. "Well, come home and we'll talk it out. But... hang on a minute, did you have to check in at the guard shack again?"

I switched over to my Bluetooth and pulled out of the Piedmonts' driveway. "Yep, same as last time. The guard verified that I was on the list and let me through." Suddenly, a light bulb went off in my head. "Oh my God, Vivian, so for Rhiannon to get through those gates..."

"Someone would have had to put her on the approved visitors list. Damn, P, forget following the socialites, I think we're stumbling onto much bigger and better things. How soon will you be home?"

I glanced down at the dashboard clock. "Forty minutes or so. Why, what have you got in mind?"

Vivian chuckled mischievously. "Well my friend, I think it's about time we get a copy of that approved visitors list and see just who's allowed through those gates. Got any ideas on how we can lure the guard out of his shack?"

I smiled, shaking my head. "Oh, I can definitely think of a few."

THE NEXT NIGHT VIVIAN AND I FOUND OURSELVES AROUND

the block from the Piedmonts' gated community, nailing down the final details of our plan.

"Okay," Viv began, zipping up her black leather jacket. "Obviously you'll be the one to play the helpless victim, since you're so blonde and cute."

I smacked her arm. "Shut it. So while I'm flirting and crying, you'll be hanging out in the bushes ready to maneuver your way into that shack?"

"Uh-huh. Hopefully, we'll be able to find out who exactly gave Rhiannon approval to enter through these gates. I feel like we're missing a big piece of the puzzle, and it's really starting to annoy me that we haven't figured it out yet."

"We'll get there, Viv. You know these things take time." We hopped out of the van and I knelt down by one of the back tires, removing the valve stem cap and pushing a flat-head screwdriver against the metal pin inside. "At least we know we won't get busted by the Piedmonts. The charity dinner they're attending won't be ending for at least another two hours."

"Thank God for that. You sure you don't just want me to slash it? It's going to take forever to let the air out." Vivian gestured toward the tire.

I rolled my eyes. "And ruin a perfectly good tire for the sake of you taking out your aggression? Please."

"Cheapskate."

"Sociopath."

We high-fived, both of us laughing as Vivian disappeared into the night. In the meantime, I waited impatiently for the air to be completely released from my tire. Once it was good and flat, I hopped into the van and thought of dead puppies and sick children until I was officially sobbing.

I pulled up a short distance away from the guard shack and put the van into park, wiping my eyes as I walked toward the same guard I'd seen yesterday afternoon. Didn't this guy get a day off?

"You again, hello there!" he smiled, leaning through the open window. His smile fell when he saw me upset and pouting. "What's the matter, honey?"

"I just don't know what to do! I have this delivery to make by eight o'clock and I'm already late, and my tire's flat and I don't know how to fix it!" I rambled as I cried, my hands covering my face as he stepped out of the shack.

"Come on now, sweetheart. I can help you with your tire. There's no point in such a pretty girl being upset by a little problem like that."

I smiled and let him lead the way to the van, thankful he was a kind grandfatherly type and not a sleazy pervert.

I sniffled and turned my head just in time to see Vivian heading toward the shack. She pulled on the door handle, but of course it was locked. I could almost hear the frustrated curse come out of her mouth as she looked around for a quick moment and then dove through the tiny window head first.

My best friend was one of a kind.

The next fifteen minutes consisted of the guard putting on the spare tire, tossing the perfectly good tire into the back of the van and double checking to make sure everything was secured tightly.

"There we go," he sighed. "Good as new. Make sure you don't drive too far on this temporary tire, honey. They only last for so long."

"Thank you so much, sir. You have really been a lifesaver. How can I repay you?"

He waved a hand. "No need, sweetheart. Call it my good deed for the day. I've seen you quite a bit this week, you gals must be doing a good amount of business in this neighborhood."

I nodded, smiling radiantly. "Yes, Lisa Piedmont is one of our best clients. Well, thanks again!"

He waved goodbye, and I climbed back in the van, waiting until he made it back into his shack and opened the gate for me. I completed my fake delivery and made a U-turn at the end of the cul-de-sac, then waved to my new senior citizen friend as I pulled out onto the main road. I met Vivian in the same spot we were earlier.

"Good thing you decided not to eat that second doughnut this morning, Viv. Your ass might not have fit through that little window," I laughed, smacking her butt as she jumped into the van.

Her smile was sickeningly sweet as she flipped me the bird. "You're one to talk, flirting with that little old grandpa."

"All in a day's work," I grinned. "So, what did you find out?"

Vivian pulled out her small high-tech camera, flipping through the crystal-clear photos of each visitor's page. "Well, Rhiannon was authorized by one of them. If someone is logged as visiting them, it's because either Jack or Lisa added them to the approved visitors list."

"Probably the husband, if Lisa didn't even know who she was."

"Unless she was lying," Vivian pointed out. "But what's really interesting is that this woman, Angel Wright, has been here three times already this week. Luckily for us, the previous weeks were in the log as well. I snapped photos of the last two months' worth of visitors."

I whistled softly. "Damn, you're good. So you think this Angel chick is a person of interest?"

Vivian shrugged. "She's worth looking into. What business does she have here three or more times a week?"

"Sounds like we need to see what Rhiannon and Angel are up to."

Viv nodded. "We sure do. Let's head home and get to work, hopefully Angel Wright will be easy enough to track down."

"Famous last words," I smirked.

5

VIVIAN

Some people may get their best thinking done in the shower, or during a long contemplative walk, or while driving cross-country. Luckily, both Parker and I were excellent at brainstorming while multi-tasking, which came in handy when we were in the thick of a case.

Parker sat with the printed and enlarged photos I'd taken of the Piedmonts' visitor list spread across her lap, cross-referencing every name that had been logged for entry. I was skimming through the recordings that the bug in Jack Piedmont's office had made and wirelessly transmitted to my computer. Thankfully, my software could scan all the conversations for me, flagging ones that included keywords. Words such as love, fuck, hotel, wife, and of course, Rhiannon Simons. Now, to be on the safe side, the list also included Angel Wright.

I felt a pang of sympathy as I listened to and then dismissed a conversation where Jack ended a phone conversation with his screaming wife by hanging up and then cursing loudly. Some people might have felt qualms about listening in on such private moments, but working for the

CIA was designed to wring those morals right out of you. It was a good thing I had Parker to keep me from resorting back to even more shady stuff.

It didn't stop me from feeling bad for Jack, though. My gut reaction after meeting him was that he was a decent guy who was married to a flaky and semi-hostile socialite. It didn't mean he wasn't cheating... that might be the reason *why* he could be cheating, actually... but I didn't dislike him as I had some of the past men we'd investigated.

Parker huffed and scratched a giant check mark against another name. "That's the last one. Every single person the Piedmonts approved was friend, family, or hired help. All except for Rhiannon and Angel Wright."

"How many times have they gone in over the past two months?"

"Rhiannon, just today. Angel though... sixteen times."

I hummed thoughtfully and deleted another one of Jackson's harmless conversations. "I wish we knew when they were added to the approved visitors list. I mean, Rhiannon could have been added a month ago but just visited for the first time today."

"I'd offer to sweet-talk Grandpa Guard Shack again, but he might start to wonder about the frequency of the flat-tire thing," Parker said seriously.

"Eh, if it came down to it, we could just ask Lisa to call down there and have him give us a copy." I came to the end of the recordings, having found nothing useful, and stood to stretch. "I just don't like the idea of giving her a heads-up on what we're looking at."

My best friend nodded. "You're getting the same vibe I am?"

"Yeah. Jack may be a cheating dog, but she's no wronged angel. Without ruling anything out completely, we can safely say that Jackson approved Rhiannon, right?"

"Definitely. He's meeting with her and Lisa says she doesn't know her."

"So why was Rhiannon tailing Lisa, then? Trying to size up her competition, maybe?"

"Maybe," Parker mused. "You don't think she'll go all psychotic-stalker on her, do you?"

I shrugged my shoulders. "Anything is possible, but Lisa isn't paying us to be her bodyguards."

"Do you think we should tell Lisa we saw Rhiannon outside the house?"

I considered that for a long moment, weighing any potential risk of blowing our cover against possible danger toward anyone involved in this case. "Not yet. Evidently Jack cleared her to get through the guard shack, for whatever reason. He can't have been too worried about her having proximity to his wife, even if it just means boning her in the house every once in a while."

"Rhiannon wasn't exactly stealthy about it either," Parker pointed out. "I'm surprised even Lisa and her dingbat friends didn't notice her on their tail."

"They don't strike me as the sharpest knives in the drawer. We should keep a close eye on Rhiannon then, huh?"

Parker stacked and then paper-clipped the guard shack lists together. "Definitely. Okay, next person of interest... the mysterious Angel Wright. Every single time she visited was during regular business hours, during the week, while Jackson was presumably safe at work. What the hell is up with that?"

"Good catch," I murmured. "What *is* the point of that? Is she in there trying on Lisa's clothes and perfume or something creepy like that? Was there any pattern to her visits?"

"Not really, aside from the weekday business hours thing. I sense a possible stakeout in our future." She grinned at me.

I grinned back. "Yeah, you're right, if Angel has already

shown up three times this week, we should be able to catch her no problem."

"Did you find any trace of her online?"

"Nothing, not a damn thing. Weird, but I'll dig a bit deeper tomorrow... look for name-change petitions and stuff. Okay, back to the Piedmonts, and then I'm ready for bed. Let's assume Jack is cheating. People have been cheating on their spouses since the beginning of humankind, so there's no shocker there. We can't automatically assume Rhiannon or Angel is the girlfriend, so we may not have found her yet. Maybe those two fit into this some other way. But what about Lisa? You said she flipped from devastated spouse to retail therapy butterfly in a split second. There's something more going on with her. What does she have to gain from Jack cheating on her?"

Parker held up her hand and began ticking off points on her fingers. "First off, money. Her family is very middle class, and she had a go-nowhere career when she met him. Now she's married to a senator's son. Their prenup clearly states if *he* cheats, she gets half his portion of the Piedmont fortune. If they get divorced for any other reason, she gets a fixed settlement that is peanuts in comparison. If she can prove he's cheating, she gets a bigger payout. If he is cheating, I can't really blame her for wanting to screw him for every penny she's due."

"I wouldn't blame her either. What else?"

"To save face," Parker counted off another finger. "You should have seen the bimbos she drove off with today. They may be her friends now, but I bet they'd disappear overnight if Jack and Lisa get divorced for anything other than scandalous reasons... scandalous in her favor. Coming out of it with half of Jackson's money and the tragic divorcée image would be much more to her advantage."

"What if she doesn't want a divorce?"

Parker held up a third finger. "Something to hold over him, then. If we find proof that Jackson cheated on her, she's got the ultimate power. She could stay Mrs. Lisa Piedmont, beating him over the head with the knowledge that she could take him to the cleaners and embarrass his family any time she wanted. Hell, when Jackson's parents die, he's the sole heir to the entire Piedmont fortune. Lisa doesn't strike me as the type to let a little cheating get in the way of so much money... but she would make sure she's got insurance against anything threatening it, hence her desperation to find proof. Jackson's a comfortable millionaire already, he'll be one *many* more times over when his parents die. Lisa knows that, and we can't forget it either."

A FEW HOURS LATER IT WAS THREE O'CLOCK IN THE MORNING and I was still wide awake. I'd forced myself to stop thinking about the case since Parker and I had dissected it to death, but now I found myself with a lot of nothing to think about.

I hated sleepless nights.

Rolling over in bed, I clamped a pillow over my head and tried to count sheep, which of course didn't work.

Half an hour later I was semi-resigned to getting up and watching some late-night infomercials to bore myself to sleep. I'd just thrown back the covers when the burner cell phone on the bedside table lit up and buzzed softly.

I went completely rigid before reaching over and snatching it up. There was only one person who had that number, which was why I never turned it off. I hit the answer button and then waited.

"*Privet moya dorogaya,*" he said simply.

I let out a long breath. David Coburn. The man who would always call and greet me in "our" language, as we'd laughingly called it. The only Scotsman I knew who spoke Russian as though he'd been born there. The last link to my prior career and life; a British Military Intelligence officer and also one of the most brilliant people I'd ever known. Handsome without being vain, carrying the confidence and calm that only a man with his life experience could possess. He was also the only man I could say in all honesty that I'd ever loved.

"David."

"It's good to hear your voice." His faint Scottish accent still colored his words, even after years of living in England.

"Right back at you. What are you up to at seven-thirty a.m., your time?"

He chuckled softly. "I just got home, actually. I'm knackered, but I can't sleep."

"So you had some desperate yearning to call me? I haven't heard from you for, let's see... one year, three months, and fifteen days. You're not just calling because you miss me. Spill it."

"Your name came up today," he said, after a short pause.

I sat up in bed. "Where? In *London?*"

"During a phone call to Langley. It was in passing, really. A casual 'Does anyone know what Carmichael is up to these days?' sort of thing."

"Who asked?"

"We did."

A chill went through me. "And the answer was?"

"'Not sure, we'll check.'"

"Lovely. Well, even though what I'm up to is nobody's business, it's not like I'm hiding. I have a perfectly legal cover business for another perfectly legal business. I don't owe anyone anything." Despite my casual words, I clenched the sheet tightly in my free hand.

"Don't give me that. You know if they've asked out loud, they'll have eyes on you there next."

"I don't care," I replied hotly. "What can they really do to me, David? They already ruined my life once, what are they going to do, go for round two?"

"You, more than anyone, know how possible that could be."

His quiet words, and the warning behind them, brought everything back. Sitting in a dim, richly decorated office, facing the people who represented the country I'd dedicated my career to. Risked my life for. Only to have them throw me under the bus to cover their own asses, a tactic I'd seen too many times before. It was a whole different experience, though, when it had happened to *me*. I'd been lucky that they'd stopped at just ruining my career.

"Are you not telling me something?"

"No, Viv, you know me better than that. I just... I couldn't hear it and not warn you. I have no idea why they're interested in you now. You're not up to anything new, are you?"

"No." A cheating spouse case paled in comparison to some of the things I'd taken on before.

"Keep your eyes open, then, for your sake and my sanity. I can't lose you again, you know that."

I swallowed against the lump that was quickly forming in my throat. David truly had been and still was one of one of my best friends... one of my *only* friends. One of exactly three people in the entire world that I trusted. "Thank you for the heads-up, David. I'll be careful."

"Are you going to tell Parker?"

"Tell Parker what? That my ex-bosses have potentially sent people to spy on me, or put the screws to me? I think I'll wait until I have something a little more substantial for her to worry herself sick about before I dump *that* on her."

"I wish you'd..."

"David, thank you for telling me. But it's not your job to worry about me anymore. I don't want you ending up where I was."

He sucked in his breath sharply. "You really think I've ever stopped worrying about you? *Ty nuzhna mnye.*"

I need you in my life. Hearing the words he'd said to me so many times, in friendship, in fondness, and then in love, almost did me in. The lump in my throat had nothing on the ache and regret that was pounding through me now. "It's not fair to you. Thanks again for the warning. *Ya tebla lyublyu.*"

I hung up before he could say anything else and dropped the phone beside me. I definitely wouldn't be getting any sleep that night.

6

PARKER

I was feeling out of sorts today, totally distracted from anything other than the arrangement in front of me and the circle of names I couldn't seem to get out of my head.

Jack and Lisa Piedmont.

Rhiannon Simons.

Angel Wright.

And then of course there was Viv.

All she had told me was that she'd received a call from David a few nights ago. She didn't elaborate, but the far-off look in her eyes as she loaded the van with deliveries told me her mind was swimming with memories of the past. Vivian hadn't divulged a whole lot about David Coburn, but it wasn't hard to tell just how much he'd meant to her. My heart ached for my best friend. It was so unbelievably hard for her to let anyone past the barriers she had set up around every emotional bone in her body. Only I could see that she was aching for them to be knocked down.

It was a slow, typical Tuesday. Vivian had stepped out to make a delivery, Gran had gone to brunch with her girl-friends, and there hadn't been a single customer to enter our shop. The businesswoman in me thought that I should be more concerned about our bottom line, but really I was happy for the time alone. I needed some space. I needed to turn my iPod up to an obnoxious volume and lose myself for a little while.

I didn't even hear the bell on the door sound as it was being opened, nor did I see our potential customer approach as I put all my attention into my arrangement and the Black Keys song blaring from behind me.

A faint "Excuse me," sent my heart racing as I looked up to meet dark brown eyes. Really dark. His blond hair was in such contrast to his eyes that it was almost shocking. Not to mention his long lashes that almost gave him a natural eyeliner look. Damn these pretty men.

He chuckled a bit and looked down at his feet, a signal that the music was still blaring, and I was still slack-jawed.

I reached back quickly to turn the music down and then wiped my hands against the green Pistils apron I was wearing. "I'm so sorry." I smiled apologetically. "I guess I was in the zone. Can I help you?"

"Well, I'm not sure, are you Parker Chase?"

I smirked playfully, the sound of his voice saying my full name making my stomach flutter just the tiniest bit. "That depends, who wants to know?"

He smiled widely, revealing pretty white teeth. This was a very important feature in my approximation. "My name is Carter, and I'm looking for a Ms. Parker Chase because according to my old college roommate, she makes the best floral arrangements in town. I just so happen to be in need of one."

"Ah, so you must be the one that charmed my grandmother."

He looked confused. "Oh, you mean the other day, that was your grandma?"

I nodded. "She said someone had stopped in here looking for me, and that he was slicker than a can of grease."

His face reddened, and it was kind of adorable. "Well I hope that's a good thing. I'm assuming you're Parker then, it's nice to meet you."

He held out his hand and I took it for several seconds, letting his warmth sink into mine before releasing it. "I suppose I'll own up to being Parker Chase, mainly because my arrangements are pretty spectacular. So Carter... is it just Carter? Like Prince? What exactly are you looking for?"

Was I talking too fast and too much... and was it hot in there?

He chuckled and ran a hand through his hair, rubbing the back of his neck briefly before letting it fall. "Even though I can pull off a purple jumpsuit like no other, I do in fact have a last name. It's Conlin. Carter Conlin. And I guess I'm not exactly sure what I'm in search of. Do you have any examples of your work?"

I looked at him quizzically for a moment and then waved my hand around me. "I hate to state the obvious, Conlin, Carter Conlin, but you're standing in a room full of my work."

He blushed again, and I was suddenly well aware that I was flirting with him and being way too snarky toward a potential customer.

"Hmm. I'll just have a look around then."

He turned his back to me and maneuvered around the displays. My stomach was doing somersaults, and I didn't know if it had to do with the way his hair curled just a bit in the back or the fact that I had been slightly rude to him.

I took off my apron and walked around the counter until I was standing by his side. "What's the occasion? That might narrow down our options."

He slid his eyes to the left and looked down at me with a

smirk before focusing back on the flowers. "They're sort of a thank you to my friend's wife for allowing me to crash in their guest bedroom while I'm in town. Since I've already been here for almost a week, I'm kind of late on showing my gratitude."

Do not swoon, Parker. No swoonage.

"In that case let me steer you away from the red roses, unless you plan to thank her in an entirely inappropriate way." My eyes widened as the words slipped out of my mouth, and it was my turn to feel the flush of embarrassment on my face.

I felt him behind me as I led him farther toward the back, my mind feeling the rush of something new and exciting that I hadn't felt in so long. Honestly, I had no right to feel this way. The past made me leery of all men and this one just needed an arrangement, but something felt different and there was no way I could analyze it with my mind working at warp speed.

I finally reached my destination, pulling out an all-white arrangement in a pristine square vase. "I think these hydrangeas are the way to go, Carter. They mean a bit more than a simple thank you, but this one is perfect. Hydrangeas are an expression of deep gratitude, a gesture of kindness to another person. Platonic kindness, just so we're clear."

I maintained eye contact as he took a step closer. When he spoke, his voice was a bit quieter and deeper than it had been before. "Well, in that case..." he paused and took one single stem from the arrangement, rearranging the other flowers to fill in the gap. "Please accept this as my token of gratitude, Ms. Parker Chase. Unless... I can always go back to the other display if you'd like one of those red roses."

I laughed and took the flower from his hand, holding it against my chest as I watched his eyes crinkle delightfully. "We better start with this expression of your kindness,

Conlin, Carter Conlin. But thank you, that's sweet. And thank you even more for adjusting that arrangement. I felt a split second of horror when you manhandled my work of art."

He was about to say something but decided otherwise, smiling and shaking his head as we walked slowly back toward the register. "Since we're on a first and last name basis, and you're still twirling that flower in your hand, I was wondering if I could ask you one more favor."

I stepped behind the register and somehow managed to hit the correct buttons, ringing him up. "And what might that be?"

"Well, I'm only in town for the next week or so and I know exactly three people, one of them being a toddler. I'd love to have a new friend. You can never have enough of them, or so I hear."

I giggled. "That is what they say."

"Plus, I have so many questions." He fumbled for the wallet in his back pocket, and I just then realized that the color of his sweater matched the deep coffee of his eyes.

I processed the credit card he handed me, watching him surreptitiously as he signed the slip. "Such as?"

He grinned at me sweetly as I gave him his receipt. "I'm curious about the name of your shop, the pink in your hair, that little sliver of ink peeking down from beneath your bright white polo sleeve. You are a very intriguing woman, Ms. Parker Chase."

"Just Parker. And you might want to get to the point, new friend, before my pristine white hydrangea starts wilting."

He didn't hesitate. "Dinner? Tomorrow night?"

I heard the ding of the bell on the door, feeling light as a feather as I went to help my next customer. "Lakeside, seven o'clock."

"Seven p.m. tomorrow, I'll be there. May I have your number?"

I glanced over at my new customer, who seemed to be content browsing for the time being, and took Carter's receipt from his hand, scrawling my number down.

"There," I smiled up at him.

"Lakeside?"

I nodded.

"Seven o'clock?"

I nodded again.

"You know, I went by that place the other day with my friend. He couldn't explain to me why it's called Lakeside when there's no lake from what I could tell."

I smirked, turning my head to look at him as I walked away. "It's irony, Carter Conlin. There is no lake."

He walked backward toward the door, laughing and watching me intently as he very nearly took out a tableful of tulips. "Irony. Huh. All right, see you then, Just Parker."

He turned and walked out before I could say another word.

I glanced back at my single white hydrangea sitting on the counter and smiled broadly.

Gran and Viv were going to love this.

7

VIVIAN

I sat in the Pistils van in front of the Piedmonts' home yet again, and gave myself the luxury of a few minutes before heading inside and doing more patient follow-up with Lisa Piedmont. Parker was more skillful at this than I was by far, but it was only fair for me to step up, no matter how tired or preoccupied I was at the moment.

And God knows David's phone call from a few nights ago had put me squarely into that frame of mind. My brain was grinding through his words over and over... *Your name came up today.* That was like seeing the IRS on your caller ID... it wasn't a polite inquiry.

I would never be able to forget or dismiss my seven years with the CIA. They were present every day whether I was assessing strategy on a case, analyzing the stare of a stranger as being either dangerous or simply curious, or even when I recalled something those years had taught me.

There was so much I wanted to forget, though. So much I wished it was safe to pretend had never happened. Not just for my safety, but for the safety of my best friend and her grandmother... all the family I had now. Ensuring theirs meant I was never ever allowed to forget or disregard a single damn thing.

God, sometimes I wished I could just erase everything in my memory from age eight up until three years ago. With the exception of Parker's family and David, I wouldn't miss much else.

I scrubbed the heels of my palms against my forehead, pulling myself back to the present. *Get it together, Carmichael. You've got a job to do. Stop being a little bitch.*

It was only the muscle memory of the CIA's best training that got me out of the van, smile innocently in place, slipping into the role that was so essential for me to play. *Just pretend she's a foreign asset. She has secrets she may not even know about. Get them out of her.*

Lisa answered the doorbell dressed in tennis whites, a racket already over her shoulder. "Oh! Vivian! I wasn't expecting either of you, or I would have…"

"I won't take but a moment of your time," I said smoothly. "I do apologize for not calling, but you can never be too sure about who's listening to a phone conversation." *I should know, I could bug your cell with my eyes shut and both arms behind my back.*

She bit her lip and nodded, twirling the racket in her hand. "I was just headed out to the courts to meet a friend but… they can wait. Let's go out into the garden."

The backyard of their home was, quite frankly, stunning. Gran would have keeled over and had the big one at the sight of all the gorgeous flowers arranged in flawlessly manicured beds. Not a piece of mulch was out of place. "Your gardens are lovely, Mrs. Piedmont."

"Thank you, we just hired a new gardener and I think it really shows. Over here… there's a bench where we can sit."

"Should we be expecting the gardener to be around?" I queried automatically.

"Oh no, today is his day off. So… did you find anything new?"

"Nothing solid yet, but we're eliminating certain factors and that's definitely a step in the right direction. I just wanted you to help us with that. First of all, I visited your husband at work and he did pick out the flower arrangements for the anniversary party. He didn't have time to talk for very long…"

"Did he hit on you?" Lisa asked quickly, leaning toward me.

I bit off my words and stared at her, lifting one eyebrow and letting my gaze frost over for a long moment before I answered her question. "Why would you assume that?"

She swept a hand up and down in front of me. "Well, you're gorgeous, and I just assumed that you would… you know…"

"Dangle some bait in front of him and see if he'd take it?"

Lisa nodded eagerly, apparently too oblivious to hear the edge of sarcasm in my tone. I bit my tongue and counted to ten, willing myself not to rip every salon-toned hair right out of her head. "Mrs. Piedmont, you hired us to find out if your husband was being unfaithful, and to provide evidence if he was. Neither Parker nor I ever said anything about setting him up. I'm sorry if you misunderstood that."

She flushed a dark red, realizing too late her verbal faux pas. "I'm sorry, I didn't mean… I just assumed that it was part of the process."

I shook my head. "If he's cheating on you, he might be more likely to make a pass at other women too. And if he does make a pass at either of us, we'll let you know in due course. But for the time being, we're not setting him up."

"I apologize," she said meekly. "Was there anything else you wanted to ask me? Otherwise I'm going to have to head out."

This woman really was a piece of work... one second she was practically crawling down my throat to find out what I knew, the next she was kicking me out to go play tennis. "Just a couple of questions. Parker asked you about Rhiannon Simons. You're certain you don't recognize her? Or that her name doesn't ring a bell?"

"No, definitely not."

"She's not possibly a business associate of your husband's? Or one of their wives?"

"I've met all of Jack's associates' wives, at holiday parties and such. I'd know."

"This may seem like an odd question, but are either of you involved in an insurance claim right now? Home, business, vehicular, or otherwise?"

"What? No, definitely not, unless there's something at the firm that Jack hasn't told me about." Her lower lip quivered. "We don't really chat much these days."

"I understand. My last question... are you acquainted with someone named Angel Wright?"

Lisa's head jerked up. "What?"

All my investigative senses went into overdrive at her reaction, but I kept my expression neutral. "As I mentioned before, we're trying to eliminate anyone who is definitely not intimately involved with your husband."

"Oh! Oh no, Angel is my therapist. Jack doesn't know... he already thinks I'm a jealous, paranoid headcase as it is. You won't tell him, will you?"

"It's not my business to tell."

She cleared her throat. "If you don't mind me asking, how did you find out about Angel? I'd rather none of my friends or the society pages find out either."

There was no way in hell I was spilling my guts about our raid on the guard shack. "We have our sources. You do understand that we have to keep some of them confidential."

Lisa looked nonplussed with my answer. "Well... I suppose so. As long as Jack doesn't find out."

"If you're seeing a therapist, that's entirely your business. I won't ask again since it clearly makes you uncomfortable."

"It's just so embarrassing..."

"There's nothing embarrassing about seeking help if you need it, Mrs. Piedmont, just as you sought out our help."

She looked slightly relieved. "Yes, when you put it that way, it makes sense. Vivian, I'm so sorry to cut our visit short, but I really must go."

I stood as she did. "No, I understand that you had a previous engagement, I appreciate you taking the time to speak with me. We'll be in touch as soon as we have more information for you."

She gave me a bright smile just as her cell phone chimed. "Oh, thank you! You don't mind seeing yourself out, do you?"

"Of course not," I said drily. She bounced away before the words were completely out of my mouth.

I pulled out my own cell phone as I climbed into the van and speed-dialed Parker.

"Pistils Phone Sex Hotline, Parker speaking, what's your fantasy?"

I chuckled as I put the van in gear. "One of these days it's going to be Gran borrowing my phone when you answer like that, you know."

"Where do you think I picked it up from? So what's up, buttercup?"

"Just left the Piedmonts'. Guess who the mysterious Angel Wright is?"

"Lay it on me!"

"Lisa's therapist. Although I thought she was going to have a stroke when I mentioned her name. She's desperate for Jack not to find out."

"That's understandable," Parker mused. "Jack's attorney

would try to paint her as mentally unstable in the divorce. Shitty move, but definitely wouldn't be the first time."

"Yup. I double-checked with her about Rhiannon Simons too. She still swears she has no idea who she is. She also said they're not involved in any insurance claims that she knows of, so that eliminates Rhiannon hanging around in a business capacity."

"Doesn't explain why she'd be tailing Lisa, though."

"Nope. Listen, I'm going to swing by the Grantham House and do a courtesy visit with the event coordinator about the Piedmont party, but that shouldn't take too long. Want to do a stake-out on Rhiannon Simons tonight?"

"Sounds good, when do you think you'll be back here?"

I couldn't help but notice that Parker's voice was even brighter than usual. "A couple of hours, probably. Why, what's up?"

"Nothing!"

"Don't make me go all human-lie-detector on you, P."

"I'll tell you when you get back. Maybe. Gotta go!" And with that she hung up on me. I shook my head, laughing, as I pulled out of the Piedmonts' neighborhood... Parker in a good mood was always contagious, no matter my own state of mind.

The visit to the Grantham House went smoothly, as we'd done a couple of smaller parties there before and were familiar with the house rules and overall floor plan. By the time I'd returned the Pistils van to the shop, picked up my own car, and arrived at our apartment, it was late afternoon. Parker was already waiting with chicken alfredo.

"Oh my God, that smells amazing," I moaned, tossing my purse onto a side table. "You spoil me, you really do. What's the occasion?"

She plunked two plates down on our kitchen table and flung herself into a chair. "No occasion, it just crossed my mind that we eat too much takeout. There's so much fat in that crap."

I shook my head even as I picked up my fork to attack dinner. "P, there are probably more calories in chicken alfredo than in a burger value meal."

"Yeah, but fast food makes you bloated. And gassy."

If I hadn't been busy digging into dinner, I would have laughed. Both Parker and I had been blessed with good genes, but we both also worked out regularly. Imagining a bloated Parker was beyond the realm of my imagination. I allowed myself two more delicious bites before I spoke again.

"I'm sure it does, but if that were the case, we'd both be Macy's Thanksgiving Day balloons by now. What gives?"

A slight flush spread over her face, but her cheeks lifted in a smile. "I'll have you know that I have a *date*, and I'd rather not blow up to parade balloon proportions beforehand."

My eyebrows shot up. Aside from occasionally going out for a round of beers with the guys from the target range, our social lives were sadly lacking. It wasn't as though we were short on offers by any means, but neither of us had found a guy that made the entanglements of long-term dating worth it. Sure, every once in a blue moon we'd find someone especially nice to scratch the itch. Parker had a thing for blond guys while I was still hung up on dark-haired men, but they were never any more than one-night stands.

A *date*, though... "Well have fun, my dear, when did this pop up?"

"It's not really a date, more of just a we-clicked kind of thing. He came into the shop and said he'd heard my arrangements were the best." Her voice softened. "We got to talking and one thing led to another... he gave me a hydrangea..."

I snorted. "Let me get this straight. He came in, and gave

you a flower, one of *your* flowers? I bet you didn't charge him for it either."

"Well, he… I… shut it, Vivian!" The laughter in her voice told me she wasn't serious. "I sold him a forty-dollar arrangement, so I figured I'd let him slide on one stem."

There was nothing else in the entire world that I wanted more than for my best friend to be happy, but caution made me ask. "Is this the same guy that came in looking for you before?"

"Yeah… his name is Carter Conlin and I'm meeting him at Lakeside at seven o'clock tomorrow. You can come rescue me with guns-a-blazin' if you get an emergency text, okay?"

I grinned in spite of myself. At some point Parker and I were going to have to loosen up, or we really would end up spinster sisters with twenty cats, just as Gran kept threatening.

Darkness found us in relative anonymity behind the tinted windows of my car, across the street and two houses down from Rhiannon Simons' home. Several of the houses on her street appeared to be empty or in foreclosure, so we were able to observe her evening routine with ease.

Around nine-thirty, a car pulled up and a young teenage boy bounded out the front door, waving to Rhiannon as he clambered into the backseat. She leaned against the front doorjamb for a moment as the car headed down the street, away from us.

"P, not to be a bitch or anything, but I think it's about time for some Mistress Bingo. Because Rhiannon is failing miserably."

Parker laughed. After our first few infidelity cases, we'd noticed a definite trend in the mistresses we tailed. Tight skimpy outfits, an overdose of makeup, visits to sex shops, repeated drive-bys of the boyfriend's home… we'd actually made up a Bingo card to keep ourselves amused when the stakeouts dragged long into the night.

"Yeah, I'm with you on that, we need an anti-Mistress Bingo card for her! You go first."

"That's easy… she apparently has a teenage son. Baggage!"

"She's wearing… I don't know what that is. A sweatshirt and stonewash jeans? Fashion fail."

"Jackson is at least ten years younger than her, so unless he's into cougars, she's pushing the envelope."

We both laughed, I knew we were being bitchy, but it was all true. Rhiannon was not fitting into any kind of mistress mold we'd ever seen. As soon as she straightened up and headed into the house, we both pulled out binoculars.

Rhiannon puttered around the house for a bit, appearing to tidy up the kitchen. I was just about to check the location of Jack's car from my laptop when Parker let out a squeal. "Oh my *God*, what the hell is *that*?"

I dropped the binoculars and squinted into the night. A multitude of shadows, slinking close to the ground, were appearing from behind trees and under nearby porches, all making a beeline for Rhiannon's side door. "Holy shit!"

Parker slapped at the passenger side door, making sure it was locked, as I half-dove into the backseat for my night-vision goggles. If some kind of zombie possums were roaming the neighborhood, I definitely wanted to see them before we got out of there.

"Viv, what the *hell*? Can we go now? Are those rodents of unusual size or something?"

I snapped the goggles over my eyes just as we both saw the side door open and Rhiannon step out. The shadows moved in faster, crowding around her as she bent over. Parker let out a squeak just before I dropped the goggles into my lap, lowered my head to the steering wheel, and started snickering uncontrollably.

"What's so funny?" Parker snapped, snatching at the goggles. She stared through them for about five seconds before she started giggling too. "Oh, my God. Oh, my *God*. That's it, she just broke the anti-Mistress Bingo card. And set it on fire. She's a crazy cat lady."

There were at least a dozen cats crowded around Rhiannon's ankles now, and our giggles slowly trailed off as we stared in disbelief. She arranged two large pans on the ground before stepping back and watching as the cats climbed all over themselves to get at what must have been food inside.

"P, can we safely assume that Jackson Piedmont, esteemed millionaire architect and son of Senator Randall Piedmont, is not having an affair with this woman? I mean, *damn*."

Parker shrugged. "I don't know... everyone has their kinks. Maybe stonewash and cat fur get Jackson's motor running."

"I guess you're right," I shuddered. "We can't rule her out completely until we know for sure. But this is like some *Willard* type shit, just replace rats with felines."

"Well, at least she loves animals," Parker protested weakly. "They're hungry, look at them!"

"She's also contributing to the population explosion of feral cats in the neighborhood," I contradicted. "Unless she poisoned that food, in which case this whole thing takes a hard left turn."

We both watched silently as the cats polished off the food in record time. Rhiannon hunkered down after a moment, watching them, occasionally reaching out to pet one when it came within reach. After the shadows began to slip back away into the night, she slowly collected the pans and stood up, pausing for a long moment in the dark before going back inside. After a few more minutes, the lights in the house flipped off one by one.

We sat for thirty minutes more, to see if Jack would make an appearance, but traffic was apparently light in that neighborhood and Rhiannon had headed to bed. It was getting late, and we decided to do the same.

8

PARKER

I stared at myself in the bedroom mirror while Duran Duran's "Hungry Like the Wolf" blared from the iPod dock on my nightstand. A fun fact about Parker Chase: When I'm nervous, I spin 80s pop music like no one's business.

My phone chirped, signaling another text.

I couldn't help but smile. Carter and I had been texting on and off all day, just innocent little flirtatious messages that had us acting like teenagers. We were pretty cute, I couldn't deny it, but with every message he sent, the more my nerves went into overdrive.

I didn't enjoy feeling this way. For the past two years, ever since going into private investigation with Vivian, I'd had this insane amount of confidence that I'd never really acknowledged before. I guess that's what happens when you find your true calling... self-assurance is suddenly your greatest asset.

But one thought back to Carter Conlin's dark chocolate eyes had reduced me to a sixteen-year-old girl. I flopped back on my bed, staring at the ceiling while

"Take My Breath Away" played faithfully in the background.

This was getting pathetic.

I'd barely seen Vivian since returning home several hours before. She was giving me the space she knew I needed while preparing for my first date in... when was the last time I'd gone on a date? Shane wasn't exactly Don Juan for the last few years of our relationship. Had it really been since my mid-twenties that I'd gone on a good and proper date?

Wow, that was embarrassing.

I stood from my bed with a huff, jabbing at my iPod and yelling at Berlin to stop singing me sappy, stupid, *Top Gun* lovey-dovey crap.

Apparently being nervous had also put me in a shitastic mood.

I took one last look at myself in the full-length mirror, wearing a little black dress I'd purchased about a year ago but had never removed the tags from until tonight. I'd finally found a reason to cut them off, which made me both happy and sad. I was happy because as scary as it might be, I was finally putting myself out there, and sad because it had taken this long to wear it in the first place.

Despite all of that, I was pleased with the reflection staring back at me. My eyes were smoky, my hair was smooth and tipped up a bright pink, and showing off a little bit of tat never hurt anybody.

Did I want Carter to like what he saw? Hell yes, but even though I was hard up, I really didn't want tonight to lead to sex. If he was meant to be in my life for any certain period of time I wanted to feel that slow buildup, the need that two people feel burning in every part of their body, that heavy anticipation when the intensity is stifling and the relief is just out of reach. The wait made it so, so sweet.

I missed that feeling, but if Carter was only in town for

the next week, would I really even have time to move at that slow burning speed?

I grabbed my clutch and walked out of the bedroom, finding V on the couch in a pair of yoga pants and a hoodie, laptop sitting on her folded legs and a pint of Ben and Jerry's in her hand. Even in her lounge clothes, she looked like she'd just walked off a runway. If that runway were full of scumbags who needed a good ass-kicking, but still. I feigned shock as I walked toward her. "You hussy! A threesome right here on the couch, and you didn't even wait for me to leave?"

She moaned and her eyes rolled back. "Damn straight, P. Ben and Jerry are doing me real good right now. I can't even tell you."

I laughed and leaned down until she put a spoonful into my mouth. "Oh wow. Forget Carter, I'm getting in on this action."

She yanked the spoon back and glared at me. "No way. You're going on a real date with a live man who has blond hair and big hands and an even bigger…"

My mouth dropped open. "I don't know how big his you-know-what is! What, do you think I dropped to my knees right in the middle of the shop?"

She grinned and took another spoonful of ice cream. "Why not?"

I shook my head. "You need to get some action, girl, you keep turning every real-life scenario into a cliché porno movie." I slammed her laptop shut and pointed a finger at her. "Take the night off and do something for you. Go out, find a smokin' booty call, or stay home, draw yourself a bath and have some *me*-time. If you know what I mean. And I think you do."

She shrugged, setting her computer on the coffee table. "Yeah, actually I think I could use a break."

I sat on the couch and leaned my head on her shoulder.

"Do you want me to cancel? We can go out together. I'll be your wingman."

She put an arm around my shoulders and squeezed me tight. "Thanks for the offer, but I think you hit the nail on the head with the *me-time* thing. I've just been so wrapped up in this case..."

"I know. Speaking of which, what was that I saw on the screen before I closed your laptop? Is there anything new?"

She shook her head, standing up and pulling me with her. "Oh no, if I'm taking the night off, then you definitely are. Don't think of anything other than enjoying yourself tonight. I'll catch you up tomorrow. Now get out of here, you're going to be late. Maybe I'll go raid the battery drawer, I'm sure BOB will be thrilled to be resurrected from the dead."

Vivian waggled her eyebrows, and I laughed, saying goodbye as I walked out the door and headed to my car.

The banter between me and my best friend was a great distraction from my nerves, but now that I was alone, I felt like I was walking toward the guillotine.

Don't be a pussy, Parker.

I gave myself a quick pep talk and then pulled out of the parking lot. Destination: Lakeside.

I COULD SEE HIM FROM WHERE I PARKED, PACING SLIGHTLY IN front of the restaurant entrance. I watched him as he glanced at his watch and then ran a hand through his hair. He almost appeared more nervous than I was, which was an enormous relief.

"Take My Breath Away" was still stuck in my head as I walked up to meet him, and I mentally vowed to delete that song from my iTunes the second I got home. But then Conlin, Carter Conlin was right in front of me, staring like he was mesmerized by what he saw, which made me smile and giggle and turn beet-red because I really couldn't handle that level of scrutiny.

"Parker... you're beautiful."

He took my hand and kissed it gently, his lips soft and my heart frantic. He didn't let go of it as we headed inside and were led to our seats by the hostess. Carter looked extremely handsome in a charcoal gray suit and crisp white dress shirt, and I somehow had missed the deep dimple in his left cheek, which was now all I could focus on. "Did you remember how to get here easily enough?"

"I did," he smiled, reaching across the table for my hand once more. "Is this okay?"

I nodded, our ring, middle, and index fingers intertwining loosely as I stared into his eyes a beat too long. The waitress came with a carafe of lemon water and Carter ordered us two glasses of wine, never letting go of my hand. When she retreated we got into a bit of a staring match again, which was perfectly fine with me until he broke the silence.

"I'm completely blaming you for my apparent inability to speak right now, Parker. Honestly, you knocked me off my feet yesterday, and I shouldn't be surprised that you continue to do so."

"Well, thank you. But you need to stop making me blush, it's embarrassing," I laughed, averting my eyes to the tabletop.

"Your blush is stunning," he murmured, squeezing my fingers before breaking our contact. He took a sip of his water and folded his hands in front of him. "So, Ms. Parker Chase... tell me everything."

"Everything?"

"About you. I'm desperate to know," he grinned.

I chuckled, my hands fidgeting in my lap. "All right, as long as you do the same when I'm done."

He promised he would, and I started talking, not sure that anyone truly knew how to explain everything about themselves. "Well, I'm originally from Charleston. I went to Duke, majoring in psychology for the love of it, but not really going into it with a career in mind, which probably doesn't make sense to most people. My best friend Vivian and I have been inseparable since birth. I moved here two-and-a-half years ago with her and my grandmother to open up Pistils. Ummm…I like long walks on the beach and candlelit dinners?"

He laughed. "All right, that's definitely a start. Hmm, what else? Favorite song?"

Not "Take My Breath Away."

"Can I plead the fifth on a song in particular and just choose The Beatles? My parents would sing me to sleep with a different Beatles song every night. I think they're implanted into my DNA," I laughed.

"Good answer," he smiled. "My mom was a huge Gwar fan. She could really nail those gnarly death metal tones, and her head banging was top-notch."

My mouth was hanging open, and I really had no idea what to say, until he let out a bellowing laugh.

"I'm kidding, Parker. That was my failed attempt at humor."

"Oh!" I giggled a little louder than normal, appreciating the awkwardness of a first date for what it was. I reached out for his hand this time, feeling calmer when his skin was touching mine. "It was funny. Really."

The waitress returned with our wine and we glanced at the menu, ordering quickly so we could go back to holding hands like we were in the freaking eighth grade. It was just so… *nice*.

When our waitress had left and our fingers were tangled, I settled in to learn more about the elusive Carter Conlin. "Okay, your turn."

He cleared his throat and started. "Well, when I was little my mom and I moved around quite a bit, but when I was eight we ended up settling in Cleveland, which is where I've been ever since. I'm an editor for a marketing company there. More like a slave for them, actually. I have no one but myself to blame, but for the eight years I've been with them, I've been a bit of a workaholic. I had all this vacation time built up and decided now was a good time to take a long overdue break."

"Sounds like you needed it," I sympathized. "So your mom still lives in Cleveland as well?"

"She does," he nodded, his face falling a bit. "She's actually recently been diagnosed with congestive heart failure. She's only fifty and has lived a pretty healthy lifestyle, so it was kind of a shock when we found out."

"I'm so sorry," I murmured, squeezing his hand.

He squeezed back. "It's okay. She's dealing with it on a day-to-day basis. The doctor said she's got a lot of life to live yet, and there are ways to manage it. But after her diagnosis she told me some details about my family that I'd never known before, and I felt like this was a good time to learn about my genealogy."

"Is that why you're here?" I asked.

He hesitated a bit, clearing his throat. "Kind of. A few leads led me to the area, and since one of my best friends lives here in Savannah, I thought I might as well spend some time with him."

"Killing two birds with one stone. I like that. So what about your dad, does he live in Cleveland too?"

I could practically see the blood draining from his face, and I immediately regretted asking the question. If he'd wanted to mention his dad, he would have. I could totally empathize. I'd loved my father more than anything, but talking about him still left this deep ache inside me that I couldn't stand to feel.

Carter held my hand a little tighter and maintained eye contact before he began speaking. "My father has never been in my life, and for good reason since he's not exactly what you'd consider a decent person. He was actually a big deciding factor in this whole search into my family tree. I've only very recently found out who he was, and when I did, it was easy to see why my mom never told me about him despite years of me asking for any details she could give. Even now, part of me wishes I'd never found out. But I felt it important to at least learn about the family I do have on his side, and the people he's impacted by his choices and actions. I guess in a way, that's all a part of me too."

His eyes glassed over a bit and I felt terrible for even bringing it up. This was obviously a huge deal, brand new revelations that he was actively trying to come to terms with. I really didn't know what to say, but there was clearly a lot more to the story that I didn't know and I definitely wasn't going to pry. "I'm sorry, Carter. I really am."

He smiled weakly. "It's all right. Everyone has a past. Mine's just a little more complicated." His expression fell again, and it looked like he was readying himself to ask another question. "What about your parents?"

My stomach lurched, but then my heart felt warm and full, which is what typically happened any time someone had asked about or brought up my parents. "They were amazing. My dad was an accountant by day and a comic book geek by night," I laughed, smiling fondly and trying not to let the tears well up in my eyes. "He instilled a love of superheroes in me from the very beginning. It was kind of our thing, you know? We'd always play Batman and Robin versus The Joker, because for some reason I disliked him more than all the other villains and really wanted revenge on him. I mean, hell, my name is even derived from my father's love of super-heroes. Parker...Peter Parker? Yeah, I'm named after Spider-man," I chuckled.

Carter smiled but maintained a level of seriousness. "That's so amazing Parker, truly."

"Yeah. I miss him every day. He died, when I was five. A robbery gone bad and believe me, the irony is not lost on me. He was mugged in broad daylight, and really not even that far from our house. He um...he fought back, screamed at me to run, and I ran without even looking back. I still regret it. I know logically, what could a five-year-old little girl do to a man with a gun but...Robin left Batman high and dry while The Joker took his life, you know? He was abandoned by his sidekick."

I didn't even realize the tears were running down my face until Carter got up from his seat and enveloped me in his arms. "I'm sorry, Parker. I'm so unbelievably sorry. God..."

I felt stupid crying in the middle of a restaurant, but with Carter's warm hand running slow passes along my hair, and the other wrapping me up so tight, I'd never felt more safe or more accepted.

I ran the back of my hand underneath my eyes, thankful I'd worn my waterproof mascara. His face was mere inches from mine and the butterflies in my stomach were flying fighter jets, battling on inside me as I looked deep into his eyes. The emotion I saw there, the raw, honest regret he had for the loss of my father...it was nearly more than I could take.

"I'm sorry, Carter. I wasn't trying to turn this into a therapy session. It just kind of happens when I talk about my mom or dad. I lost her to cancer when I was twenty-four, and that's still a pretty fresh wound, too."

"Hey…" He put two fingers beneath my chin until I met his eyes again. "Don't ever apologize for opening up to me. I'm honored you find me worthy enough to hear so much about your past, Parker. I'm so sorry this had to happen to you and your family."

My heart was beating fast, and I knew then that I was going to kiss him. I needed to feel his lips against mine because he was so unbelievably sweet and sincere and he was right there, smelling so good and touching me just right…

And then the waitress came with our meals, effectively snapping us out of our emotional exchange. It was probably a good thing she did, even though the need to kiss him never lessened. I just realized that doing it in a crowded restaurant after crying my face off probably wasn't the best way to go.

After I explained to him how amazing my mom and I were together for the remainder of my adolescent years, and gave him a few more details on how she passed away, Carter and I vowed that we would only talk about happy things for the rest of the night. We didn't regret the real emotions we'd exposed to each other. In truth, doing so made me feel that much closer to him. Plus his smile was so wide and his dimple so perfect, all I wanted from that point forward was to bring it out as much as humanly possible.

"So you taught self-defense back in Charleston? That's kind of awesome, Park."

In the time between our dinner was eaten, and we'd traded in our wine for dessert, and our dessert for coffee, Carter had begun to call me Park. It made my heart do back-flips for some reason.

"I did, and I loved it! I guess it stems back to my love of all things superheroes, and the importance of making sure women know how to handle themselves when faced with the threat of danger. But basically I just thought it would be fun to kick some ass. Well, hypothetically at least. I didn't realize it would be such a precursor to my current life, but I guess that was just another sign that I needed to know how to protect myself in my line of business."

He chuckled, running his finger along his jaw. "You mean all the floral emergencies we have in this day and age? I understand totally, it really is an epidemic."

My eyes widened a bit as I realized my slip-up, but I recovered quickly, slapping his arm for making fun of me. It was way too early to tell him about P&V, Inc. "What I meant was, being a business owner, it's important to be able to stick up for yourself. Plus, I have Gran to look out for, as well as the fact that I need to keep up with V, which is a feat in and of itself," I laughed.

He grinned sheepishly. "I should be worried about meeting Vivian, shouldn't I? I bet she's really protective of you considering how close you say the two of you are."

"Yeah, protective is probably an understatement but don't let her scare you. I'll make sure she draws the line at Chinese water torture." During dinner Carter had asked a few basic questions about Vivian, and since I couldn't divulge her actual past, I went with her tried-and-true cover story about having a military background and left it at that. There was no way I could deny that she might give him a hard time, though.

"I appreciate that, Parker."

His eyes were dark and extremely intense, and his smile could only be described as downright sexy.

Unf.

"I don't want to leave, but the wait staff is staring daggers at us right now. I'm pretty sure they're about to close," I smiled timidly.

He glanced at the check that had been sitting on the table for a while and then threw a few bills down. "I could use some fresh air anyway. Would you like to take a walk with me?"

I nodded, accepting his hand as he stood to help me up. There was a slight breeze when we stepped outside, making the humidity in the early summer air just a little less intense. It was a beautiful night, the moon bright and full as Carter slid his hand over mine. I leaned into him as we started walking, completely content for what could have been minutes or hours.

"You're quiet," he observed, leaning down to murmur in my ear. "What's going on in that beautiful mind of yours?"

I smiled, glancing up at him briefly. "There isn't anything in particular. I've just had a really great time tonight. You're quite the conversationalist."

"Is that what I am?" He chuckled deeply, lifting my arm and twirling me until I was walking backwards in front of him. "I thought maybe I was more like the best first date ever. Prince Charming? No frog kissing necessary?"

I didn't even realize we'd stopped walking until I felt the cool scratch of brick that I was pressed up against. "Hmm, sounds to me like Conlin, Carter Conlin has a bit of an ego." I grinned up at him as he took a step closer, and my arms wrapped naturally around his neck.

"No," he shook his head, leaning down until our foreheads were pressed together. "I just feel like this night was one for the books, Parker Chase."

"Which book?" I whispered, drunk with his scent and close proximity.

"The big one."

"The Bible?"

"No, just my metaphorical book that highlights any significant moment in my life. Birth, graduation, meeting you, going on a date with you. Maybe even...."

"Kissing me?"

His lips were on mine before I could even finish the sentence, demanding and soft as he held me there, learning what it felt like to kiss me for the first time. I reached up on my tippy-toes and suppressed a moan as he grabbed me tighter, his mouth moving chastely over mine, but his movements were slow and deliberately sensual.

I was very seriously considering climbing him like a tree right there against whatever building we were in front of, but a loud chime coming from my clutch snapped us out of the moment.

We were both panting, our lips still an inch apart as we mutually chose not to move away from one another. "I think you have a message," he whispered, still slightly out of breath. I could taste him on my lips, and I wanted more.

"Yeah, but I'm sure it's nothing." I grabbed his lapel and kissed him with a little more force this time, a short groan escaping his throat as his hand went to the back of my head.

Another chirp.

Grrr.

Carter chuckled, reluctantly putting a little bit of space between us. "Maybe you should get that, Park. Could be a floral emergency."

"Hey!" I poked his chest. "Those come up more often than you think, buddy!"

I fished my phone out of my clutch. Two messages from V, as she had apparently decided against the whole *taking a night off from the case* thing.

Figures.

Up for a little B&E? J Piedmont's office, ten minutes.

If you're not busy and naked, that is.

I looked up at Carter regretfully. "Actually, I guess I do need to go. Vivian needs some help with a certain project we're working on. Where are we anyway?"

"Somewhere on the earth, I think." Carter sounded a little dazed from our whirlwind make-out session.

I looked around and realized we really weren't that far away from where I'd parked. "Come on, walk me to my car?" I pulled on his hand and he grinned bashfully at me as we made our way to the parking lot.

"So Ms. Parker Chase..." He leaned me against the driver's side door and put his hands on my waist. "It has been an absolute pleasure. And that is a vast understatement. Do you think we should do it again sometime?"

"I know we should," I whispered, leaning up to kiss him once more. "Just call me, okay?"

"Like in five minutes?" he murmured against my lips.

I giggled. "You might want to wait a bit longer than that. You don't want to seem too overeager."

"But I am eager, Park. I'm trying not to be, but, I'm kind of all caught up in you. And you never told me about this tattoo." His fingertips slid down the exposed ink on my arm, and I kissed him chastely.

"Okay, I'll throw you a bone," I teased. "Since this one has been exposed to you all night, I'm sure you can see what it is: a sparrow, carrying a key in its mouth."

"It's pretty," he observed.

"Yes, V and I got tattoos together after she was out of the military for good. She has a subtle little lock along her shoulder blade. I guess the meaning is pretty self-explanatory."

He nodded. "I really like it. Thanks for sharing."

I stuck my tongue out as he squeezed my hand. "Well, that's all the tat explanation you get for a first date."

"Does that mean there are more?"

I smirked. "Next time."

One more kiss and a promise that he'd call, and I was

dreamily sighing as Carter Conlin walked away from me and our perfect night together.

I let out another sigh, because apparently that was all I could do since he walked into my life.

How the hell was I supposed to break and enter when my mind was still focusing on Carter's impeccably soft mouth?

It didn't matter, because it was time to put my game face on. A hot make-out session and a little law-breaking had the formula for one hell of a perfect night.

9

VIVIAN

After Parker left, I reluctantly swapped out the Cherry Garcia for a piece of the lasagna that Gran had made for us earlier in the week, slowly scrolling through my e-mails as I ate. Although I'd been dying to tell my best friend that the screening software had flagged a few conversations from the bug in Jackson's office, I'd seen the nervousness in her eyes and the way she tugged on her sexy black dress. P deserved to have a nice night off with a good-looking guy, an evening that didn't involve wiretaps, suspicious behavior, and the infidelity that made such a profitable second job for us.

The screening software was still open, and my eyebrows went up as I read the description of the file.

3:45pm

Keywords: Rhiannon, Simons

Oh shit, this could be good. I'd only be able to hear his side of the conversation, and I made a mental note to break into his office and bug his work phone if need be. I pressed play and listened to what was apparently an outgoing phone call.

"Rhiannon Simons please... yes, thank you." A few moments of silence. "Rhi, hey, your cell keeps answering as disconnected... oh shit, really? Okay, I was just getting concerned... yeah, I know, those things are expensive as hell to replace. Sorry to bother you."

A few beats of silence. The bug was so sensitive that I could actually hear the very faint murmur of Rhiannon's voice from Jack's desk phone, but I couldn't make out any individual words.

"No? Yeah, those are her friends, and I use that word loosely. A bunch of blondes with more Botox than brain cells. They mainly exist to help Lisa spend my money, not that it matters... no, don't worry about it... yeah, that might be a good idea."

I was seriously cursing my failure to have not already bugged that damn phone by now.

"Just my parents' anniversary party, and she'll be on her best behavior for that." A few more moments of silence, and then Jack chuckled. "Oh yeah, trust me on that. Listen, I don't want to keep you while you're at work... yeah, I know, but still. You're the best, I mean that. Hey, is everything else okay? Why don't we get together for lunch tomorrow, I've got time in my schedule. I probably won't be able to get away for a while after that."

My earlier kindly disposed thoughts toward him were rapidly evaporating.

"Oh hell, they called animal control again? Yeah... Rhi, yeah, I know, but you've got to stop feeding them. You're a good person for taking care of them, but those cats are... okay. I know."

Huh, and here Parker and I had figured the crazy-cat-lady thing would have more than likely ruled her out as a mistress. Maybe she was back in the running after all.

"Okay, I'll see you then... yeah, you too, bye."

Oh Jackson, I think it's about time I start putting the screws to you a little bit. No point in dragging it out.

With a few keystrokes and the click of a mouse, I booted up the tracking software that told me to within a few yards exactly where Jack's car was parked. I wasn't sure whether I was more surprised or disappointed when, within seconds, it placed it in the parking lot of a downtown hotel.

Ten minutes later, I'd changed into a professional but sexy dress, shook my hair out into loose waves, and touched up my makeup. I wouldn't look like I'd been at the hotel for wicked in-room ventures, but I'd fit in fine with the white-collar business class that frequented the bar there. A bar that afforded a view of the lobby, as well as the comings and goings of the hotel's patrons.

I spotted Jackson's car almost immediately and parked two rows behind it. He'd been there at least two hours, according to the tracking software, but I had no way of knowing if he was planning on spending the night. I sure as hell wasn't. I gave myself three hours, tops, of lurking at the bar.

Locking the car behind me, I let myself sink into the role I had to play tonight. *I'm in town for business. No thanks, I've already started a tab. Yes, I'm married. No, I won't bang you upstairs on your corporate-card-paid king-sized bed.* Businessmen on trips were entirely too predictable. I'd have to make friends with the bartender, though, they always provided a rescue from guys who couldn't take the hint.

I strode confidently through the lobby, my heels clicking sharply as I made straight for the small restaurant and shook my head with a smile at the maître d'. "No thanks, I'm just waiting for a friend at the…"

Oh shit. Jack Piedmont was at the bar.

Assume, make an ass out of you and me, Carmichael. I'd assumed that Jack was up in one of the rooms, getting his freak on with his potential girlfriend, and the sight of him sitting there changed up the game completely. But thinking on my feet was something I could do automatically, and I glided past, ignoring him as I slid daintily into a seat on the other side of the bar, putting me only about ten feet away from him.

He hadn't noticed me, which gave me a chance to surreptitiously eyeball him as the bartender went off to pour the merlot I'd ordered. Jack looked tired, his jacket was tossed over the back of his chair and his collar and tie were loosened. His fingers tapped moodily against the glass of amber liquid in front of him, and he stared down at his smartphone.

The bartender smiled kindly as I settled onto the barstool. "Would you like for me to start a tab for you?"

"Oh no, I'll just be having a glass of wine. I'm supposed to be meeting a friend here, but she's such a flake! Oh well, if she doesn't show up, *c'est la vie!*" I made sure my voice carried, but was light and sweet, and I finished my little performance for the bartender with a lilting laugh. At the sound, Jack looked up and over at me.

Men. So predictable.

He blinked and cocked his head to one side, and then a cautiously optimistic look came over his face, as though he weren't sure how the next few seconds would go. "Uh, Vivian?"

I looked up with a careful look of surprise. "Yes? Oh! Jack, hello! I didn't see you sitting there!"

Taking it as a tentative invitation, he picked up his drink and belongings, walking over to me but not sitting down. "I wasn't sure if it was you."

"Well, I'm not in work clothes now," I chirped dryly, and he laughed. I did notice that he didn't ogle my outfit, which was a bonus point in his favor. "Would you like to sit down?

I'm waiting for a friend of mine, but running late is the norm for her. If you aren't busy, I mean."

He shook his head and sat down next to me. "I had dinner here with a client earlier. We're renovating an old antebellum house for him downtown, and he was in a hurry to get back and show his wife some of the sketches I came up with."

"You do residential work then too? Not just commercial?"

The tired lines of his face disappeared as he smiled and lifted green eyes to meet mine. "We do a bit of both, actually. Commercial definitely pays most of the bills, but smaller jobs like this are the reason I wanted to become an architect."

I gave my outer thigh a wicked pinch to refocus my brain, because Jackson Piedmont was one great-looking guy when his face lit up like that. Parker, damn her, was spot-on: I was seriously hard-up. "That's wonderful! Do most people want you to restore the old details, though, or gut it and make it all modern inside?"

Jack made a wry face. "A bit of both, actually. Although I try to convince them that there weren't pot fillers above the stove back in the eighteenth century. No one really uses those damn things."

We both laughed, and I felt myself relax incrementally. I was still on guard, but Jack was being every inch the friendly innocent gentleman and I was curious to see how far down his guard would go. "I'd never use one, I only know what they are because my roommate watches a lot of HGTV. She's obsessed with *Property Brothers*."

"Oh God, don't get me started on what those two have done to me," he groaned. "If I had a dime for every time someone comes in crying because I can't do a complete renovation within three weeks... or when a wife says 'Well Jonathan can do it...' I just want to scream."

I shook my head and smiled. "Yeah, I could see where that could get old real quick. There are probably reality shows out there about florists, but we haven't seen them yet, thank God."

"I can't wait to see what you do for my parents' party," Jack said, after a sip of his drink. "I mean, not to turn it around back to business, but…"

"Oh, it's okay." My mind hopped, skipped, and jumped. An idea presented itself, and I went for it. "I'm really here on business tonight anyway."

"Yeah?"

I contorted my face into its best sad-but-not-crying look, trying to remember Parker's tips. "Yeah," I sighed. "We're having a serious work issue… one of the girls we call in for big events got into an accident in our van on her way to a delivery. Now she's trying to claim worker's comp but… I don't know. I hate to think the worst of people, but still."

"Oh hell," Jack murmured. "That's not a good situation."

I shook my head and took a sip of wine, then bit my lip for good measure. "It's just hard, being a small business and having to deal with something like this. The friend I'm meeting tonight is some kind of insurance claim detective. I don't know exactly what she does, but she said she might be able to help us out."

"Hey, listen…" Jack touched my hand lightly, and I was surprised again, as I had been at our first meeting, at how *warm* this guy was. "I don't know if this would be combining business with business or whatever, but I have a friend who does that sort of thing for a living. Insurance fraud investigation. She freelances, and she's really good at what she does. I could give you her name and number, maybe she could help you out."

I almost fell off my barstool at that point; surely it couldn't be so easy? "Yeah?"

Jack shifted enough to pull his wallet out of his back pocket. "I've known her for years. She's been out of the game for a little while because her kid was in an accident and she's been taking care of him, but she's good." He shuffled through the wallet before finally coming up with a slightly battered business card. "Her name is Rhiannon Simons. Just tell her I recommended you to her and she'll take good care of you."

"Thank you, I appreciate it," I murmured, my brain going a thousand miles an hour. "She's your on-call person for the firm, then?"

He shrugged and threw back the last of his drink. "We very rarely have the need for an insurance fraud investigator. If I needed one, yes, I'd call her for sure. But I've known her for enough years to know she's very good at what she does. Trust me on that one."

I smiled automatically and tucked the card into my purse. "Wow, I definitely got lucky running into you tonight." The words were out of my mouth before I realized the double entendre. *Yikes.*

"Well, any business I can throw her way is a good thing. And it was really nice talking to you again. My wife has nothing but wonderful things to say about your business."

If you only knew... "That's kind of her to say."

The relaxed look on his face tightened slightly. "Yes, well... anyway. Vivian, it was an absolute pleasure running into you again. Do you think your friend will be showing up anytime soon?"

I pulled my phone out and screwed my lips into a pout. "She said she's an hour away. Oh, to hell with her, since I have this recommendation from you, I don't need to see her, right?"

Jack chuckled, but the tense look on his face remained. "Are you okay to drive? Or can I have the front desk call you a cab?"

"Oh, I'm fine." I gestured toward my half-finished glass of wine. "You?"

He sucked in a deep breath and looked away for a moment, just before his shoulders slumped incrementally. "I think I'm staying here tonight, actually. Lisa's book club meets at our place once a month and I was informed a long time ago that my presence is unwelcome." He gestured to the bartender.

"She kicks you out because of her book club? Ouch!" I tried to keep my voice light.

He shrugged, then handed the bartender enough cash for both our drinks.

"Oh, you don't have to," I started to protest.

"I know I don't have to, but I insist. You're a very easy person to talk to, Vivian, and I guess I just needed that."

If he only knew that particular skill was learned from the government, not inherited. "That's very kind of you. Thank you."

"My pleasure. And let me walk you to your car at the very least."

Jack took my arm as he escorted me out into the parking lot, but it was a polite gesture, the kind that Southern men who were brought up right did automatically. "Well, unless we happen to run into each other again, I'll see you at my parents' party in a couple of weeks, right?"

I smiled as I fished out my keys. "We're there for the set-up and such, and one of us usually stays for the duration of the party, in case of any last-minute situations."

He smiled and ducked his head, and there it was, whether either of us intended it or not. That awkward back-and-forth goodbye moment between a male and a female who probably shouldn't be alone together. I broke the brief silence first. "Goodnight, Jack, I'll see you in what... ten days?"

"Yes, definitely. Goodnight, Vivian." He took a couple of steps back as I started my car and put it in reverse. Even as I drove away, I could see that he was still standing in the same spot, watching me as I left. When I was far enough away to be out of sight, I stopped the car and typed out a quick text to Parker.

Up for a little B&E? J Piedmont's office, ten minutes.

I hesitated, then grinned and sent another. *If you're not busy and naked, that is.*

By the time my partner in crime had found me, parked two dark streets over from Jackson Piedmont's architecture firm, I was busy strapping on the low-profile black harness that kept my .45 snuggled tightly against my ribs. Parker raised her eyebrows as I pulled a short jacket on over my dress, hiding the gun from sight.

"You're really serious about the breaking and entering thing, huh?" she queried, walking over to retrieve her own harness and gun from the trunk of her car.

"It's only *slightly* illegal, which falls under my own personal moral ambiguity code. It's getting to be balls-to-the-wall time, P. Speaking of balls, how was your date?"

"I got a text just before I had a chance to find out, cock-blocker."

"Liar. You would have ignored the hell out of me if you were rounding third base." We both laughed quietly. "So I had my own interesting date tonight with our boy of the hour."

"Jack?"

"I tracked him down in a hotel bar. We chatted, we drank, we played footsie… and he told me about Rhiannon Simons."

"What?" Parker squeaked, barely keeping her voice down. "How did *that* happen?"

"I told him we were embroiled in a worker's comp claim because some lying whore of an employee wrecked our delivery van." We were circling around behind the old Victorian office now. "He recommended we call his good buddy Rhiannon, the same Rhiannon he had a cozy chat with on the phone this afternoon. He gave me her card and everything, right before he told me he was spending the night at the hotel to avoid Lisa's book club."

Parker tilted her head to the side quizzically. "She can read?"

In the shade of an oak heavy with Spanish moss, I pulled out my phone and started typing in the code that would disable the building's security system and freeze the images on all the security cameras. We kicked our sexy date shoes under a bush, and I looked at Parker. "Ready?"

She tucked her hair back behind her ears, looking incredibly bad-ass for a hot blonde in a little black dress. "Let's do it."

I pressed one last button to confirm the override, then took a deep breath and walked quickly to the back porch, Parker hot on my heels. Picking the lock took all of fifteen seconds and, once we were in, a glimpse at the security pad by the door confirmed that the system still appeared to be on and functioning normally, although I knew we were passing through it like ghosts in the wind.

"This way," I murmured, hurrying to Jack's office.

"Not to be dense or anything, but what are we looking for?"

"I'm giving us a deadline, P. My gut is telling me that we're wasting our time on this case, and I don't want to deal with Lisa Piedmont forever. We haven't found a single scrap of solid evidence that Jack is cheating on her, although I'm amazed he hasn't yet. We're looking for that scrap, and if we don't find it soon, we quit this bitch. What do you think?"

She nodded slowly. "I think you're right. What's our deadline, then?"

I thought for a moment. "The anniversary party. We're still tied to the Piedmonts for the flowers, so we've got to stick around at least until then. If you and I haven't found anything after that, we're done."

Parker nodded again, and we started our careful search of Jackson Piedmont's office, working together like a well-oiled machine. I went straight for the computer while she started riffling through drawers.

Despite all my years of experience, it never failed to blow my mind how unbelievably careless people were at work. They could sign agreement after agreement that computers and phones were to be used only for company business, they could attend in-services lecturing them about a dreaded "reply to all" mess, they could hear about coworkers being fired for inappropriate texts on company cells and they *still* would do stupid shit at work.

Jack, despite my recent kinder feelings toward him, was no different. Granted, he was the owner of the company, but being careless made him vulnerable. In less than a minute I'd discovered that he checked his personal e-mail account at work, and made my job a million times easier by not bothering to log out of it. When I saw the most recent unopened e-mail, I sat back in his luxurious leather desk chair and chuckled. Parker looked up at me from where she was carefully breaking into a locked file cabinet. "What?"

"I swear I almost feel like we're being led on here. This is too easy." The e-mail was from RJ Simons, the subject line was *Pics*, and a little icon indicated that there were several attachments.

"Are you kidding me?" Parker scooted me over enough so that she could perch next to me on the chair. "Viv, if these are naked sex pictures of those two, I'm going to need some serious brain bleach."

"I don't know, I wouldn't mind seeing Jack in the buff," I teased, clicking the e-mail.

"Fair enough, but none of Rhiannon, please."

Jack, these were taken tonight. Call me whenever.

"Oh gross, they're totally going to be nude selfies, or cat pictures, or both," Parker groaned as I clicked on the first attachment and the virus scan began.

"I think we may need to crack open a bottle of bubbly when we get home," I agreed. "Because if these are our smoking gun..." Just then the picture loaded, and both our jaws hit the floor.

"Holy shit," Parker gasped. I was already clicking on the next attachment. Another one, except with a lot less clothes on. By the time I'd clicked the third one, where Lisa Piedmont was getting busy on her knees in her beautifully decorated living room with an unidentified guy, I'd started to wheeze with laughter.

"Parker... oh my God, we are the shittiest private investigators ever!" I choked out. "We were chasing the wrong Piedmont!"

Parker had both hands clamped over her mouth, desperately trying to smother the laughter that was coming out in undignified snorts. She shook her head frantically when I went to click on the last picture.

"We've got to... ohhhhh, my God. I can't unsee this. Oh, gross." There was absolutely no mistaking the climax that had been captured so skillfully by the estimable investigator Rhiannon Simons.

"That is one awful boob job," Parker managed from behind her fingers.

I cringed, jamming my portable flash drive into the CPU and downloading the incriminating evidence. "Lisa's book club, huh?"

"I told you she can't read!" Parker shuddered and hopped up, returning to her file cabinet. "I can't believe neither of us caught on."

"We knew something wasn't right." I scanned the rest of

the e-mails, noting that there were several more with attachments from Rhiannon. I saved them to my drive and, after finding a few months' worth, called it quits. There wasn't much else of interest in Jack's e-mail account, but God knows what we'd found was enough. I didn't even bother with bugging his work phone. "What have you got?"

Thickly bound legal documents were stacking up around Parker from the locked cabinet. "Looks like his legal stuff... last will and testament... here's their prenup... old trust fund stuff. Nothing recent."

I glanced at my wristwatch. "Let's do a quick last sweep and get out of here, then."

When we'd decided to our satisfaction that there was nothing else of interest in Jack's office, we swept it clean of our tracks, both virtually and physically. After we slipped out the back door and I reset the alarm system, we were sliding into our discarded shoes no more than thirty minutes after we'd first entered the house. The Savannah streets were quiet as we made our way back to our cars and, in unspoken unison, we both headed back home after re-stashing our guns.

As soon as we walked in the door, Parker threw her clutch onto a chair and headed straight for the freezer. "Vodka, Vivian, vodka. I know you don't normally, but I need vodka for this."

"No argument here. So holy hell, this changes things a bit, doesn't it?"

Parker pulled out the icy bottle of vodka and grabbed two tumblers. "Well, I won't lie, my knee-jerk reaction was that Rhiannon is blackmailing him or something. But if he was talking to her on the phone, and then recommending her to you for business earlier..."

"Exactly." I took the glass Parker handed me and clinked it against hers. "She's working *for* Jack. She's a professional investigator. Granted, a bit out of her usual element, but she was getting evidence that Lisa was screwing around on him. Why the hell didn't he go with someone more specialized, though?"

She shrugged and took a chug of her vodka, then winced. "He told you he'd known her for years, right? So she's an old friend, someone he can trust."

"Those e-mails went back a few months," I mused. "I wonder why he's waiting... oh. Oh, I get it. It's a re-election year for his dad."

Parker made a face. "He's staying with that wretched bitch to save face for his *dad?*"

"His family," I corrected. "Everything we've found on him says that he's very close to his family. I'm willing to bet he wanted to have all his ducks in a row, waiting until after the election before dropping the Big D on Lisa. God, what a life."

"I hate to be the buzz-kill here, but technically he could still be cheating too," Parker pointed out.

"Yeah, but I'd bet my Mossberg that he'll keep it in his pants if he's planning on keeping his nose clean while divorcing Lisa. *If* that's what he plans on doing... he could be planning to keep her around for all the same reasons we thought Lisa might, you know?" I very rarely drank liquor, and the buzz of the vodka was already hitting me hard.

"I hear you. What's our next step, then?"

I shrugged. "Ostensibly, we're still on the clock, working for Lisa, looking for evidence that *he's* cheating. Any ensuing mess after that is not our problem, unless we're called to testify in court. We'll stay the course for the next ten days and then present our findings to Lisa after the anniversary party. The end, case closed. We've already cashed her check." I was quiet for a long moment before giving myself a little shake and then shooting her a lascivious look. "So seri-ously...how was your date?"

10

PARKER

After staying up far later than I should have, playing secret agent girl with Vivian and recounting to her my fuck-awesome date, the next morning proved to be a rough one.

The vodka surely didn't help, but after getting an eyeful of Lisa Piedmont's phony melons in mid-bounce while her mystery man nailed her from behind... well, alcohol had been justified.

Not only was our case getting more and more interesting, but the Piedmonts' anniversary party was closing in, and preparations on our end needed to begin. Even though the celebration was considered small for the likes of a senator and his wife, it would still be a bigger event than what we would normally agree to do. When situations like these occurred, we had no choice but to outsource through a local temp agency. It was important to have a few extra hands on deck, because even though this was our cover business, it was still *our business*, and our presentation at the party needed to be executed flawlessly.

Since the majority of the manual labor had to be done in

the days immediately preceding the party to keep the product fresh, our main project of the day was to plan out every detail, every bloom, and every aspect of that day. Gran and I had our arrangement designs sprawled across her desk, as well as a blueprint of the general layout we'd be dealing with in the Grantham House. Even though the mansion was gigantic, thankfully the festivities would be confined to one great room. That left arrangements to be made for the huge foyer, sunroom, and the various tables and grand displays exhibited throughout the room.

Easy, right?

Yeah. Right.

Vivian had snuck away sometime mid-morning, claiming she had some business to attend to. I wasn't exactly sure what was going on with her, but you had to handle her carefully. She'd let you in on what she was doing, but on her timeline. I'd been subjected to her process of dealing with things my entire life. I could just imagine us as babies, chilling in the playpen while Vivian contemplated whether she needed to go number one or two, and me sitting idly by while she decided.

She'd let me know when the time was right.

"Ooh, look at these calla lilies, sweet pea." Gran pointed one wrinkled finger at an arrangement from our book. "These would be perfect for hiding recording devices throughout the room of that big old mansion."

I laughed at her. "Could you imagine all the scandalous gossip we'd hear if we bugged a room full of rich political types? Talk about hours of entertainment."

Gran gathered up our designs and put them into a file labeled *Piedmont,* huffing as she plopped back into her chair. "Well, that's mostly sorted out. Now we just have to worry about the busywork left to do next week. If only we could somehow give our Vivian a green thumb; that would sure help us out!"

I laughed, standing from my seat as I heard the front door chime, signaling a customer. "Aww, leave poor Vivian alone, Gran. She's a great supply handler, card writer, and arrangement carrier."

She started to reply but drifted off mid-sentence, freezing as she fixated on something behind me. "Well hello there, young man. It's nice to see you again."

My heart started beating faster, and I turned to see the very handsome, very smiley Carter Conlin staring back at me.

"Hi," I said dumbly.

"Hi," he replied, not sounding any more intelligent than I had.

And then silence.

The kind of heavy silence between a man and a woman that you don't necessarily want your grandmother to be present for.

God, he looked good.

"Well!" Gran exclaimed a little too loudly, snaking her way between me and Carter. "I'll go man the counter. Looks like you two could use some privacy."

I face-palmed as Gran retreated, watching in pure mortification as she gave Carter a shove into the office and closed the door behind him. "Well, that was embarrassing," I murmured behind my hand.

I looked up to see him grinning. "She's awesome."

"Yeah she is," I agreed. "So what's up? Need more flowers to express your gratitude?"

He walked slowly forward until I was backed up against the desk, his hands on my hips. "No, not this time. It would probably be in poor taste to give a florist her own flowers twice in three days."

"Mmhmm. Definitely not impressive," I whispered as he leaned in to kiss me. When his lips met mine, I breathed a sigh of relief. I didn't care if the blinds were open or if Gran had busted out her binoculars and Beltone to figure out what was going on in her office. I just wanted him to kiss me. Again and again and again.

Unfortunately, logic won out. I put my hand on his chest, separating us marginally. "We have to slow down," I breathed.

"Like, you want me to move in slow motion?"

I glared playfully at his shit-eating grin. "No, I mean this is the third day I've known you and already I want to—"

"Want to what?" he asked excitedly, his eyes widening.

"Nothing!" I insisted.

"Tell me."

"No."

"Park."

"No!"

He started tickling me until I cried uncle, finally giving in. "Fine! You make me want to, like, do stuff to you."

"Stuff?" He was positively beaming now. "What kind of stuff?"

I shrugged in reply and he shifted, leaning against the front of the desk next to me, our shoulders pressed together. I couldn't tear my eyes away from the dark wash of his stylish jeans and just how muscular his thighs looked beneath them.

See? Stuff.

"Stuff is good," Carter agreed, shifting nervously. "But non-stuff is good too."

"Non-stuff?"

He nodded. "As much as I want to do all the *stuff* with you, Parker, spending time with you is equally important. Even more so, actually."

I leaned more of my weight against him, taking his hand. "Okay. But you're not making me want to do the stuff any less, just for the record."

He chuckled, leaning down to kiss my temple. "How about we just go with the flow for the rest of the week? Starting with tonight... are you available?"

My mouth twisted into a frown, knowing that Vivian and I had plans to do a little recon that night on Jack Piedmont. "I really want to, but we have a work project we have to complete tonight. How late does your offer extend?"

He used one finger to tuck my hair behind my ear. "Hmm... not a minute after the sun comes up, how about that?"

"I can make it work," I giggled. "But the real question is, are you ready to meet my best friend?"

He paled a bit, standing up a little straighter. "Didn't you mention something about Chinese water torture?"

I shrugged innocently. "Hey, I said I'd draw the line there. That's got to count for something."

He wrapped me up in a one-armed hug, placing a sweet, lingering kiss on my forehead. "Truth is, Parker, there isn't much I wouldn't endure if it meant I got to spend time with you." He took a few steps toward the door, then turned back to face me. "Call me when you're ready for me."

As usual, Carter Conlin had managed to put me in a complete and utter daze. "Definitely," I murmured.

He winked, grinning like a little boy. "I can't wait. Later, Park."

I didn't move until I noticed Gran standing in front of me, snapping her fingers. "Yoo-hoo, are you in there, grand-daughter of mine? I see that fine young man hasn't charmed the pants off of you. At least not yet, anyway."

"Gran!" I yelled, turning a deep shade of red. "That's inappropriate!"

"Oh, please!" she laughed. "You act like it's my first time around the block. I used to be a young woman too, you know."

"Yes, Gran, I know."

"So? Spill the beans! Are you going out with him again tonight?" she asked eagerly.

"Well, Viv and I have some work to do on the Piedmont case. Carter didn't seem to care what time we got done, as long as he got to see me. So I figure when we're all wrapped up, I'll have him come over."

Gran's expression turned serious. "Parker Marie Chase. You're going to subject that sweet boy to Vivian's third-degree interrogation?"

I laughed. "She won't be that hard on him."

She gave me a skeptical look, and I realized that maybe she was right. "I'll talk to her. I learned so much about him last night, Gran. He really is a great guy."

"He's a great guy who lives hundreds of miles away," she pointed out sadly.

My heart lurched. It probably wasn't wise of me to develop feelings for a man who was only temporarily in Savannah, but it was too late now. For better or for worse, for the first time in years I was letting my gut instinct lead the way when it came to matters of the heart.

"HEY, GIVE ME SOME OF THOSE BONBONS." I REACHED OVER into Vivian's lap to grab a handful of chocolate, setting my binoculars down. "It would be great if something interesting could happen sometime this *century*."

Vivian sighed, looking at the laptop that sat on the center console. "Jack is almost home according to the tracker, but he sure is taking his sweet ass time. I just want to hold out a little longer to see if he brings anyone back to the house. What the hell is he waiting for, anyway?"

I perked up. "Maybe *that*?"

Viv looked to where I pointed to see a car backing out of the Piedmonts' garage. I was positive it didn't belong to either one of them, nor any of their staff since we'd had access to the makes and models of their cars.

"Who the hell is that?" I questioned, trying to peer into the car's windows. "It's just too dark, and the windows are tinted. Damn it."

"Well, I have the license plate recorded, at least," Vivian conceded. "Maybe it's Angel Wright leaving from an evening therapy session with Lisa?"

I shook my head. "Why would she work so late, and why does she even see Lisa at home? Doesn't she have an office? *And* office hours? Plus, why would she be parked in the garage?"

"If you're rich enough people will do whatever you want, apparently. But you're right about the garage thing. That doesn't make sense."

"Maybe it's Lisa's boyfriend, leaving after taking her down to pound town?" I joked.

Vivian snorted. "Wow, that's lovely, P. I guess there's only one way to find out."

Without warning, she peeled out of our parking space, whipping a U-turn in the opposite direction of the unidentified vehicle. Vivian drove like a bat out of hell, turning down sidestreet after sidestreet until she stopped at the end of a road that intersected the main one out of the gated community. The unknown car had no choice but to cross our path. "Way to keep a low profile, Vivian! I think you left half of our tires back there on the pavement!"

She chuckled. "They'll never know it was me. We need to get a look inside that car."

Before we knew it, headlights shone brightly as a car pulled onto the street about five blocks down. Vivian jumped into action, speeding out onto the main road. The mystery car was now our oncoming traffic. "Better hang onto those *oh-shit* handles, P. I'm a woman on a mission."

We were speeding toward the car, and I had no idea what Vivian's grand plan was until she began slowing down the closer it got. She waited until the last second before turning directly in front of them and onto another side street. "Parker, look now!"

Our headlights shone directly into the car as Vivian cut through their path, and I caught sight of a blinded Lisa Piedmont in the passenger seat, and a male with tan skin and dark hair in the driver's. "I can't be one hundred percent sure, but that looked an awful lot like Lisa and her piece on the side."

"You're positive it wasn't Jack?" Vivian questioned.

I shook my head. "It definitely didn't look like him. Besides, isn't Jack en route to his house right now?"

Viv nodded. "Yeah, he was at least. Let's swing by the house one more time, just to cover our bases."

"We do have the plate number on that car," I reminded her.

She tilted her head to the side. "True, but if it was just Lisa having her cake and eating it too, it really has nothing to do with our investigation on Jack. Even if that does make her the sleazier of the two."

"That's a good point."

We came around the bend just in time to see Jackson getting out of his car in the driveway. Vivian whistled softly. "Lisa sure likes to live on the wild side. Talk about cutting it close. Well, let's hang out for a little while to make sure Jack isn't having someone over for his own little rendezvous, and then we can go home. I have a sexy man to meet. And then question. And then beat to a pulp if he doesn't answer to my liking."

"Come on, V!" I whined, watching through binoculars as the lights in the Piedmont house went out one by one. "You promised you'd be nice to him!"

"I will be," she insisted. "Unless I get a Shane-like vibe from him. Then he's getting a junk-punch."

I gave her a pointed look. "Vivian, I've learned my lesson. You know that."

"I know," she said, squeezing my knee. "But it's my job to take care of you."

I smiled at her fondly. "I know it is. Well, I think it's safe to blow this popsicle stand. It looks like Jack has closed up shop for the night."

My best friend gave one long look toward the Piedmont house, and judging by her expression, she was deep in thought. After what seemed like forever, she finally looked my way. "What? You're ready to go?"

"Um, yeah. What did I just say?" I teased.

Viv made a noise that closely resembled a squeal, and I had to do a double take. "Hell yes, let's get out of here! I'm ready to meet your man!"

AFTER DOING A QUICK ONLINE SEARCH FOR THE LICENSE PLATE just for the hell of it, we discovered it had been a rental car in Lisa's name. We decided it wasn't worth looking into it any further, even if it was tempting as hell to dig a little deeper since she was obviously up to no good.

"Vivian, Carter is going to be here any minute. Can you please put the laptop away?"

She looked up briefly before glancing back at the screen, her keystrokes never slowing as she smirked. "Rawr, someone's cranky when they're nervous about their best friend meeting their *booooyfriend*."

"I just haven't dropped the bomb on him about our little side business yet. Don't you think he's going to wonder why you're surrounded by a bunch of high-tech gadgets that look like they just came off the set of *Mission Impossible*?"

She shrugged. "Tell him I'm reliving my old *military* days. Wait, did I even come up in between make-out sessions and forehead kisses?"

I nodded. "You did, and I had to give him the military cover story. That way if you start giving him the third-degree he'll just think you're normal-crazy versus bat-shit-crazy."

She glared at me. "You'll thank me one day, P."

Our eyes met as we heard a car door slam. There was no going back now. Vivian had a smirk permanently planted on her face as she stashed our gear and made her way toward the front door, waiting for the doorbell to ring.

"I can get it," I insisted.

Viv shook her head. "Oh no. I got this."

THREE HOURS LATER, AND I WAS STILL IN AWE. EITHER MY BEST friend had decided to keep her friends close and her enemies closer, or she genuinely *liked* Carter.

I prayed that it was the latter because without Viv's stamp of approval, there would be a lot of awkward and uncomfortable moments in our future. I hung back purposely, letting them lead the conversation and interact on their own. It brought me more joy than I could possibly explain.

Every now and then Carter would meet my eyes, something inside them changing from mere friendliness to warmth and sweetness, like he had a secret only we knew.

I wanted to hold his hand, but since he was out of reach to me, I'd just have to patiently wait.

"Well, this has been fun but I'm pretty sure the sun's about to come out," Vivian yawned.

Okay, maybe I wouldn't have to wait that long after all.

She pecked Carter on the cheek just before giving him a sweet smile. The evening had gone far better than I ever could have imagined. She came over to give me a hug goodnight, whispering in my ear, "Don't do anything I wouldn't do."

"Doesn't rule much out," I smirked.

Vivian retreated down the hallway and before she even had her bedroom door closed, Carter was next to me on the loveseat.

"Hi," he murmured, wasting no time by leaning down and giving me one slow, lingering kiss.

"Hey you. Looks like you made quite an impression," I smiled, finally entwining our fingers.

"Do you think she liked me? It seemed like she did. She wasn't nearly as scary as you described her."

"No, she wasn't!" I agreed, shaking my head in disbelief. "But I think the fact that she was so nice just goes to show how much she really did like you. Besides, what's not to like about a Gwar-loving, flower-stealing marketing editor?"

He rolled his eyes. "I was kidding about the Gwar thing, Park."

"Liar. Your love of Gwar is real and true."

He was tickling me again, and it made me want to grab him by his collar and throw him down onto the cushions. But this night was about non-stuff, and I had to resist the urge. "So did you have a good time?"

"I did," he admitted, sandwiching one of my hands between both of his. "It was pretty amazing watching the two of you together. Kind of like the way a tree branch sways with the wind. You and Vivian are completely in sync. I assumed you were exaggerating when you said you'd been best friends since birth, but how long have you actually known her?"

"Since birth! I wasn't kidding about that, we were even born on the same day. Our moms were best friends, and had got pregnant very close together. We've been together since diapers and baby bottles, even though our moms' friendship ended up withering away. Vivian and I... we both had it tough in our own ways. I had the loss of my dad to deal with and then when we were eight, her dad took off without a trace. That led to her mom hitting the bottle pretty hard. She never stopped. My mom did everything she could to get V's mom on the right track, but in the end, there was only so much she could do. By the time we were in the sixth grade, Vivian was spending nearly every night at my house, and her mom never really seemed to care. My mom, Vivian, and I were like three peas in a pod. Well, with Gran it was four because you definitely can't forget her. We were our own little makeshift family. That's why losing my mom has been so hard on both me and Vivian. She was really the only mother she knew, and because V had been overseas, she couldn't even be there during the time she had left. They wouldn't even let her come back for the funeral."

"Wow. That's terrible, Park. Has she ever heard anything from her dad, or patched things up with her mom?"

I shook my head. "We have no idea where her mom is, and her dad seems to have fallen off the face of the earth. Vivian doesn't like to talk about it, and I never bring it up. Our past has a lot of painful elements to it, but everything has fallen into place since then. We're so happy with where we've ended up in life."

"Yeah, I know the feeling," he murmured softly. "Even though recent revelations from my own mother have kind of turned my world upside down, I've never been happier. Ever since a beautiful girl with pink highlights and mysterious ink entered my world."

"The feeling is mutual. And for the record, I plan on revealing the rest of my ink when you can see every last bit of it." I leaned in and grabbed his collar like I'd wanted to do all night. This kiss was unlike others to date, breaths hitching, lips demanding, and clothes pulling and twisting in our fists.

I wanted him. There was really no other way to put it. It didn't matter how long I'd known him, or how insistent I was that we take things slow. Everything about him fit perfectly with me mentally and emotionally. At this point, I was only wasting time not knowing just how well we fit together physically.

Bring on the stuff.

Unfortunately, it was Carter that had stopped us this time. He pressed our foreheads together as we both panted wildly into each other's mouths. "You have no... idea... how badly I want to ask you to let me stay. But maybe we should wait. I don't want you to misunderstand my intentions."

"I know you have good intentions, Carter," I insisted, holding his hand against my chest. "But since apparently you're the king of willpower and we aren't having a sleepover, why don't you tell me what exactly your intentions are."

He chuckled, kissing my hand. "Isn't it obvious?"

I shook my head. "Nope. I'm incredibly dense."

He rolled his eyes again; he was really adorable when he did that. "I'm in it for you, Parker. Just you. Every day. In whatever capacity you'll let me have you. That's what I want."

He was just the sweetest thing ever.

We stayed on the couch until the birds started chirping and the sky lightened to a wispy pink, kissing sweetly, talking quietly, and building our own little cocoon that I never wanted to leave.

As the night turned to morning, I found myself asking one question... was love even a possibility after three and a half days?

11

VIVIAN

I heard the front door of our apartment shut just before dawn as Carter left. This meant one of three things: my best friend was the queen of self-restraint; Carter was a monk-in-training; or Parker really *really* liked him.

I had a feeling it was the third.

And after the evening the three of us had shared, I didn't blame her. Carter was a likeable guy; fun to talk to, witty, intelligent, and very easy on the eyes. The fact that he was head-over-heels for Parker was obvious, and Parker seemed right in step with that plan. I knew she'd been anxious for me to like him, and I did. He'd seemed genuinely interested when I told him about the years I'd spent in Russia and Bulgaria, and even attempted a few simple Russian words and phrases, laughing when he inevitably tripped over the pronunciation. He was well on his way to winning me over.

And for Parker... she'd practically been glowing as Carter and I chatted. Even if she would never admit it, I knew how important it was to her that I like this guy, especially since Shane had been the one sore spot between us for so many years. The fact that she had someone to help her banish the specter of that douchebag from her life forever made me happy. The unspoken problem was that Carter lived over eleven hours away, but even that certainly wasn't unsolvable.

I sighed as I rolled over again, punching my pillow into something approximating a comfortable lump. My body and mind were screaming from exhaustion even as I lay in bed, but I hadn't gotten a decent night's sleep since David's phone call. It wasn't his fault; I was grateful to him for the warning. But now my brain was set into permanent alert mode, and I was sadly under-equipped to cope with it.

Parker would have my ass if she knew about David's warning, along with my subsequent decision not to tell her about it. I felt guilty about it myself. But as far as I knew, they had zero interest in Parker or Gran. Unless that changed, I wasn't going to burden them with the knowledge that my old life was creeping back up on me for some reason.

I'd felt like a total jerk for ducking out on them the morning before as they did some logistical prepping for the Piedmont party, but Parker knew from experience that if I wasn't telling her the reason for my actions, then it was a reason I couldn't share just yet. And Gran would probably have a stroke if she'd known what I was doing.

It took a few hours, but before reporting back for flower delivery service, I repeated my actions from the Sunday before. Once again, I swept Gran's cottage, our apartment, all three of our cars, and the delivery van for bugs, making a mental note to re-check the shop as soon as possible. I dismantled phones to examine them, and then went through every nook and cranny that could conceivably hide a camera. I double-checked that the motion-detectors I'd installed on our own discreet security cameras were working.

Yes, I was probably overreacting, but doing *something* was the only thing that kept me from hauling ass out of Savannah, leaving a wide-enough trail so that they'd follow me and leave Parker and Gran alone.

Does anyone know what Carmichael is up to these days?

Simple words, with a myriad of possible meanings behind them. Why should they care? It had been made clear I'd never work for the CIA or any government agency again. I hadn't seen or spoken to any of my former colleagues in years. I wasn't up to any nefarious schemes. Why the hell did they care what I was doing?

And why had they just used my last name, as though "Carmichael" had been a topic of discussion recently?

Not knowing was a lot scarier than knowing, that was for sure.

I took a deep breath, trying to remind myself that I could only influence things within my control. I could lie in bed panicking, or I could be productive.

After a few more long breaths, I pushed thoughts about the CIA out of my mind and concentrated on the Piedmont case. It seemed to have gotten even more clear-cut, although even I was amazed at the depths of Lisa's stupidity. She'd hired private investigators to bust her husband, who in all likelihood hadn't been unfaithful. In the meantime, she was screwing around right under her husband's nose, so blatantly that a second-rate PI like Rhiannon had been able to capture extremely detailed photos of them. If Jack had gone home that night instead of staying at the hotel, he'd have had all the evidence he needed for a cut-and-dry divorce.

I rubbed my forehead, frustrated. There was something we were missing, I knew it. One of the things that had been drilled into us in training was to trust your instincts, to follow up on anything that just seemed *weird*, even if there appeared to be a perfectly logical explanation. In just a week and a half, we'd be informing Lisa Piedmont that there was no evidence of her husband having an affair, and as per the contract she'd signed, our fees were non-refundable. Why did I give a damn if she screwed the pool boy, the gardener, hell, even the housekeeper or her therapist if she were so inclined?

The memory of the dark-haired man in the car with Lisa the night before came back to the forefront of my mind. Her lover, obviously. And apparently Lisa had been slyer than I'd given her credit for, getting him in and out of the community undercover. She must have been with him in the car each time, therefore no need for an ID check or visitor log-in. He'd slipped completely under our radar.

And the problem was that I didn't *like* things slipping under my radar.

Although there was no way to completely absolve Jack Piedmont of any wrongdoing, I had to admit that I'd pretty much given up the possibility that he was having any kind of normal affair. Cheaters got ridiculously complacent after a while, and I'd seen nothing of the kind in him. He was obviously unhappy; it appeared he'd hired an investigator to confirm what he must have already known, but there was absolutely no evidence that he was fooling around. We'd nabbed Lisa cheating in a couple of different ways, but had absolutely nothing on Jack. And I could accept that... not every person we'd been hired to investigate had ended up being guilty.

Lisa's own motivations for desperately trying to find evidence that Jack was cheating were obvious: despite her guilt, she wanted to cover her ass. So to speak. Even though it made her a world-class idiot to carry on her own affair while trying to blackmail her husband for the same thing.

I groaned softly and rolled over again. In black-and-white, Lisa and her lover weren't my concern, even if I felt bad for her husband. Contractually, we would continue to investigate Jack for any evidence of cheating until the anniversary party, and then we were through. The fallout after that was none of our business, unless Jack wanted to hire *us*, which we would have to decline because of the conflict of interest.

Jackson Piedmont would be okay in the long run. The sooner he shook Lisa loose, the better. He had a successful career, a loving family, and being hot as hell didn't hurt a bit.

Now where did that come from, hmm?

Throwing back the covers and swinging my legs out of bed, I squashed that thought before it had a chance to go anywhere. The world was full of good-looking men. You saw them every day. Yes, Jack Piedmont was hot as hell, and nice, and smart, and...

And I stripped and hit the shower before I even went there, at all.

———

THANK GOD FOR ROUTINE CASES. PARKER AND I HAD BARELY stepped into the Pistils shop before Gran was tossing notes at us, cackling something about easy money. Since I could wither a flower just by frowning at it and the Piedmont party was rapidly approaching, I was dispatched to capture yet another cheating husband. This one favored hookers and was too cheap to spring for a hotel room. I had pictures and video back at the shop before noon, they were summarily delivered to the wronged wife, and another case was in the bank.

The next week was much of the same. Parker and Gran were busy with the final logistical details of the Piedmont party setup as well as daily shop duties, so I made myself useful in as many administrative ways as possible, picked up the two quick and easy cases that came in, and did routine checkups on the Piedmonts.

Nothing had changed there either; I caught Lisa sailing past the guard shack with her lover in tow, and once even followed them to what I assumed was his hotel room. Creepily enough, it was only a few miles from our apartment, and after that I gave up watching her completely. Parker fielded her sporadic tearful calls asking for progress, Jack worked long hours and went home, and even Rhiannon seemed to be satisfied with the full-on intercourse pictures she'd captured, as I never saw her again. It was the proverbial calm before the storm.

But it was a Southern electrical storm… you could feel it. No peep of activity from my former employer, no change in Lisa's obliviously stupid affair, no hint of indiscretion from Jack. The only good thing was the building chemistry between Parker and Carter. The sparks they threw off were palpable, and like any good roommate, I tried to give them as much time alone as possible.

The inescapable truth, though, was that Carter was due to leave town in a matter of days, on a plane departing the morning after the Piedmont party. Parker was obviously unhappy about it, although she funneled her frustration into her work. Gran fussed over her more than usual, and I finally accepted the fact that I was being one shitty best friend by not letting her blow off some steam.

Things finally came to a head two days before the Piedmont party. Parker and I were both exhausted from the larger-than-usual event we'd taken on, in addition to its covert mission. Even Gran had pled off dinner, claiming a headache. All three of us were worn out and cranky, and it was over tuna and sake at our neighborhood joint that P and I finally went head-to-head.

"Suuuuushi," Parker moaned, digging into the enormous platter of fish we'd ordered. Our mutual love and semi-addiction to sashimi was just another thing we shared; we ate leftover sushi for breakfast the way some people ate cold pizza.

"*More*," I agreed, and for a time we were occupied with stuffing down as much delicious fish as we could hold. It kept us quiet for a while too.

"So," Parker finally groaned, setting down her chopsticks and reaching for her cup of sake, "What's up with you?"

"What do you mean?" I snagged a piece of yellowtail.

"Whatever it is that you're not telling me. And before you have time to come up with what you think is a plausible lie, just don't. I love you Vivian, but you're more nervous than a long-tailed cat in a room full of rockers, and you have Prada-sized bags under your eyes."

"Harsh, P." I dropped my chopsticks onto the plate and scowled at her.

"I could have said Birkin bags. I didn't want to grill you because you'd have normally spilled to me by now, but it isn't happening. What aren't you telling me?"

"When have I ever been able to lie to you? Successfully for any amount of time, anyway?"

"Exactly my point. And keep in mind that a lie of omission is still a lie." Parker set down her sake and gave me the look that let me know I wouldn't be able to bluff my way out of this one. "The only thing I've been able to remotely consider is that you know something about Carter, and you're not telling me."

Stung, I sat back. "Really?"

"What else would you even think about keeping from me?" she shot back. "Now talk, before I take a lesson from your book and jam wasabi under your eyelids."

There was a long silence between us before I finally decided to come clean with her; she was on to me and there *was* a huge difference between withholding information and flat-out lying. "David called me."

Her eyes softened. "You mentioned that. And?"

My throat closed up for a moment, and I had to clench my teeth together to get myself under control. "He... gave me a heads-up about something."

Parker swallowed, but her expression remained neutral. "Okay."

"They, uh, the agency... well, British Intelligence actually. There are people asking about me. What I'm up to." I took a deep breath before quietly continuing. "They wouldn't ask for no reason. If your ass is booted out, they have zero interest in what's left of your life, unless you're causing a problem. I hadn't heard from David in ages, so for him to take a chance on contacting me, to warn me, it's something serious."

"He couldn't tell you what it was?"

I shook my head. "That's what freaks me out the most; he would have found some way to tell me if he had any more details. I know it seems backwards... you would think it's not that bad if there aren't details, but it's the exact opposite. This was an MI6-to-CIA inquiry, even if it was unofficial, which is weird as hell. Why would *London* be asking Langley about me? Hell, there could be official inquiries that David doesn't know about, even with his level of clearance."

Parker chewed on her lower lip. "What do we do?"

I laughed a little before poking at some eel. "There's nothing *we* can do. I have absolutely no idea why they're interested in me now. If push comes to shove, I'll split and try to figure out what's going on."

Fury descended over my best friend's face. "You'll split for *hell*."

"You want me to stay here and put you and Gran in the middle of whatever it is?"

"That is *bullshit,* Vivian."

"*Shhhh,*" I hissed, noticing other diners' stares. "I'm sorry if trying to keep you and your grandmother safe is *bullshit* to you."

"Don't even!" Parker's eyes were narrowed now. "If you're trying to imply that *your* safety is an afterthought, as opposed to ours..."

"This is *exactly* why I didn't tell you!"

Parker sucked in a sharp breath. "Wow. Want to twist that knife a little bit deeper since it's already in my back? Fuck that, Vivian. You're my best friend, you're my *sister*. I love you. And you keep something like that from me? Is it because you think I'm stupid, or you just don't trust me enough?"

If she'd shot me right in the heart, Parker couldn't have hit me harder, and I lashed back more cruelly than I normally ever would have. "I know I don't actually have to answer either of those, right? How exactly are *you* going to help me outrun the CIA?"

She snatched at her purse, yanking out a stack of bills and throwing them on the table. "Whatever, V. When you decide to be honest with me, starting *now*, let me know. Otherwise, I'm out. I can't believe you'd keep something like that from me. I can't..." She choked, then turned to sprint out of the restaurant.

Goddamn it. I pounded back the last of my sake and then reached over to polish off the rest of Parker's too.

It was two hours later when I unlocked and entered our apartment. The lights were all off, but Parker's bedroom door was open, and the flickering of the television told me she was still awake. I sighed, dropped my purse on the floor, and squared my shoulders. It was make-up time.

The volume was on low, but I could tell immediately that

Parker was watching *Beaches*, in her most comfortable flannel pajamas. I was in deep trouble.

"Was that on TV, or did you rent it?" I queried, pushing the door open.

"It was on Lifetime, fuck my life," she muttered, before shoving the pillows up behind her. "V…"

"Shut up," I replied, before hopping into the bed next to her and giving her the tightest hug I could without actually putting her in a chokehold. "I'm an asshole. I'm sorry. I love you, and I really really hope you're not still mad at me, even if I deserve it."

Her arms wrapped tightly back around me. "I'm an asshole too. I have zero tact and the delicacy of a rabid honey badger. And I love you too. Just don't keep this shit from me, okay? You can't *not* tell me this stuff. I may not be a CIA-ninja like you, but I need to know if those guys are on your tail. Because *your* tail is *our* tail, in case you haven't noticed. Just don't *keep* things like that from me." She drew in a shuddering breath. "What do you think it would do to me and Gran if you…"

"I know. I'm sorry." I hugged her tighter. "Just promise me if I tell you that I need to burn rubber out of town for a little bit, you'll roll with it. Promise?"

She was quiet for a long time. "That's a tough thing to agree to."

"For Gran?"

"If I didn't…" Parker took a deep breath. "For Gran, I would. But you have to keep me in the loop, okay? No more martyr bullshit, Viv. We need you."

"We need each other. I don't know what the hell is going on, but you'll be the first to know when I do. In the meantime it's just day-to-day."

That said, we settled back and watched *Beaches*, crying a little at the end just as we always did.

12

PARKER

What. A. Week.

It seemed like everything had been coming to a head. The Piedmont case was in a holding pattern, which meant that Jackson was more than likely not cheating. This was a good thing, of course, but it always made me wonder if there was something we were missing, and I didn't like to doubt myself. It also occurred to me that thinking this way meant I wasn't giving the men in these cases the benefit of the doubt. Apparently they were all condemned to a certain stereotype in my mind whether they were unfaithful or not. I didn't like that revelation, nor did I like what it said about my cynicism and opinion of men in general.

Nevertheless, I couldn't deny that Carter was proving me wrong in every single way. It turns out a man can be sweet and not be looking to gain something out of it. A man can look you in the eyes and genuinely laugh at what you're saying because they truly think you're funny, not because the harder they laugh, the better chance they have of getting in your pants. A man is capable of ignoring the bombshell walking past your table because he's too wrapped up in the contours of your face and the light in your eyes. Carter wasn't perfect, not by a long shot. But in just over a week's time he had proven to me that it's okay to have hope. It's okay to put your faith in someone, even though it's scary. It's okay to be in love if you're honestly and truly feeling it.

And boy, was I feeling it.

He had already stayed in Savannah four days longer than planned, opting to stay at a hotel so he wouldn't inconvenience his friends with an extended stay. This had given us ample opportunity to um... physically express our feelings toward one another, but other than a few heated make-out sessions and some dry humping like a couple of teenagers, we hadn't taken our relationship to the next level. I was ready, and I knew he was too, but there had been such anticipation building that I almost felt like we were *nervous* about it.

Even though there wasn't any sex to be had as of yet, we were still having an absolutely amazing time together. I couldn't believe how much we had in common, and every day I couldn't wait to see him again. We'd been pretty inseparable ever since I'd made his acquaintance. I was lucky that Gran was picking up my slack at the shop, and Vivian was putting up with my absence every evening and well into the night. I seriously owed my grandmother and my best friend, and soon I'd have plenty of free time to make it up to them. Carter and I had purposely not been talking about the fact that he was going back to Cleveland, but one morning over coffee he had mumbled dejectedly that his departing flight would be the upcoming Sunday at eight-thirty in the morning. I didn't like what it was doing to the inside of my stomach. There was a constant nagging ache reminding me every second of every minute that he was leaving, and would be hundreds of miles away from me.

Realistically, he was only a half a day away. Twelve hours

that I could easily endure in a cramped car to see him again. But was a long distance relationship conducive to my life right now? I was an incredibly busy girl. Pistils was one of the most popular flower shops in town, and what we lacked in size we made up for with heart and an immaculate product. The people of Savannah were quickly realizing that, and we were proud of all that we'd accomplished with what we had only intended to be our cover business.

And then of course there was P&V, Inc.

Flowers were beautiful, and I loved arranging and working with my grandmother just as I had my entire life, but it didn't hold a candle to the thrill that private investigation gave me. I poured every single piece of me into the work I adored and the family I breathed for.

When would I even have the chance to make time for Carter?

These were normally things I'd go to V for, but she'd been so bogged down with her own issues, I really didn't want to bother her. The thing about Vivian was that she almost always had the answer. She was the security blanket I could never do without, the only person on this planet who knew me almost as well as I knew myself. You can claim that someone *knows* you, but the truth is that who you are around other human beings is never the same when you're alone with yourself.

But what Vivian and I had was different, and the fact that she'd been keeping something so potentially life-altering from me hurt more than words could say. She was self-sacrificing to a fault. In her mind, the well-being of Gran and I meant way more than her own, and in a way I could understand where she was coming from. I would end my life in a heartbeat if it meant I'd be protecting the two of them, but I'd also do everything in my power to save us all when it came down to the wire. The fact that Vivian wanted to tackle this

CIA issue by herself rather than dealing with it as a team was a real kick to the gut. Sure, there was nothing I could realistically do to keep her past at bay, but we were Vivian and Parker. We handled these things *together*.

While our argument hadn't been the first in our lives, it was certainly one of the ugliest. After I stormed out of our favorite restaurant, I bee lined home, changed into my comfiest pajamas and inhaled what was left of the Cherry Garcia. Of course during my channel-flipping I came across the most heartbreaking movie known to mankind, *Beaches*, and with my sugar coma and my depressing film, sobbed for absolutely everything I couldn't control in my life: Vivian keeping vital information from me and not trusting me with the truth, and Carter disappearing from my life and me being totally unable to stop it.

I was so thankful that Vivian came home when she did, apologizing to me even though we'd both said and done things we shouldn't have. We stayed up most of that night talking and reconnecting, realizing that even though we worked and lived together, real life had the tendency to make even the best of us go on autopilot. After we made up we had returned to our usual dynamic, resorting back to the little girls in pigtails who wouldn't play with anyone else and spoke a language only they could understand.

Now Vivian and I were stronger than ever, and we had to figure out what we were going to do if the CIA was in fact after her for some unknown reason. Honestly, there was nothing we *could* do until we had more information. In the immediate future, we had a few hurdles to get through before we could really talk logistics about what their interest in her could potentially mean for us. First, we had to wrap up our investigation on Jack Piedmont, scouring one last time through our recordings, photographs, and whatever data we'd collected on him to make sure there was nothing we'd missed. Truthfully, Jack was heavily and expertly surveyed by us. We would have found something by now if he was up to no good, and I had no qualms about going back to Lisa and telling her as such, especially since it turned out she was the dirt bag in this scenario, not Jack.

Once the case was closed and the Piedmont anniversary party complete, I'd have to say goodbye to Carter. Knowing me and Vivian, I was sure the day or two following would consist of takeout, pajamas, tears, and lots of 80s rom-coms until I could put my big girl panties on and deal with it like an adult. Viv and I both agreed not to accept any cases for a while after the Piedmont case was wrapped. Not only did we have major shit going on in our personal lives, but there was a potential for danger that we were clueless about at this point. Finding out why the CIA was interested in Vivian again would be priority number one. The douche-faced husbands of the greater Savannah area would have a few more weeks to continue with their seedy activities.

We had a more important case to solve... our own.

It was the day before the Piedmont party, and things were hectic at the shop. The two girls we'd acquired from the temp agency were a great help, one of them having already worked in a flower shop for many years. Considering how efficiently she worked and how easily she could keep up with our snark, Vivian, Gran and I were very seriously thinking about making her an offer to stay on with us permanently. We'd have to crunch a few numbers and see if it would even be something she'd want to do, but having another hand on deck full-time would be a great relief for Gran, as well as Vivian and me when we were swamped with a case.

"Parker!"

I snapped out of it just in time to see a brick of floral foam flying at my head, and I stuck a hand out to catch it. "Death by foam. Real nice, V," I laughed, catching the rest she decided to throw my way. Our supply delivery had been twice what it normally was, and with my iPod playing a Sinatra-themed station at Gran's request, we put away our inventory while having some fun with it. With all the preparations complete and the arrangements made for the anniversary party, we could finally allow ourselves to let go a little bit.

We'd closed over an hour ago, but with all the lights on and the radio playing some straight up classics, we were in too good of a mood to chase out a customer who just needed a bouquet of roses to give to her daughter after her dance recital that night.

She even joined in on the chorus of "New York, New York" with us, and for that, Gran gave her a fifteen percent discount. I looked around the room, smiling so brightly my face ached, watching Gran shake her booty, Vivian sing into her broom handle, and Janice, one of the new girls, twirling as she changed our display in the corner. Despite the potential danger we were facing, despite Carter leaving in just a couple of days, in this moment I was so unbelievably happy.

Like clockwork, Carter walked through the door and I turned to jelly. My stomach was warm and my heart was fluttering as he sauntered over to place a kiss on my forehead before heading toward Gran. The song changed to "At Last," and Carter held one of Gran's hands to his chest and the other in his as he swayed to and fro with her, the girls belting out the chorus while I laughed so hard there were tears in my eyes.

I felt Vivian watching me, so I turned to look at her. She was smiling widely, pretending to fan herself over Carter and his adorable slow dance with my grandmother. I walked over and swung an arm around her shoulder. "What do you think? Should I be worried he might leave me for Gran?"

She chuckled. "I'm not sure, P. That's some stiff competition." We both laughed as Gran kissed Carter on the cheek, blushing as he spun her in front of him.

"Yeah. Good thing he's leaving in two days," I sighed.

Vivian pulled me closer, giving me a one-armed hug. "You guys can make it work, Parker. I know you can."

"We'll see," I murmured softly. "So hey, do you want me to stay with you tomorrow night at the party to make sure things run smoothly?"

She shook her head. "Nah, I'll be fine. As long as you, Gran and the girls are there to help with the final setup, I can hang around to keep things under control."

"But Vivian, flowers *hate* you. What if you look at one funny, or they decide to revolt and start the zombie flower apocalypse?"

She chuckled loudly. "Well, in that case I'll call you to come save me. Along with those *Walking Dead* guys. The redneck is pretty hot."

"Hmm… I prefer my men a little cleaner-cut." I licked my lips as I met Carter's eyes from across the room. He smiled at me crookedly, wordlessly flirting with me and then some. "Damn, I need to get a piece of him before he goes home."

Vivian shook her head. "That's another reason why you won't be sticking around the party. It's your last night with that man and you *still* haven't sealed the deal."

"I know, but—"

"No buts!" she stated firmly. "I understand that your big plan was to hold out on the sexin' because Carter meant more to you than just a fling. But it's been over a week, P. He obviously has serious feelings for you. What's the point in denying each other the pleasure of a little bump and grind?"

I stole the broom out of her hand and started singing a

soulful rendition of R. Kelly's "Bump n' Grind." She smacked the back of my head and stole her broom back, laughing as I pouted at her. "I'm serious, Parker Marie! After we're all set up at the Piedmonts' tomorrow, your ass is headed to Carter's hotel room and you're going to give it up, got it?"

"Yes, ma'am."

"Good, now let's finish putting this stuff away so we can close up shop and go relax. Tomorrow is going to be one long ass day."

VIVIAN WAS RIGHT ABOUT THE LONG ASS DAY PART. WE SPENT hours transporting the grandiose displays from the back of our shop to the Grantham House and then assembling them once we got there. Many of them needed to be pieced together onsite since they wouldn't have fit in the back of the van otherwise. This was definitely the biggest event we'd ever done, and I was pretty damn impressed that we'd pulled it off so flawlessly.

Lisa was there the entire afternoon, bossing around caterers and the majority of the hired help like she was the queen of the universe. She was even snippy with us, which made it so very tempting to print out one of the photographs of her in mid-thrust with her lover and accidentally leave it laying around the mansion.

No, as tempting as that was, we were professionals. We took Lisa's demanding tone with a grain of salt, knowing how important it was to be the bigger person in a situation like this.

It also didn't hurt that we knew she'd be getting hers once Jack took action with the pictures of her caught in the act.

Karma was a bitch indeed.

After everything was in place, our whole crew left the

Grantham House. Gran had poker night with her girl-friends from the senior center but promised she'd be available if anything came up. In the meantime, Vivian and I both went home to doll ourselves up. Viv had to be immaculately dressed at the anniversary party, and I had some very real plans with a very handsome man. Every time Carter's face popped into my head, my stomach lurched. I knew this night was going to be special, but that didn't change the fact that he was leaving in less than twenty-four hours.

What would happen after that?

Vivian stepped out of her bedroom wearing a sexy suit, and I let out a low whistle. "Wow girl, you look absolutely un-freaking-believable. Are you going to try to pick up a senator or something while you're there?"

She rolled her eyes. "Oh yeah, for sure, P. My life's been feeling a little dull lately, so I thought becoming involved in a nice sex scandal might spice things up a bit."

"Good call!" I clicked my tongue. "Just make sure you aren't going after a total geez, Viv. Even amidst a sex scandal, you should still have standards."

"Nope, you're the one who likes the ancient ones, remember?"

I feigned shock. "Leave me and Grandpa Guard Shack alone! Our love was real, you hater!"

Vivian shook her head. "Shouldn't you be getting ready for your hot date? Or are you going to wear that because you know it'll just be ripped off of you anyway?"

I stuck out my tongue. "I've got time. I was waiting until you were done getting ready so we didn't have to fight for the bathroom like always."

"Liar. You just wanted to wait till I was gone so you could play 'Take My Breath Away' at top volume."

"I... shut up, Vivian!" I kissed her on the cheek and

headed down the hall before looking back at her. "Have fun tonight and call me if you need anything."

"I'll do my best. I want all the kinky details when you come back home tomorrow. No holding out on me, woman."

I smirked at her but made no promises, closing my bedroom door and sighing up at the ceiling.

Now what the hell was I going to wear?

EVERYTHING WAS DIFFERENT ABOUT THIS NIGHT; FROM THE way he held my hand, flexing our fingers together in a rhythmic pattern almost sensually, the way he would kiss my lips and just linger there, giving me more and more until we were making a scene, and the sparkle in his eye promising that our night together held so much more in store.

Carter had taken me to dinner at the restaurant in his hotel, and I thought it was perfect. Still in public so we could at least control ourselves, but close enough that if the need got too intense, we were only an elevator ride away from his king-size bed.

I could barely taste the food as I ate it. The energy between us was so alive you could feel it in the air. He didn't let go of my hand, nor did he take his eyes away as I took one slow bite at a time.

He hadn't even touched his food yet.

"Carter?" I murmured.

"Hmm?"

"Are you going to eat something?" I smiled softly.

He chuckled, looking down at the table for a few moments before meeting my eyes. "Maybe later."

Liquid fire coursed through me, and I needed to get the hell out of there and devour this man.

"You need your strength. You're a growing boy," I smirked.

Carter shook his head. "Parker, you're killing me with the way you're phrasing things tonight." He leaned down to kiss my hand and then regretfully let it go. "I'll eat, if that will make you happy."

"It will make me very happy," I nodded, popping a shrimp into my mouth.

He sighed deeply, taking me in for a long moment. "That's all I ever want to do, beautiful."

After that I was the one who didn't want to eat, opting instead to watch him and the way his lips moved with each bite. I was so in love with this man, and it terrified me to no end. He was leaving, I was staying, and yet I couldn't think of anything other than finally being alone and naked with him. I needed to make him understand how deep my feelings were for him because even though the words were constantly on the tip of my tongue, I just couldn't bring myself to say them so soon.

"Ready?"

I asked the question when he was mid-bite. I couldn't wait. It was too much. Tears were in my eyes and my heart was beating so fast. He was the one I'd been waiting for since I was a little girl, marrying Barbie and Ken in my bedroom while Vivian sat in the corner and rolled her eyes, insisting that Barbie should marry GI Joe instead. It was too soon and I couldn't control it. It's true what they say—when you know... *you know?*

Carter threw some cash on the table and stood up immediately, never breaking eye contact as he moved to crouch down in front of me. He took my hand, kissing it over and over, pressing it against his cheek as his other hand tucked a pink piece of hair behind my ear. He nodded and smiled as his brown eyes shone happily. "I'm ready, Parker."

Before he had a chance to stand I wrapped my arms around him, drunk on his scent as my nose pushed into his neck and I willed the tears to stay in my eyes. He was my anchor then, keeping me real and there in the moment. He wrapped me up so unbelievably tight, somehow sensing just how much I needed him to press me against him. In the middle of that crowded restaurant on a Saturday night, Carter and I wordlessly confessed our love to one another.

Because now I knew there was never any doubt.

We'd ended up in front of the elevators in a daze, his arm around my waist and my head on his shoulder. Our ride was quiet, and we were thankfully alone, a peaceful moment between us as my forehead pressed into his chest and my hand slid inside his jacket, wrapping around his back.

"Parker." His whisper was so full of emotion, and his warm hand found the back of my neck, holding me against him until the elevator sounded and the doors opened.

I felt his fingers tremble as he took my hand. Apparently this was a big deal to him as well. We both chuckled nervously as he tried and failed to open the hotel room door, the light blinking from yellow to red each time.

"Let me try."

He handed me the key and came to stand behind me, hands on my hips and breath on my neck as I slid the card through the reader.

By some miracle, I only messed up once.

The silence was heavy but not awkward as the door closed behind us. My heartbeat was frantic, and I watched with bated breath as Carter removed his suit jacket and threw it in a nearby chair.

"Come here, sweetheart." He looked out the window while holding a hand out for me. I slipped out of my heels and padded on tip toes until his hand was in mind, gazing out into the beautiful Savannah night.

I stood in front of him, both of us silently captivated by the breathtaking view from the top floor of the hotel. "It's so beautiful from up here," I whispered.

"How could I ever leave a view like this?" he asked seriously. He slid two fingers along my jaw until I looked up at him, and I suddenly realized he wasn't talking about the scene outside the window.

"Carter…"

"Tell me this is real, Park."

I held his palm against my face. "What do you mean? Of course this is real…"

He swallowed thickly, his hand going to my waist as he stared intensely down at me. "Tell me when I go back to Cleveland that it's okay for me to leave my heart here with you. Tell me that I can brag to my mother and my friends that I've found this gorgeous, vibrant girl who loves superheroes and loves life… and let me tell them that she's *mine*. Please, Park…."

A tear slid down my cheek and fell onto his fingers. I was finding it difficult to speak, so instead I pressed my lips to his and didn't break away until tears were on both of our faces. We stood there together in front of the window until I was sure my heart would burst, and then I slowly pulled him toward the bed.

I leaned on one arm as he sat next to me, taking his hand and running it beneath the strap of my dress until he was touching the back of my shoulder.

"Right here… this one is a pink Superman emblem. Pretty self-explanatory. It's for my dad, and for me too. I asked the tattoo artist if he could add some sparkle in there. He said as soon as glitter ink was invented I'd be the first to know."

Carter chuckled softly, leaning forward to admire the tattoo. My eyes fell closed as he placed three slow wet kisses against the design on my skin.

"What else?" he whispered.

Without a word, I turned until my back was facing him, and I moved my hair to the side. He took my cue, slowly sliding the zipper down on the back of my dress as far as it would go. Just a hint of pink and gray peeked out between the parted zipper, and chills ran throughout my entire body as he traced it up and down with two fingers.

"You're so beautiful, Parker," he whispered reverently.

"That's just a piece of it," I murmured, turning my neck until I was facing him. "The lotus flowers are a bright pink, but the lily pads are black and white. I love the contrast of it. The tattoo goes across my lower back and wraps a little around my side, right here." I moved his hand until it was on my waist, wishing the dress wasn't in between my skin and his fingers.

He moved then, the room so silent that the shifting of clothing and the bedspread was loud in my ears. He slid over me, careful not to let our bodies touch as he stared down at me. "Can I see more?"

My eyes didn't leave his as he peeled the dress off my body, and never had I felt more in love. Every move he made was an emotion, and Carter Conlin had me absolutely drowning in it.

My heart was racing and I couldn't seem to catch my breath. I was in nothing but my bra and panties and his eyes were more intense than I'd ever seen them; so hauntingly dark and devastatingly beautiful.

Suddenly I was rushed and frantic. I wanted to take it slow, but he was just wearing too many layers, so I unbuttoned his shirt and pulled it off of him as quickly as I could. Our hands explored newly exposed flesh, goose bumps rising on my skin as my fingers slid over the light patches of hair on his chest.

Silently he laid me back, waiting to connect our bodies

while I fought with the buckle on his belt. A thin layer of sweat began to form on my skin, the anticipation of what was to come mixed with the beautiful sight of him bare becoming more than I could take.

His pants were gone. It was down to thin layers and nothing left to the imagination.

This time when he settled back over me, he made no effort not to line every part of him up with every part of me.

Just like that, the clothing that remained couldn't be removed fast enough.

Three soft kisses on my already swollen lips.

His hot breath fanning over my heated skin.

The sweet love he never hid in his beautiful coffee eyes.

Some memories were made to last a lifetime, and I knew this was a moment I would never forget.

AT SOME POINT I DOZED OFF, EVEN THOUGH IT REALLY HADN'T been that late when I practically dragged Carter up to the room like a cave woman.

Totally worth it.

I groaned and stretched, feeling little aches in parts of my body that had been sadly neglected for far too long.

The truth was… Carter had managed to scratch an itch that no man had ever really been able to.

And he was so gloriously mine.

I shifted to face the alarm clock, his very warm, naked body sliding up against me until he was the big spoon and I was the little one.

Yum.

He placed kisses along the back of my neck, causing me to giggle but also sending a streak of warmth shooting straight down my body. It was a little past midnight, which meant we had at least seven hours before Carter would have to leave for the airport.

I didn't plan on wasting a single second.

"It's still early," I whispered, turning to face him.

"That's because someone couldn't even wait until I was through with my dinner to get me up here and have her way with me."

I slapped his arm, and he pulled me closer, placing kisses all over my face. "It's not my fault," I laughed, running my fingers slowly through his hair.

"It's not?"

I shook my head. "You're the one that's so handsome. And you've denied me for so long!"

He feigned shock, grabbing me around the waist until I was perched on top of him, straddling his stomach. "That's not even true! Our decision to wait was mutual. And I deserve a freaking medal for resisting you, Miss Parker Chase. Seriously, you don't know how hard it was."

I wiggled a little on top of him, smiling widely. "Mmmm... but I know now."

He growled as he flipped me over, laying his body over mine as he kissed me hungrily.

I heard my phone chime somewhere in the room, but there wasn't a chance in hell I was answering it when I had this gorgeous, perfect man on top of me.

But then my sense of responsibility kicked in. What if there was a problem at the party?

Carter felt me stiffen, and he broke our kiss. "You need to get that, don't you?"

I crinkled my nose apologetically. "I'm so sorry. I really don't want to, but I pretty much abandoned Vivian tonight. We supplied flowers for a huge anniversary, and she's flying solo just so we could have our special night. If it's her with a crisis, I'll just get ahold of Gran, send her over there and we can keep on… you know."

He laughed. "It's so cute how you can't bring yourself to say dirty words."

I stood, wrapping his light blue dress shirt around my shoulders. "You'd be surprised what dirty words can come out of my mouth, Conlin, Carter Conlin."

He watched me hungrily as I walked away, fumbling through my clutch until I found my annoying, cockblocking phone.

And then everything stopped.

Absolutely everything.

Jinx angel isn't whoetnk 0—erd

My heart raced as I stared down at the text from Vivian, knowing that something had happened, and it was bad.

Jinx was our word.

The word that meant, *Hey, buck up right now because some real shit is going down and I need you NOW.*

angel isn't whoetnk 0—erd

Getting a text like this from Vivian was more than alarming. Miss Grammar Queen never even missed an apostrophe, let alone jumbled up a word like that. Okay, Angel isn't… that was easy enough. Whoetnk. Sounds like who we think? The rest was obviously just a bunch of accidentally typed characters from texting too fast. I couldn't call her, there was no way I safely could. If she was in danger and her phone rang, I could potentially make the situation even worse for her.

Jinx.

We'd never even had to use it before.

I snapped into action, dashing across the room and doing a mad search for my clothes. "Carter, I am so sorry but I have to go."

He slid his boxers on and came to stand beside me. "Hey… Park, what's going on?"

"Floral emergency," I mumbled, looking under the bed for my bra.

"Come on, Parker. Do you really expect me to believe that? Look at yourself, you're terrified. Park, honey, *stop*."

Tears welled in my eyes as he took my hand, reaching between the sheets with his other to recover my discarded bra. "You need to tell me what's going on. I've known you for twelve days, and the number of floral emergencies you've had to leave me for just aren't feasible. What the hell is going on?"

I squeezed his hand, begging him with my eyes to just let me go so I could deal with this. "I promise you I'll explain everything when I get back, okay? Right now I just need you to help me find my panties, because I really need to go."

"Why won't you open up to me?" he demanded. "I've confessed how much I… how much you mean to me. Parker, you can trust me."

Once I was fully dressed and my heels were slipped on, I threw my arms around him. "Please please please let me go deal with this, and as soon as I can come back, I will. I'll tell you everything. Just please, Carter. I have to go."

He looked so hurt that I could barely look into his dark brown eyes. He nodded stiffly and stepped back. "If you need to go, then go."

Walking away from him in that moment was one of the hardest things I'd ever done, but I had to put it on the back burner for now. Vivian was in trouble, and there was no way in hell I would stop until she was safe.

13

VIVIAN

Nine-thirty p.m., and the Piedmonts' anniversary party was in full swing. The senator himself, accompanied by his wife, complimented me personally on the beautiful floral arrangements, and I made a mental note to pass all the appreciation on to Parker and Gran. P wasn't joking when she said I could probably bring about the zombie flower apocalypse just by scowling at one... she'd bought me a cactus for my fourteenth birthday, and the poor thing died within a week. That was some sad shit right there.

The crowd was almost entirely upper-crust and elderly, with some representation from the younger generations. Jack and Lisa appeared together, looking every inch the elegant young society couple. Jack in particular looked unbelievable in a tux, and I was able to appreciate that fact from the corner in which I'd stationed myself. *Damn, if he wasn't married...*

But he was, I firmly reminded myself, and snapped back into Pistils-mode. That meant unobtrusively slipping business cards to those who approached me and carefully fixing any arrangements that were mussed from amorous old rich men yanking out blooms and gallantly presenting them to their coiffed-to-the-max wives. I briefly wondered if Parker was having a good time at that moment, although I was fairly sure she was, and grinned to myself a little.

Carter would be lucky if he could walk tomorrow, if Parker took all that bottled-up sexual frustration out on him tonight.

Ten, and then ten-thirty came; the party reached its mellow stage. Many drinks with hearty hors d'oeuvres had been consumed, the chatter became lower and more intimate, and there was a lot of quick laughter. It would have been boring as hell if I hadn't been watching a few things for the past hour.

For one, Lisa Piedmont was well and determined on getting extremely drunk. I'd watched as she'd snatched flute after flute of expensive champagne from the waiters' trays, then switched to the harder stuff from the bar.

Second, Jack was well-aware that his wife was approaching a disaster of *Real Housewives* proportions. He'd gently taken her elbow a few times to guide her into a quiet alcove, or around a corner, murmuring to her even as his lips hardened and his jaw grew tight. Lisa was rapidly heading for what I personally called "the point of no decorum," where her snappy replies to him were getting more and more shrill.

At one point, Senator Piedmont jovially clapped a hand over his son's shoulder and pulled him away from the group they were chatting with. His mouth smiled, but I had no doubt what the subject of their terse conversation was. Jack nodded quickly before smiling gallantly at the grandmother-type that tottered up to him.

Parker totally gets the next party after this one, I thought to myself, just before slipping into the solarium. There were only a few arrangements there, but party guests had a nasty habit of discarding their half-empty glasses, dishes, and napkins around Parker and Gran's hard work. It looked like crap and that didn't fly with me, so I didn't mind picking up a little bit of the wait staff's slack by tidying up.

I'd just finished in the solarium when a hard hand came down on my shoulder, nails digging in deep. My mind went blank, and I reacted as I always had after so many years of training and experience in the field: I snapped my arm up and prepared to break that hand off right at the wrist.

"*Bitch!*" The snarled word hit my ears even as I whirled around to find Lisa Piedmont wobbling behind me. She blinked as though confused at my sudden movement and at finding her arm bent half-back, but the fury in her face didn't abate. "What in the *hell* do you think you're doing?"

I forced myself to release her wrist immediately. "I'm sorry, but you startled me."

"You were supposed to get me proof on *him!*" She reeked of straight booze, both from her breath and the glass she clutched tightly in her free hand. "What the hell am I *paying* you for? Just these stupid flowers? Where is the evidence you *promised* me?"

I clenched my teeth together and counted slowly to three. "We never guaranteed we'd find proof, only that we'd do our best. This probably isn't the best location to have this conversation though, Lisa, so…"

"That's *Mrs. Jackson Piedmont* to you, bitch!" Her face was twisted in such ugly lines, even I was taken aback for a moment. Her makeup had caked and settled into furrows around her eyes and mouth, what little lipstick that hadn't bled away was faded to her lip line, and if we hadn't suspected forehead Botox injections before, I was sure of them now. "Now *where is my evidence?*"

"We never…"

"Bullshit!" she snapped, waving her drink around until its

contents sloshed over the edge. "I don't care what you have to do, I need *proof!* I need answers, I need…"

Lisa was tap-dancing on my last nerve now; in some ways it had been easier dealing with trigger-happy terrorist-types than this spoiled drunken socialite. "Mrs. Piedmont, we don't have any proof. Per the investigation conducted by myself and by my partner, we have found no evidence whatsoever that your husband is cheating on you."

That silenced her, and in that moment, I couldn't help but notice that one of her expensive false eyelashes had started to work loose. Lisa Piedmont, elegant Savannah socialite, was falling apart before my eyes.

"You mean to tell me…"

"Again, we've found no evidence of infidelity on Jackson's part."

Lisa shook her head a little, more a gesture of denial than confusion. "But he is, I *know* he is. You just didn't look hard enough. I should have known better than to hire some hack back-alley hillbillies who still have dirt under their nails from digging their way up. Consider yourself fired, Veronica."

Red flared in my vision, and for the first time in many years, I felt myself losing control. "My name is Vivian. And just because we didn't get any pictures of Jackson cheating doesn't mean we didn't get any pictures at *all.*" I let the ice in my voice thicken over the last few words.

Lisa, even through her drunken haze, caught the meaning in them. "What did you just say?"

"Nothing. Only that the camera never lies… regardless of the subject."

She paled, and for a moment genuine fear cut through the boozy fog over her eyes. "What do you mean?"

"Not a thing, Mrs. Jackson Piedmont, not a thing. I'll be sure to update our records that our official working relationship with you ended at this time tonight." With that, I deliberately turned away from her, examining one of Parker's beautiful arrangements.

I could hear her swallow down the last of her drink, ice cubes clinking together, before she walked and then half-ran away from me. Good. She'd made her bed, it was about time she lay in it. Jackson Piedmont wouldn't need our help for that.

Luckily, the hour was growing late enough for guests to start taking their leave in a steady stream, politely ignoring where Lisa Piedmont sat sniffling in a corner divan. She'd huddled into it just after our spat, clutching her cell phone like some kind of pathetic modern-day Blanche DuBois, arguing in dramatic whispers with whoever was on the other end. I didn't know if it was her boyfriend, her therapist, or a cab company, but I was past caring.

The catering company began clearing up the clutter of abandoned dishes and silverware, and I shifted from one foot to another. Technically, I wasn't supposed to start loading up Pistils' vases and equipment until the party was truly done, but based on everything I saw, it was pretty much over at that point. I set my mental countdown for ten minutes before I busted this place down like no one's business and left the Piedmonts behind.

"Vivian?"

A tired voice from my right, and I turned to see Jack Piedmont standing there, looking red-eyed and exhausted. Jesus, the poor man. If this was a typical night for him, I genuinely hoped he and Rhiannon had enough evidence to ship Lisa off with no scandal or money attached.

"Good evening, Mr. Piedmont," I replied automatically, and a slight smile cut across his face.

"Jack, remember?"

"Good evening, Jack. I hope you and your parents had a nice time?"

He rubbed a hand over his jaw, looking to where his parents were bidding the last of the guests goodnight. "I think they did, yes. I've had better."

"I'm sorry to hear that," I murmured, fighting every instinct in my body to tell him that his wife was a cheating whore and that he deserved so much better. Hell, if he kicked her to the curb and just needed a quick rebound, I wouldn't say no.

Jesus Carmichael, get hold of yourself! "Is everything all right?"

Those bright green eyes met mine. "I don't want to make you uncomfortable."

"It's okay."

"It didn't escape anyone's notice that my wife's behavior tonight..." He stopped and then forced another brittle smile to his face. "I shouldn't dump this on you."

What the hell did I have to lose at this point? "She looked upset, and maybe had a bit too much to drink. I hope it didn't ruin your parents' celebration."

"Not in the way you'd think it would, they just..." He sucked in a deep breath. "But the party's over, and apparently my wife prefers the company of a cab driver to her husband. At least, I presume that's who she called and drove away with. Do you have a ride home, Vivian?"

Those last words, had they been spoken at another time, in different circumstances, would have prompted a completely different reply from me. As it was, though...

"The Pistils van is parked out back. I just need to break down the arrangements and load them up, then I'll be on my way."

He swallowed, then nodded gamely. "You and your pistil-packing partner did an incredible job tonight. Please be expecting many references from my various business associates, and more business from me."

"We always appreciate it," I said quietly. "Have *you* got a safe ride home tonight?"

This time, his smile was more sad than anything else. "I'm fine. My car is here, and I've had nothing but fancy sparkling water to drink all night."

As soon as I was sure that the last few guests and the Piedmonts wouldn't notice, I pulled my suit jacket off and went after the floral arrangements like a woman on a mission. Breaking down took only a fraction of the time that setting up did, so forty-five minutes later I was finally on my last trip out to the van. My feet ached, my head swirled, and I wanted nothing more than to get home. I'd pop a couple of aspirin, give myself a nice scalp massage, take a hot shower, and then...

A hard arm went around my waist and locked down tight, harder than steel. I didn't think, I reacted; arching my back, both arms flew back to aim my fists at my attacker's head, even as my legs sought to entangle and trip his. The crystal vase I'd been carrying exploded against the rough ground.

There was a guttural curse in my ear when my slimmer build allowed me to twist in the man's arms, bringing the full force of my arms and fists into play. I managed to bring down one ringing blow to the side of his face and felt the force of it stagger his body. My mind was completely detached now, just aiming to incapacitate and eliminate this threat to me. One more solid punch to the head should give me enough leverage to get a knee up and...

"Jesus bloody Christ, Vivian!" The muted shout rang in

my ears, amplifying the shock of hearing my name, and the familiarity of the voice. "Leave off a man's balls, will you?"

"Get off of me," I growled.

"Like hell I will, woman," David snarled. "After crossing this bloody ocean *again*, and this time because you're up to your arse in alligators, as you too often said. No trouble at all, eh? *That's* what you tell me?"

My mind and body were still shut down into rapid calculation and self-preservation mode. "My ass and my alligators are none of your concern, now get *off* me!"

David and I flung each other apart at the same time, both panting, both unbelievably furious. "You tell me you're not in it, Viv, then I find out it's this bad? What in the hell is *wrong* with you?"

I slumped against the back brick wall of the Grantham House, my breath coming in gasps. "What are you talking about?"

"I asked you straight out, after calling you and telling you…" David stopped and shoved his hand through his short brown hair, a frustrated reaction I hadn't seen for years. "And you *lie* to me? To *me*, Viv? Really girl, I know those at the CIA do brainwashing for fun, but that's a bit much, wouldn't you say?"

"What the hell am I lying about?" David's sudden appearance, along with his accusations, had my brain in a complete tailspin. "I'm a small-town florist chasing down small-town infidelity cases, David. Were you mad I didn't tell you about the latest who-nailed-who case?"

That answer was the wrong one, I could tell as soon as the anger flattened his eyes and thinned his lips. This was MI6 officer David Coburn, the man who could make life-or-death decisions in a heartbeat and carry them out without hesitation. "Listen to me, Viv, and curb your sass. The FBI is at the front door of this house as we speak, investigating a death threat against the senator. If you're caught in it now, there's nothing I can do to help you."

"Help me *what?*" I demanded, even as he yanked off his black jacket and wrapped it around me, zipping it up to my chin. The scent of him, so recognizable even after so many years, was enough to rock me back on my heels.

"Lie to me, Viv, and I'll twist that pretty head right off your neck, as much as I love it. Tell me the truth now, what have you been up to?" His arm wrapped tightly around my waist and he began guiding me out of the back alley at a surprisingly slow pace; we could have passed for lovers. Of course, that was one of the primary rules... don't ever *run*.

"I have nothing to lie to you about." From around the front of the mansion, I could hear one quick squawk of a siren and then a few car doors slamming. Short of an actual hostage situation, I knew the FBI wouldn't dare make a scene unless there was no other option. Most likely, a generic man in a black suit was introducing himself at the front door and politely asking for permission to search the house to ensure the senator's safety. With a heavily armed SWAT team backing them up and ready to go at a moment's notice, of course. Death threats against a U.S. senator were not taken lightly.

"Well, then...*ne boysya.*"

I blinked. Why had David suddenly switched to Russian to ask me to trust him? We both spoke it fluently, of course, but it made no sense. "*Ya ne ponimayu.*"

We kept walking at an absurdly relaxed pace, but he finally looked down at me. "*Angelus Atanasov?*"

"I..."

"*Velichko Atanasov. Ty pomnish?*"

Of course I remembered, I would never forget that name for the rest of my life. My mouth went completely dry. "*Da.*"

"Then we are speaking the same language again, Viv, I

was afraid you'd conveniently forgotten." His voice was calmer now, but his arm was still hard around me, propelling me forward.

"What does he have to do with me, with us here? I haven't heard that name in years, since…"

"Bulgaria." He finished for me. "Which was more than enough for the CIA to put two and two together, eh?"

I took a deep breath. "Spit it out now, David. I haven't been to Bulgaria in years."

"I know that. They know that. But you were also actively involved in the Velichko Atanasov case, gathering enough evidence so we could put him down. And then with what happened afterward, of course."

Icy cold settled in my chest, memories that I'd sworn to keep away were coming at me too fast to comprehend. "We caught him, David, he's in prison and…"

"And his son, Angelus Velichkov Atanasov slipped through our fingers. He vanished into thin air, and it was only five months ago that one of our officers got lucky with a lead and found out that he'd been in Chechnya. The man is a ghost, he managed to legally enter the States without anyone finding out about it until just a few weeks ago. He's been here for months."

"David, *stop.*" This time I managed to hook a heel into the street and yank against his strength. "This is crazy! I haven't had anything to do with that since I left!"

"Does the name Angel Wright ring any bells?" he finally snapped. "Because that's what he's going by here in the States. The fact that was spotted in the same city as you made quite a few people very nervous. Too close for coincidence, you might say."

Angel Wright. Lisa's therapist, except apparently not. Oh God, how could we have made such a stupid assumption that Angel was a woman, and why in the hell was Lisa dealing with the son of a convicted terrorist? One from *my* past, no less. If not her therapist, then Angelus could only be… and then my thoughts froze as realization hit me like a bucket of cold water. "David… if I go with you, will you listen to what I have to say to you, sixty seconds or less, then go from there?"

David put his hands on my shoulders and looked at me square-on. "Viv, tell me what in the world I can do to get you clear of this. I'm trying to keep you out of hot water, because mark my words, they'll boil you alive this time."

I yanked my cell phone out of my back pocket and tapped out a rapid text to Parker, using our red-alert-oh-shit code-word for the first time. I prayed that she'd read it not just with her eyes, but also trust that weird, freaky connection we'd had since birth, and discern at least part of what was going on. As soon as I was finished, I took a deep breath. "Angel Wright is screwing around with Lisa Piedmont, Senator Piedmont's daughter-in-law. We knew she was having an affair, but that's it. She told me that Angel Wright was her therapist, and we assumed she was a female."

David's blue eyes narrowed. "He's screwing the daughter-in-law to get to the senator."

"What?"

"Senator Piedmont is the chairman on the Judiciary Subcommittee on Human Rights. They've been hammering away on Chechnya, going after the crime families, and the Atanasov family had close ties to the Chechen mob. The subcommittee is throwing their full support behind taking them down, and that's increased the spotlight on all the insanity over there. Special ops has been inside for a while, trying to nab the ringleaders one by one."

My jaw dropped. "So, you think he came here specifically to go after the senator? Is he crazy?"

"Yes," David said shortly, leading me toward a dark sedan parked in the shadows. "But he is also extremely intelligent, and that makes him very dangerous. The FBI has been looking for him, but he's been very careful until tonight."

"What happened tonight?"

"Got into a bar fight earlier. There was some bit about the senator and the committee on the news, and he had words with someone about it. It got to the point where he was yelling that he'd kill Piedmont himself. The bartender called the police, but Atanasov got a phone call and took off before they got there. Not sure how the FBI caught wind of it, but they confirmed it's him from the surveillance footage. Plenty of witnesses heard him threaten the life of a United States senator, so he'll be arrested now... if they can find him. The man is slippery as an eel."

"A phone call," I breathed. "Lisa must have called him, I saw her arguing with someone on the phone. Jack told me that she'd just left, it must have been with Angel."

He nodded. "Where would they go, then?"

The long list of Angel Wright's passages through the gated community popped into my mind. "I'd guess back to her house, she was really drunk. She's not in any shape to be out in public."

"I've never doubted your instincts and I'm not going to start now. Tell me where to go."

I gave him directions automatically, my mind still going a mile a minute as the puzzle pieces finally clicked together. "So Angel was just using her to slide his way in, while she was busy falling in love." In the briefest terms possible, I filled David in on our investigation, along with the terms and conditions of Lisa and Jack's prenup. "That's why she wanted proof that Jack was cheating so badly. She would have had a bigger payout if she'd caught him cheating, more money for the two of them to ride off into the sunset together after the divorce."

"While in the meantime he doesn't care for her except for

the access she provided. She could have walked him right into the senator's house and introduced him as anything from a damn tennis instructor to a lobbyist. Christ, is the woman that dumb?"

"Unfortunately, yes," I replied. "David... you still haven't told me what you're doing here."

His hands clenched around the steering wheel. "MI6 has been trying to track him down since he went off the radar in Chechnya. I was called when the FBI finally located him here in the States, they knew he'd be up to no good. My intel and experience with the Atanasovs were seen as assets."

"You weren't the only officer involved in that," I reminded him.

"Oh, you want me to say it then? All right, Vivian, I volunteered to come. The second I heard they'd identified Atanasov, and that he was in Savannah, it all made sense. I'd been turning it over and over in my mind, trying to understand why they'd be asking what you were up to. I stood by once and let them throw you to the wolves, I wasn't going to let that happen again."

"Given our history, I can't believe they'd let you..."

"I think they were planning on our *history* being an asset, actually," he said flatly. "We knew each other well, they probably hoped you'd open up to me if you had anything to share. Although why is beyond me, seeing that you told them everything we'd done was just a cover."

His words were like a physical slap and I turned my head away, staring out the window. I knew that what I'd chosen to do so many years ago had hurt him, but I'd also hoped he'd come to understand *why* I told the Deputy Director what I had.

After a few more turns in the road, his warm rough hand reached over and caught mine. "I'm sorry Viv, that wasn't fair."

"It's okay. It's probably true anyway." I was still staring out the window.

"To them, probably. But not between us."

I squeezed my eyes shut, then turned to look at his face, silhouetted against the dark night beyond the sedan's windows. One of three people in the entire world I trusted with my heart, and with my life. "Not between us," I agreed.

As we pulled up to the guard shack, I somehow wasn't surprised when Parker's old friend leaned out the window. "Evening folks, can I..."

David quickly flashed his MI6 identification. "I'm a federal officer, and this is urgent," he said in a flawless American accent. "Open the gate immediately, please."

Grandpa Guard Shack blinked, obviously flustered. "Well, I... I hadn't heard anything about this."

"Open the gate now, please."

"Okay, sure! Shouldn't I call the police, though?"

"No. I've already notified them and they're on their way. For your safety, I'll ask you not to become involved in the situation. Now, the gate?"

Grandpa was still sputtering even as he leaned back into the shack and the gate slowly opened. David floored it and followed my directions through the community.

"It's the next one, up there."

He pulled over immediately and killed the headlights. "Let's go see what's going on, shall we?"

"Don't you think the FBI may actually show up?"

"They can't even find the man. They traced him here a few weeks ago based on an ID he used to rent a car, but he turned it back in the next day, and the address on the ID was fake. If we can verify that he's here, I'll call them in, but I'm not giving him a chance to run again."

It wasn't even a question in my mind that he was authorized to use deadly force if necessary.

"We saw him with Lisa in a rental car, but it was registered in her name. He must have talked her into paying for everything to keep under the radar."

"Right," he said shortly. "Need a gun?"

"You didn't exactly give me a chance to grab mine out of the van."

He chuckled as we exited the car and he popped the trunk. "Take your pick."

I immediately zeroed in on a Glock and loaded it up. I pulled off David's jacket, and he helped me slip into a harness, and then quickly adjusted it for my smaller frame. "This feels just like old times," I murmured, making sure the gun was snug against my side.

"Just about, but…" He put his hand under my chin, pulled my head up, and then planted a quick hard kiss on my lips. "*That* feels like old times. For luck, eh?"

I swallowed hard; his kiss had been shockingly familiar even after so many years. "For luck. Let's go."

14

PARKER

M y thoughts were swirling in my head a mile a minute as the hotel elevator descended at an unbearably slow pace. I didn't even know where the hell Vivian was, or whether my presence would hurt or help her current situation. All I knew was that if she was truly in danger, I needed to be by her side.

Everything about her text was confusing. Why would she use our panic word regarding something as inconsequential as the *Piedmont* case? So Angel wasn't who we thought she was; did that mean that she was screwing around with Jack after all? And if she was, why would Vivian need to use that word? *Jinx.* We'd been in some tough spots before, from me getting cornered by a group of men in a dark bar on one of our first cases, to Vivian triggering an alarm system and barely getting out before the cops showed up. None of that necessitated the use of that word, so now that she'd thrown it out there, I had no idea what to expect.

Thank God I had my gun in the lockbox in my trunk. I didn't know if I'd need it tonight, but I wasn't going to walk blindly into the unknown without one.

I ran as fast as I could manage in four-inch heels toward my parked vehicle, internally struggling over whether I should go to Vivian's last known whereabouts, the Grantham House, or try to figure out another way to pinpoint her exact location. Unfortunately, there was just no time and since her text was about Angel, my gut was telling me that whatever the issue, it had to have been linked to the case.

My tires squealed as I pulled out of the hotel's parking structure, Gran's number already speed dialed as I merged onto the busy city street.

"Parker!" Gran was obviously having a good time with her friends, oldies music was playing in the background and all I could hear was laughter. "How was your date? Does Vivian need help with the tear down?"

"Gran, listen. I don't know what's going on, and I don't want to scare you, but the Piedmont case is going south, and I need you to be aware of it. I might just be overreacting but until I know more I need you to stay in a safe place, okay?"

"Okay. I'll stay at Muriel's, she won't mind. It's getting late and she hosted cards tonight, so I'm already here. And I always keep that overnight bag in my car at all times, thanks to you girls."

That's what I loved about Gran. She didn't ask questions; she didn't panic when I told her something was going down. It was like she knew that even though there was a potentially dangerous situation, Vivian and I could handle ourselves. "Thanks, Gran. As soon as I know more, I'll let you know. Thanks for doing this, even if it might be unnecessary."

"It's not a problem, sweet pea. I know you and Viv have this under control. I love you both, do you understand that?" Her words were spoken forcefully, and the slight quiver there told me that even though she had all her faith in us, she was still terrified for her girls.

"I understand, Gran. Get some sleep. We'll see you tomorrow. I love you."

I disconnected the call, tears welling up in my eyes. There was no time to get emotional over Gran or the fact that I'd just ditched the man of my dreams right after we consummated our relationship, giving him no explanation whatsoever.

Ugh. No more of that. I needed to stay focused for Vivian's sake.

It was a miracle I didn't get pulled over on my way to the mansion, but thanks to my speeding I'd gotten there in no time. I opted for parking a couple of blocks away since I had no idea if the party was still in full swing or completely over. Plus, they probably wouldn't approve of me strolling right through the front door while I was packing.

But if Vivian was still there in any Pistils capacity, she'd be parked at the back entrance. I opened the trunk and entered the combination on my case, skipping the shoulder harness for my lacey little thigh holster. It kept my gun safely concealed beneath the skirt of my dress.

I popped the mag into my trusty Kel-Tec and stashed it against my thigh, cursing my heels as I made the trek toward the back alley of the Grantham House. After a nonchalant walk down the sidewalk, I dashed into the shadows and through some squishy and beautifully manicured grass in the yard next door. I finally made it to the tall hedges that separated the two properties, hunching down as I heard voices in the distance. I peeked through the branches to see a few members of the wait staff leaning against the brick wall at the back of the mansion, smoking and talking vibrantly in Spanish. When I was positive they weren't looking, I squeezed through a narrow opening between hedges, straightening my dress and walking up like I'd been there all night.

At least I looked the part.

Once I had a clear view of the alley that stretched along back of the row of mansions, I spotted the Pistils van instantly, my heart lurching as I realized that Vivian could possibly still be inside. But the closer I got to the van, the more I could tell that something had gone very wrong. The back doors had been left ajar, and on the ground below there was a shattered crystal vase and stems scattered amongst the water and glass.

Vivian was no klutz.

I immediately began scanning the area, looking for any familiar faces or anything that seemed suspicious. Staff was scattered throughout the Grantham House as I entered through the back door: the caterers cleaning up used plates and champagne flutes, the housekeepers already working on the floors in the sunroom. There didn't seem to be any party-goers remaining in the grand room of the mansion, and there was definitely no sign of Vivian. I was very seriously considering my next plan of action when something caught my eye. Near the foyer at the front of the house stood Senator Piedmont and his wife, talking to a tall man in a crisp black suit. He was middle-aged, looked very official, and stood out like a sore thumb amongst his surroundings. Mrs. Piedmont looked visibly shaken, and the senator's expression was grave as he carried on a quiet conversation with the unidentified man.

My mind immediately screamed *cop*, and not just a doughnut-eating patrolman killing time, but someone much higher in ranking. A detective? No, he was so impeccably dressed. I was still going off of my gut feeling, but something told me his presence had to do with Vivian's hastily typed text message. All of this somehow had to be connected to Lisa's therapist, as ridiculous as it sounded.

I grew frustrated as I made my way quickly toward the

back entrance. It was like the puzzle pieces were scattered in front of me and I couldn't make any of the parts fit. I once again considered calling Vivian, but I didn't want to risk her cover getting blown if she was trying to keep a low profile. Even the chime of a text message could out her, and I just couldn't take that chance.

I faltered for a moment, wavering on what exactly I should do. Where would I go next? I finally conceded that at the end of the day, Vivian's text still focused solely on Angel Wright who, as far as I knew, was strictly connected to Lisa Piedmont. There was no sign of Lisa or Jack now that the anniversary party was over, so logically my only next step would be to head to their house and see if that's where Vivian had ended up.

She was becoming more difficult to find than Waldo and Carmen Sandiego combined.

I hopped in the Pistils van, choosing to take that rather than sprint two blocks to my car. Plus I needed a feasible reason to get past the guard shack at this time of night, and hoped that whoever was manning it would be more likely to believe I had a floral emergency than Carter was.

My heart clenched in my chest, but I shut it down instantly, getting away from the mansion as quickly as possible and heading toward my next destination, where I prayed Vivian would be. By the time I got to the entrance, it was pushing one-thirty a.m., and I was seriously wondering if I'd even get let in at this point.

And wouldn't you know it. Fucking Grandpa Guard Shack.

"Hi there, honey." His tone was serious as opposed to any other time I'd talked to him, which immediately told me that something wasn't right.

"Hi," I smiled apologetically. "I'm sorry it's so late, but I have this delivery that the Piedmonts need first thing in the morning, so they asked me to bring it tonight. I'll just be a minute!"

He shook his head solemnly. "No can do, little lady. I'm not sure what's going on, but I just let a federal officer in not too long ago, and he seemed to be in a heck of a hurry. I don't think it would be safe for you to go through right now, and if the cops don't show up soon like he said they would, I'm going to call them myself!"

My stomach did flip-flops, but I decided not to push the matter. I had my own ways of getting in. I arranged my face into a terrified expression, portraying the sweet little floral girl I was supposed to be. "Oh my gosh! Um, okay. I guess I'll just call Mrs. Piedmont in the morning. I hope everything is all right, sir. Goodnight!"

I didn't give him a chance to reply as I pushed the shifter into reverse and got the hell out of there, parking a safe distance around the corner. My immediate thought was to assume that the man at the party and the federal officer here in the gated community meant that the CIA was tracking Viv down after all. But her text regarding Angel and the CIA had nothing to do with one another, so all I could do was stop questioning it and break into that gated community like a boss. The sooner I found Viv and made sure she was okay, the sooner I'd know what the hell was going on.

I found a secluded area not visible from the road and stared up at the looming fence that appeared to surround the entire community. With a sigh, I tossed my godforsaken heels over to the other side and made sure my gun was tight in its holster. I jumped and grabbed onto one of the bars as firmly as I could, climbing up the rail of metal like it was a rope in gym class. Thank God no one else was around because I wasn't leaving much to the imagination with my dress hiking further around my waist the higher I got.

I made it over the top and shimmied down a bit on the

other side before landing with a grunt on my feet. Once I had my bearings, I looked around, realizing I'd ended up in someone's yard yet again. Hooking a finger in the back of each shoe, I began running barefoot down the back property line, cursing as I saw row after row after row of pristine hedges separating each yard.

Great.

I grabbed the gun out of my holster, double-checking that the safety was on. I didn't think I'd need it, but if I would be hurdle jumping like this, I didn't trust my gun to stay in place.

I decided to just hop the first few hedges, which would keep me concealed from the guard shack to ensure no senior citizen interference. By the time I'd jumped my third line of bushes, I was huffing and puffing like I was about to blow someone's house down. I snuck out of the last yard and made it to the street, struggling with what to do next. On one hand, it wasn't realistic for me to hop hedges all night like Frogger on crack, but walking right out in the open on the street put me at risk of being seen by God knew who. And since I wasn't caught up on what was actually going down at the moment, I didn't like that idea either.

In the end, I decided to re-holster my piece, put my heels back on, and walk down the street until I hit the Piedmont house. I only had about a block or so to go, and if anyone noticed me, I looked like nothing more than a disheveled woman in a party dress taking her walk of shame in the middle of the night.

By the time I reached the Piedmonts' driveway, I was getting downright impatient. I surveyed the area, not caring at all that their security cameras were going to pick me up, but careful to stay out of the path of the motion-sensor lights. The only cars parked in front of the huge garage were

Jack's sedan and a car that looked suspiciously like the rental we'd seen Lisa and her lover in.

Huh.

The house was totally dark, not a single light visible from my hiding place along the driveway. I slid behind the garage to figure out my next step. I had just decided I was going to swing around the back of the house to see if there was any movement inside when suddenly someone grabbed me from behind with an arm around my neck and a hand slapped over my mouth.

My mind went into self-defense mode, and I could almost feel my blood start to boil and my eyes turn red as I prepared to defend myself. I grabbed the arm wrapped around me and clamped down, bending over until my elbow was in his gut and tossing him over my shoulder. Within seconds of his back hitting the ground, I had my heel slammed into the dirt directly in front of his balls, the sole of my shoe hovering threateningly above them. "Who the fuck are you?" I snapped.

I heard a soft laugh behind me. "Holy shit, P. That was awesome. I think I underestimated you."

Just hearing Vivian's voice made me forget about the man on the ground and the balls I'd nearly crushed, throwing myself into her arms and squeezing her tight. "Goddamnit, Vivian. You scared the shit out of me! Are you okay?"

The man stumbled up off the ground, brushing dirt off his dark clothing. "Are you off your head? Why does every beautiful woman I see tonight insist on putting me on my arse?"

Vivian grabbed me by the shoulders. "I'm fine. Parker, David. David, Parker. And now that we've all been acquainted, let's get inside that house and figure out what the hell's going on."

David stepped between us. "I'm terribly sorry to interrupt

this heartfelt reunion and Parker, forgive me for being blunt, but you need to leave immediately. This is not a safe situation for anyone to be in, especially a civilian."

I scowled at him, ready to press a finger against his chest and tell him what I really thought until Vivian did it for me. "David, she just laid your ass out in two seconds flat, and I trust her with my life. She belongs here just as much as we do."

He hesitated a moment, but eventually consented, and during that time I'd made two observations. One: he was gorgeous. And two: Vivian had him wrapped around her little finger.

"Do you have your piece?" she whispered.

"Of course I do, now what in the world is going on?"

She sighed, glancing around quickly before filling me in. "I'm giving you the quick-and-dirty version because I have no idea how much time we have. Angel Wright is not Lisa's therapist. He's her boyfriend, the one in the pictures and in the car that night."

"Angel is a *he*?" I asked, shocked.

She nodded, continuing. "Yeah, and also the son of a Bulgarian mobster that David and I happened to help put away years ago. I'm going to save you from all the political mumbo jumbo for right now and just tell you that he is dangerous, Parker. He's using Lisa to get to Senator Piedmont because Angel's got everything to gain by ending his life. Any more questions?"

"Nope, let's do this." I looked to David, who had remained remarkably quiet while Vivian caught me up. I held out a hand, which he shook. "It's nice to meet you, David. I'm sorry I almost crushed your testicles."

He chuckled, letting go of my hand and taking a step in front of me and Vivian. "The pleasure is all mine. Now, let's get on with it."

I swallowed hard, silently following my best friend and the man I was pretty sure she'd once loved, or possibly still did.

My heart was racing, the silence was thick... and I had never felt more alive.

15

VIVIAN

I was pretty sure I could hear my heart pounding in my ears as I followed David, Parker at my side. Part of me was uneasy about her being there—she didn't have the training or experience that David and I had, after all—but since she'd effectively put an MI6 officer on his ass, I figured she could handle herself. I'd taught her to shoot, and when it came to hand-to-hand self-defense, I knew my best friend was far from helpless.

As we eased around the back of the house, a faint glow from one of the rooms became visible. It was the living room, and there was movement inside.

As one, the three of us melted further back into the gardens and continued circling around the house until the scene in the living room was fully revealed through the floor-to-ceiling windows. Lisa was sobbing hysterically on one of the sofas, Angelus Atanasov was manically pacing back and forth, yanking at his hair. Jack Piedmont was sprawled on the floor with blood oozing from an ugly wound on his head. I stiffened just as Parker let out a soft gasp next to me.

David cursed under his breath. "Is that the senator's son?"

I was already reaching for my borrowed Glock. "Yes. Ready to call in the cavalry now?"

"Not until Atanasov is down. He could kill either of them at any moment if he's spooked. Is there a way to slip in?"

I searched my memory. "Nothing that I know of that won't be locked; we might want to just try the front door."

He nodded curtly. "Parker, can you shoot?"

"You bet." She was already hitching up her skirt when David put a hand on her arm. "Hold on, then. Here, take this." He unholstered one of the several handguns I knew he had on him. "It's bigger than whatever you've got stashed under there, and will have a lot less kick, but it's the same concept. No safety, though. If you pull the trigger, it's going to shoot whatever you're aiming at."

Parker frowned in confusion. "Why?"

"If Atanasov ends up with any bullets in him, I need them to come from one of my guns."

I immediately understood his meaning even as Parker took the Glock from him. "David, you can't!"

"Yes, Viv, I can," he replied simply. "If we take him down, I want the two of you to get the hell out of here immediately. They *know* I'm involved in this, but I don't want either of you dragged into it. Please. If they caught wind that you were here... I'm not letting it happen again. Now Parker," he turned to her. "Under no circumstances are you to shoot your own gun, do you understand me? And once Atanasov is down, you and Vivian get the hell out. I don't care what she tries to tell you, knock her in her stubborn head, drag her out of here, and go straight home."

Parker's eyes skipped from his to mine, obviously conflicted. "Okay," she said slowly.

An explosion of noise as Angel threw a lamp against the wall and Lisa screamed, and all conversation between us ended. We retraced our path around the house and David motioned us back, quickly yanking off his boot and a black sock before placing the latter over the security camera and then jamming his foot back into the boot.

"Jesus, is he like James Bond or something?" Parker whispered to me.

I grinned a little. "Something like that. You have to make do with what you've got sometimes." We watched as he carefully tried the front door, and when it slowly opened, he gestured the two of us forward. Parker kicked her stilettos off and left them outside.

We crept through the house, toward the noise that was escalating in the living room. Eventually we reached a spot where we blended into the dark behind a grandfather clock, with an almost perfect view of the scene. Jack hadn't moved, and I had to forcefully close my mind against the possibility that he was dead. Lisa was cringing back into the couch, still sobbing, as Angelus screamed at her in a broken combination of English and Bulgarian.

"*Tapa kurva!* How could you have been such a stupid bitch? Why, when everything was fine? *Katerichka!*"

"It wasn't my fault," Lisa wailed. "She knew, she *knew* somehow! Jack probably got to her and…"

"You can't keep your stupid drunk mouth shut?" Angelus snarled. "Everything was good, why did you have to fuck it up?" He looked nothing like the skinny eighteen-year-old that I'd gathered intel on so many years before. He was taller and bulkier now, and he had the wild-eyed, frantic look that David and I knew too well; it was the face of a man who had lost all control. "You want me to shoot him in front of you?"

"No Angel, please!" Lisa pleaded, swiping at her tears. "I don't understand! You didn't have to hit him, I'll still get money from him if we divorce, you and I can…"

"There is no 'you and I,' *kuchka*." Angelus reached under

his jacket and pulled out a pistol. "You fucked it all up, every-thing. I will kill you both, I will kill his father next."

Lisa visibly shrank away, horror blooming over her face. "What? No! You said you loved me! We can get far enough away that..."

"Far enough from this?" Angelus gestured toward Jack's limp body. "You think I will take you along, when you are so stupid? How could any man love someone so stupid?"

David tensed beside me as we both recognized that the man was reaching his breaking point. No words were needed between us as he slipped out of the shadows with his gun trained on Angelus, Parker and I fanning out behind him. Angelus caught sight of our motion and swung around to face us, gun aimed at David's head. He blinked as confusion, then anger, flashed over his face.

"*Kakvo pravish tuk?*" What are you doing here?

"It's over, give it up," David replied in Bulgarian. "You don't want to kill either of these two, it will only make things worse."

"Worse? *Worse?* Than what? Going back and saying this stupid bitch kept me from a simple job? Fuck you, *britanski.*"

David's aim didn't waver even as Lisa whimpered and squirmed deeper into the couch cushions while Angelus continued his rant. "U.S. cannot leave it alone, eh? They call in their English dogs to do the work they cannot finish?"

"Give it up, Angelus. It's over."

"*Ebi se,* I'll tell you when it's over!" With a lightning-fast move, Angelus swung his gun around until it was pointed at Lisa. A split second later, there was an explosion and her body was thrown back against the couch cushions, now coated in red.

As Angelus turned back toward us, I pulled the trigger. The loud bark of David's gun made my eardrums ring even as Parker and I fired simultaneously. At that point, everything went into slow-motion, just as it had in the very few similar situations I'd been in before.

David's bullet went directly between Angelus' eyes, throwing his head back. Without enough time to fall, Parker's shot went into his shoulder even as mine went through his chest, spinning him around. We were all in motion before his body hit the floor.

"Stay back," David hissed, before leaning over the body sprawled on the blood-covered carpet.

I guided Parker around the mess and we both looked at Lisa Piedmont. The bullet had gone through her throat, and the result was gruesome, made even more so by the still-fresh tears and shocked expression on her face. "She's gone," I told David over my shoulder, with a pang of regret. Lisa had been a self-centered cheating liar, but she hadn't deserved this. She'd been his pawn, no doubt lured in by sweet words in an exotic accent, and I knew without hesitation that she'd never counted on Jack being a literal casualty of her actions.

Jack...

I skirted around David, still crouched over Angelus' body, and knelt next to Jack. The blood hadn't clotted over his head wound yet but, to my relief, it wasn't a bullet hole that had caused it. Had he arrived home and surprised them? Had Angelus bashed him in the head? "David, he needs to get to a hospital, stat."

David came over and knelt next to me, then searched for a pulse in Jack's neck. "I'll have them bring medics in. Viv, you and Parker need to get out of here *now*."

"But I..."

"No buts. Don't argue with me. I'll take care of him, just please get out."

"I..."

"Out. Now. I'll see you before I leave, but for now, the two of you need to not be on the premises." He plucked the Glock out of my hand just before turning to Parker. "Nice shot. Gun, please?" She handed it to him without hesitation. "Good girl. Now, if anyone asks, you've been anywhere but here. Viv, I'll count on you to figure it out, all right?"

I looked at Jack one more time, taking comfort in the fact that he was still breathing, as faint as it appeared. "If you don't tell me what happens…"

"Have I ever been able to keep anything from you? Out now, get out. I'm giving you three minutes before I call the FBI, starting now. Get *out.*"

I felt Parker tugging on my arm and I stumbled behind her, vaguely aware when she snatched up her abandoned shoes from the front steps. It was only when she dragged me across the first thorny hedge that I snapped out of my stunned state. "Ohhh…owwww! Jesus, P, what in the hell?"

"Uh huh, now you know how I felt when I was chasing your ass in here… jump!" We hurdled another hedge.

"Is this how you got in here? You couldn't, I don't know, blow Grandpa Guard Shack for entry? This isn't Fort Knox!"

Parker socked me hard on the arm. "I'll remember that. You're the one who apparently decided that texting in coherent English wasn't a priority. *Jump!*"

We dragged ourselves across another hedge that the super-rich used in lieu of fences.

"So what the *hell* was all that about back there, Viv? I don't speak Russian, remember?"

"Bulgarian," I panted, as we heaved ourselves over one last hedge. "He's the son of a Bulgarian mobster."

"Were you planning on sharing any of this with me?" We collapsed next to an iron fence, and I thankfully noted that the Pistils van was on the other side.

"Yes. Jesus. I didn't know about any of this until tonight, I didn't even know David was here." I sucked in a breath, trying to appease my screaming lungs. "How the hell did you get in here, anyway?"

Parker cast her eyes upward and I groaned. "Seriously? P, we are really getting too old for this shit."

She rolled her eyes before staggering to her feet and tossing her shoes over the fence. "Come on grandma, if I made it, I know you can."

Climbing the iron fence brought back memories of my training at The Farm, but it wasn't until Parker and I were safe inside the Pistils van, flooring it to get the hell away, that I let myself sag back into the seat.

Lisa Piedmont's throat, blown to pieces. Jack's head. All that blood on the carpet… Jesus. And David left to deal with it all.

"Stop thinking," Parker commanded. "Let's go get my car and go home and then figure it out."

"Take the long way around," I groaned.

THE BRIEF REPRIEVE I'D ALLOWED MYSELF IN THE VAN LIFTED the moment we stepped into our apartment. "Scrub your hands, we've got gunpowder residue all over us. Pitch that dress and I'll chuck my suit, we can find a dumpster to toss them in tomorrow. Hopefully David will be able to hold them off until then."

Parker nodded even as she moved with me to the kitchen sink. "Are we in deep shit?"

"I doubt it, but it's better to be overcautious. David was doing everything in his power to keep us out of the equation, so with any luck they'll be happy enough with a dead terrorist to ask too many questions. Tonight was something of a blast from the past, though."

"Yeah." Parker hesitated and then wrapped her arms

around me. "Can you tell me about it?"

"I will, yeah. I'm not supposed to, but I really don't give a damn right now." I took a deep breath and forced myself to move to another topic. "Are you okay?"

She gave me another squeeze and then pulled away. "I'm fine."

"P, you can tell me, it's all right."

"No, seriously, I'm okay. I mean, I'm still in shock but I'll be okay."

I eyed her suspiciously as she moved away, tossed me a garbage bag, and started shimmying out of her dress. I knew she wasn't lying to me, but my best friend had been in an intense situation that she'd never experienced before, culminating with shooting a man and two dead bodies. I seriously doubted that she was really *okay*.

"Do you want to talk about it now?"

"Not yet, no. I think Carter was half-naked when I bolted on him, and he was kinda freaked out. I want to talk to him before he leaves."

"Uh-huh." I slowly started peeling off my clothing as well. "Did you tell him that you had another *floral emergency?*"

She scowled at me, even as she tossed her dress into the garbage bag I'd dropped on the floor. "Well, what else was I supposed to come up with on the fly? You send me this cryptic messed-up message, and I had to book it out of there. Got a better excuse?"

I sighed, knowing better than to push at that moment. "I don't know him as well as you do, so no. We'll talk when you get back home, okay?"

She bit her lip. "Should I tell him everything?"

"Well, not *everything*, I definitely wouldn't give him all the details." I started stuffing my clothing into the garbage bag as well. "But the private investigation thing... I don't see how it could hurt at this point. And if he's a keeper, he needs to know the bare minimum, at least."

Parker nodded and then dashed off to her room as I jammed the last of my clothing into the garbage bag and tied it off. When she reemerged, clad in jeans and a vintage Strawberry Shortcake tee, I couldn't help it, I started laughing.

"What's so funny? I'm behind on my laundry, okay?"

"Fine," I snorted. "That look totally screams *floral emergency* to me."

She swung her purse at me and I jumped out of the way.

"Hey, it's better than your ratty old Rainbow Brite pajamas," she growled, taking another half-hearted swing at me.

"Fair enough. Get your ass out of here and go find your man. Then get back here."

"You got it." She flashed me a small grin before booking it out the door. I couldn't help but smile a little again as it slammed behind her.

Suddenly, though, I was tired. So damn tired. I just wanted to sleep and sleep and pretend the entire night had never happened. I took enough time to stuff the bag holding our clothes under the sink before stumbling into bed and dragging the covers up, ignoring the fact that I was still clad in just my panties and a bra.

I CAME BLURRILY AWAKE WHEN THE MATTRESS DIPPED AND A warm arm slipped around me from behind. "How did you get in?"

"Your landlord doesn't seem to take security very seriously," David murmured against my hair. "I could have broken in blindfolded with a hand behind my back."

I snuggled tightly against him, reveling in his embrace, before I forced myself back to reality. "What's the lowdown?"

He sighed softly and pulled me closer. "Jackson Piedmont is in the hospital, in stable condition. Nasty bash on the head, but he'll be all right. He was just starting to come around when you left. Lisa and Atanasov are dead. The FBI seems to be okay with the story that I alone shot him, not that they care either way. It would be enough of an embarrassment for them if the whole story got out, especially with a senator's son in the crossfire. The whole thing's been classified, of course, since he was dancing around the city the whole time and never managed to get caught. They'll spin it as an armed robbery."

"And what about you?"

He pressed a gentle kiss to the back of my head before answering. "I'm on a plane back to London in two hours. They can't get rid of me fast enough."

Neither of us spoke for a long moment, I simply wove my fingers between his and clasped them against my chest, he settled his chin on top of my head. For a long time, we were both silent, and it was easy to slip back into the past, to remember how comfortable and easy our relationship had been. "David…"

"Come with me, Viv," he said quietly. "Even if not for keeps, come back with me for a bit. Just being with you, being around you, it makes me realize how much I need you next to me."

I squeezed my eyes shut, forcing back tears that I tried to never let him see. "I doubt that would go over well."

He cursed quietly. "Who gives a damn what *they* think? The CIA has already written you off and I…"

"You still have a career," I reminded him, twisting in his arms until we were face-to-face. "One that my presence would ruin."

He clenched his jaw. "When are you going to stop thinking of every bloody person on this planet before yourself, Vivian Carmichael? Can't you just let *me* worry about me, and you worry about yourself, and the rest of the world can fuck off?"

"I would give," I said slowly, "Anything in the world if it were that easy. But it's not, and you know it. I'd never forgive myself if I did anything to hurt you."

"You're hurting me now," he said, speaking with quiet deliberation.

"That's not what I mean and you know it. David…" I took a deep breath. "I love you in a way that I'll never love anyone else. I trust you with my life. But *right now*, I can't be *with* you. I would be constantly looking over my shoulder and wondering if my very presence had put you in harm's way, or even just got you into trouble. I would never be able to *stop* thinking that way. Not yet."

"Vivian…" he started, before pulling me so tightly against him that I almost couldn't breathe. "Don't, just don't." He hesitated again. "Like you said, I love you in a way I'll never love anyone else. And I'll be waiting for you to change your mind. We could still run off to the ends of the earth like we'd planned, eh?"

I smiled. "I'll keep that in mind."

"And don't do anything to give me a heart attack like this again, all right?"

I couldn't help it, I chuckled against his chest. "I can't promise that."

"Do your best then," he growled, just before reaching down and tipping my chin up, just as he had the night before. "Don't be offing yourself anytime soon, Carmichael. *Ty nuzhna mnye*, my world is much more interesting with you in it."

"That I can *try* to promise."

He smiled after a moment before pressing his lips hard against my forehead. "Then I'm off, lest I miss my flight and send the FBI into fits. And think about what I said... if you ever get tired of Savannah, there will always a place for you with me in London, or wherever we decide to go."

"Thank you, David. *Ya tebya lyublyu.*"

"*Ya tozhe tebya lyublyu.*" He kissed my lips gently before sliding out of the bed and leaving so quietly that I never even heard the front door click shut behind him.

16

PARKER

The second I was in my car and the silence surrounded me, memories from the night finally started sinking in. While in the heat of the moment, there wasn't time to think about what I'd witnessed or the things I'd done. Everything had happened in the blink of an eye, adrenaline pumping so thickly through my veins that there was no way I could process watching the life fade out of Lisa Piedmont's eyes, or the bullet that I fired with a trigger that was way too easy for me to pull. Doing so had felt so natural to me that now, after finally stopping to think, it terrified me to no end.

I sat there for a long moment, fingers curled around the steering wheel, shaking in their loose grip. My eyes fell closed as I forced myself to run over every single event that took place inside the Piedmont home. Jack, blood oozing from his head wound and soaking into the carpet. Lisa, terrified and raccoon-eyed as she begged for a life that she'd soon have taken away from her. And Angel, the biggest puzzle piece in this whole messed up situation that we had no idea we were a part of.

Even with the knowledge that my bullet wasn't the one

that had effectively killed him, I still thought that I should be more distraught over contributing to the end of a human life, but I didn't feel that way at all. Deep down I hoped that I was still in shock, or just completely unable to process everything so soon after it had happened. There was no arguing that he was a terrible person, but he was still a human being. Why didn't I feel more remorse? All I could tell myself was that we had taken him out to stop a series of events that could have been catastrophic. We had ended his life so his wrongdoings could never affect an innocent person again. To me that had been enough of a justification, so as I'd stared in shock at his lifeless form in the Piedmonts' living room, an eerie numbness had already settled over me.

As far as I was concerned, Angel Atanasov had made his bed and lain in it a long time ago.

I suddenly realized that I'd been sitting in the car for quite a long time, and I didn't want Vivian to worry about me more than she already was. I knew we had plenty of talking to do. I could only assume that she had witnessed a number of casualties in her day, but it was easy to see that this night had affected her as well, regardless of her past. This was something we'd have to process together. I knew David's absence would take its toll on her as well, no matter how tough she tried to come off; spending this time with him would be hard for her to get over.

I pulled out of the parking lot and turned on some speed metal. It sounded ridiculous, but when I was pumped up like this, I needed the fast-paced music to help calm me down and bring me back to earth. It had been one of the craziest nights of my life, but before that, it had been one of the sweetest, most loving ones.

Carter.

I needed to push all the other bullshit out of my head and focus solely on him. He was leaving in a matter of hours, I still had no idea what we even were, he was probably pissed at me for making up floral emergencies all the time, and I didn't know what I was going to do to fix it.

Whoa. Deep breaths, Parker.

It was pushing four in the morning by the time I pulled into the hotel's parking garage. I took the walk to his room slowly, anxious about not knowing what would be waiting for me when I got there. Would Carter be mad at me to the point where he was glad to be going back home? Was he even still at the hotel? Maybe he thought spending the night in a stuffy airport terminal would be an upgrade from possibly running into me again.

The hotel lobby was empty, apart from a few well-dressed businessmen stumbling drunkenly to their rooms. I looked down at my Strawberry Shortcake tee and suddenly felt very out of place. Oh well. If I was going to have my heart broken, I was at least going to be comfortable in the process.

I took calculated breaths as the elevator doors opened to Carter's floor, and I watched my feet as I walked step by step to his hotel room. Once I was there, I hesitated for what felt like forever. Now what? Did I knock? Call him and beg him to open the door? Break and enter? I had a complex set of mini tools in my purse, so I knew it wouldn't take me long to pop open the mechanism on the door and get that little light flipped to green. But that might not be the best approach when I was already on thin ice with Carter. After a long deep breath, I lifted my closed fist and knocked weakly on the door.

It took him a long time to answer, and my stomach twisted viciously while I waited for him to open the door. When it finally parted enough for me to see his face, I felt even more terrible. He had dark circles under his eyes, and his hair was a total mess.

He watched me for a moment before opening the door

wider and nodding his head for me to come in. The room was dark, the only light was shining through from the partly opened bathroom door. Carter had his suitcase on the bed, and it looked like he was almost done packing.

I sat down tentatively next to the open suitcase and folded my hands in my lap. The silence was thick between us, but this time it wasn't from sexual tension. "Your flight leaves at eight-thirty?" My voice barely registered in the silent room, it was so weak.

I hated feeling this helpless.

He nodded, folding up one last shirt and flipping the lid of the suitcase down. "I wasn't sure if you were coming back. I didn't know if I should hang around or not."

"I told you I was coming back," I murmured to the floor.

After a moment of silence, he crouched down in front of me, placing a finger beneath my chin until our eyes met. His expression was soft as he stared at me. He looked like a wounded puppy that I had kicked and, before I could process what was happening, I'd broken down into wracking, breath-stealing sobs.

"Park, hey…" He pushed the suitcase off the bed and it landed with a loud thud, sending his perfectly folded clothes spilling out onto the floor. He wrapped me up unbelievably tight in his arms, lying on the bed with me as I wept for so many different reasons. It wasn't just the fact that I had lied to Carter, but there was also the haunting image of Lisa's throat torn open, blood pouring out in waves, the inside of her neck visible to me… the scene was just so unbelievably gory, and it was one that I couldn't shake. She didn't deserve to die, and that was something that would tear me apart for what I was sure would be a very long time.

To top it all off, I was probably going to lose Carter over something I could have confessed to him at any time during our almost two weeks together. It wasn't like I was a spy or something. Private investigators were everywhere, why did I treat it like such an unholy secret?

Somehow we had migrated farther up onto the bed until my head was on the soft pillows and Carter was leaning over me, brushing tears off my cheeks with his fingertips. "I'm so sorry," I whispered, pulling him down and hugging him as tight as my arms would squeeze; his body weight pushing into me was the only thing I needed in that moment.

There was so much we needed to talk about, but more than anything I just wanted to feel him, to know that this connection between us was still there and just as strong, regardless of what I'd been keeping from him.

He lifted up a bit, looking into my eyes as his fingers brushed the hair away from my forehead. I ran my hand along his cheek, letting it slide down and around his bicep. "Please," I choked out, two tears rolling down my already damp face.

Please, just understand... right now I can't form words, but all I need is you.

He looked at me with a myriad of emotions shadowing his eyes before leaning down to place a long, soft kiss on my forehead. He balanced on one arm above me and I swore his eyes were shining wet.

"I love you, Parker."

Every part of me trembled as he lifted a hand to the back of his shirt and pulled it off his body in one movement.

My God, I love you too.

IT WAS ALMOST SIX IN THE MORNING WHEN OUR BODIES finally separated, Carter taking one of my hands and dragging me out of bed and toward the bathroom. It was the first time I'd ever showered with another person, and I was somewhat in awe as he washed me slowly, his eyes roaming all over my body like he had never seen anything more beautiful.

"I love you too," I finally whispered, hugging him until my arms were shaking.

Hey, better late than never.

SEVEN A.M., AND CARTER AND I WERE SITTING ON A PARK bench across the street from his hotel. The concierge was keeping his luggage safe, and he had canceled his ride to the airport so that I could take him instead.

I wasn't letting him out of my sight until I absolutely had to.

There was a bit of a chill in the air, even though it would be humid in no time once the sun rose higher in the sky. Carter slid his light jacket over my shoulders and I leaned into him, holding my coffee in two hands and taking a long sip.

I didn't even know why I was stalling.

"So are you married or something?"

I huffed out a laugh, turning to look at Carter. "Nope, not at all."

"Are you a convicted felon? America's most wanted? Come on, Parker, you're killing me." His lips were turned up into a small grin, but I could still see the hurt in his eyes.

I set my coffee on the bench next to me and took his hand in both of mine. "No," I shook my head. "It's really not even that big of a deal, I don't know why I waited this long to tell you. My biggest crime is keeping this from you when there was really no need to."

He looked at me expectantly, and I took a deep breath.

"Pistils is sort of our cover business. I mean, it's an honest and true flower shop, but Vivian and I have a little side business that not many people know about. We're private investigators."

His eyes narrowed a bit, like he was trying to figure out exactly what that meant. "Okay, so what kinds of things do you investigate?"

I shrugged my shoulders. "Mostly cheating spouses, but once in a while we'll get something like identity theft, crooked employees, even a few stalker cases."

"Is it dangerous?" His eyebrows pulled together, and I could see the concern on his face.

"There's always the potential," I admitted, trying not to think about the events from the night before. "But I know how to take care of myself and if push comes to shove, I'm one hell of a shot."

Carter chuckled, shaking his head. "That is ridiculously hot, Park, but also very scary for me. You have to understand that."

"I get it, I really do. But Carter, I love it so much. Private investigation is a huge part of who I am, and it always will be."

"Well, I would never stand in the way of what you love to do." He stared out at the street ahead of us. "I just don't understand why you made up so many excuses to get away. Why didn't you want me to know the truth?"

"It's not that I didn't want you to know," I countered, staring at his profile. "But it's not like Vivian and I have taken out an ad on a billboard. We are extremely exclusive, as in someone has to know someone who knows us in order to even be considered as a client. We keep this on the down-low because we want those clients to understand that we are nothing but discreet. We take it really seriously."

"So every floral emergency you've had since I've known you, they've all been related to this?"

I nodded. "We've been working a huge case, but it's safe to say that's over with now. Of course, it figures I'll have plenty of free time now that you'll be going home."

"Shh, don't talk about that just yet," he murmured, kissing my temple. "I just want you to be able to trust me enough to tell me these things. I want to know everything about you, Park."

"I'm sorry I didn't tell you sooner. There was truly no reason not to, other than the fact that our time together has been a whirlwind, and I chose to spend it getting to know you rather than explaining my super-secret identity."

"I just can't understand what could have been so important that you had to leave me right after we were together last night. Parker, that meant so much to me, and for you to just leave afterwards like it was nothing…"

I grabbed his hand forcefully. "Carter, you can't think of it like that. I wouldn't have gone unless I absolutely had to. There was nowhere I would have rather been than naked and in bed with you, loving *you*. But this is my job, this is my life. And if I'm needed for a case, I have to be there. Please tell me you understand."

Carter sighed. "I can promise you that I'll try to wrap my head around everything you've told me. It's definitely not worth losing you over, that's for sure."

I gave him a small smile. "We've got time to figure these things out."

He nodded his agreement, quiet for a moment before playfully bumping his shoulder with mine. "Does this mean I can't tell anyone that my girlfriend is some bad ass PI chick?"

My heart started beating a little faster at the "G" word. "Well, I don't know, who's your girlfriend?"

He held a hand over his heart and feigned a wounded look. "Don't do me like that, Park."

"How do you want me to do you then?"

He growled playfully, hooking an arm around my shoulders. "Don't start with me when we're in public like this, woman. But really though, do you need me to ask? Because I'll do it. I'll shout it loud enough to make every person on this street turn their head." He stood up, cupped his hands around his mouth and shouted, "PARKER, WILL YOU BE MY GIRLFRIEND?!"

True to his word, the few people around us looked at him like he was insane, and I felt my face heat as I put my hand to my forehead. "Oh my God," I groaned, laughing softly.

There was only one thing left to do, so with a sigh I stood on top of the park bench and screamed at the top of my lungs "HELL YES CONLIN, CARTER CONLIN! HELL YES!"

He laughed like a little boy and lifted me down from the bench, holding me against him as he beamed. "Thank you for telling me about the PI thing. And thank you for being crazy with me. And for being so goddamn beautiful. And for agreeing to be mine."

My only reply was to kiss him until my lips ached.

THE RIDE TO THE AIRPORT WAS QUIET AS REALITY STARTED sinking in. Carter drove my car, and I hung halfway over the center console, getting as close to him as I could in what little time we had left.

I felt so much better now that everything had been laid out on the table, but Carter leaving had set forth a whole new fear in me. Even though we were obviously crazy about each other, it didn't change the fact that we'd only known one another for a short amount of time. What would happen when he went back to his reality to, and I went back to mine? Would our feelings still remain as strong?

I had no idea what to expect, but who did when it came to those four stupid ass letters, L-O-V-E?

Carter parked in the short-term parking area and turned off the engine, dropping the keys into my hand with a sigh. Wordlessly we got out, and I felt my mouth morph into a pout of epic proportions. This really freaking sucked.

Somehow Carter managed to hold my hand securely in his while juggling his checked bag, carry-on and personal item, none of which he would let me help with. I held onto it like a lifeline, and I couldn't believe we were at the very moment I'd been dreading since practically the first time I'd met him. His presence in my life had been short-lived to date, but the impact he'd made in such a little amount of time proved that whatever hardships we would experience by doing this long-distance thing, they'd all be worth it. He was just so beyond worth it.

We walked through the busy entrance of the airport, Carter looking back at me every chance he got, like he was worried the next time he turned around I would be gone. I felt his desperation, the panic rising up with every step we took. My heart was beating faster, my stomach twisting, flames of anxiety licking at my skin as the crowd began closing in on me. By the time we reached the row of chairs lining the wall in front of his airline's check-in point, I was struggling to catch my breath.

I plopped down heavily into the plastic chair, Carter coming down to kneel in front of me as he pushed the hair out of my eyes. "Hey, I know," he whispered, snaking a hand beneath my hair and holding me against him with his palm against the back of my neck.

We didn't move for a long time, cheek to cheek as my breathing calmed and the sweet scent of his cologne consumed me. He was mine. He loved me. We were going to make it work. I was no longer scared of being burned by this man; I was simply scared to be without him.

Carter turned his head to kiss my cheek before glancing down at his watch. "This kills me, Park, but I have to get going."

I nodded, unable to do anything about the tears that were already welling up in my eyes. We both stood, and I fidgeted with the hem of my t-shirt, not quite ready to look him in the eyes. He mirrored my action, squeezing the fabric with his thumb and forefinger and sliding it back and forth between them.

I suddenly couldn't take it anymore.

With a soft cry I dove into his arms, holding him with everything I had left in me, my face buried in his neck as he hoisted me up until my legs were wrapped around him. We stayed that way, not caring how many people were around us or what they were thinking of our public display of affection. At this point, it was all we had left. Our very final moment before all that lay ahead of us were miles of uncertainty.

He sighed deeply before sliding me down his body and planting me on my feet. We still held onto each other tightly, our eye contact unwavering as we both accepted the fact that this was it until who knew when. "I never..." He stopped and swallowed thickly before continuing. "I had no intention of coming here and falling in love with you, Parker. I had no idea things would turn out like this."

The pain in his voice made my stomach drop. "I hope it was a pleasant surprise, at least."

His expression was so serious it was like he was trying to push his words right into me. "You are the most pleasant surprise of my entire life, Parker Chase."

I stood on my tiptoes and kissed him as tears rolled down my face, doing everything in my power to memorize his taste, his smell, his very presence. Before I could speak, he was talking again, this time a little more frantic. "Listen, Park. I've got a lot of stuff going on right now, a lot of change I'm not quite ready to come to terms with. I've got a dad who is a complete piece of shit, I've got a sick mother who means the world to me, I've got a life hundreds of miles away from the girl who owns every bit of my fucking heart but I promise, regardless of all that... I'm so unbelievably far from perfect, but I'm going to do my best for you, okay? I'm going to do everything in my power to prove to you every day just how in love with you I am. And know that every single thing I do, every word I give you is paved with the best of intentions, all right? You just mean so much to me, and I'm so goddamn sorry I have to go..."

I was sobbing now, my tears soaking into his sleeve as his arms wrapped around me so securely it ached. All I could do was nod, my hands pulling at the fabric of his shirt and struggling to get him impossibly closer.

He'd have to run to make his flight at this point and I knew it, so with the taste of salt from the tears on my lips, I kissed him until I knew I couldn't any longer, and pushed him away until there was an ample amount of space between us. "I love you so much. And everything's going to be all right, I know it will. You have to go now, Carter. You have to, or I'll never let you."

He nodded, closing his eyes as he slowly leaned forward to place a soft kiss on my forehead. "I'll call you when I land. And then we can make some plans for you to come visit me. How's tomorrow sound?"

I laughed, wiping my tears away with the back of my hand. "Not soon enough, to be honest."

"I don't think it'll ever be enough when it comes to you, Park." His smile faded, his face turning serious as he continued. "Thank you for the best two weeks I've ever had. I sincerely mean it, you have made my life so much brighter just by existing."

I smiled, holding his eye contact as he took a step back and our fingers disconnected. He confessed his love one more time, pressed his fingers to his lips, and turned to walk away.

I could have stayed and watched him until he passed through security, but I couldn't justify torturing myself even further, so the second he turned, I was headed toward the door. Somehow I managed to hold back my gasping sobs until I was in the safety of my car, and I sat there and cried until a security guard started knocking on my window.

"Ugh, what?" I yelled the third time I heard his insistent knock-knock-knock. "Can't you see I'm crying, dude?"

He backed off as I started my car, and I suddenly felt really bad because he was probably just checking to make sure I was okay.

Great, another reason to cry—guilt over being a bitch to an airport security guard.

I peeled out of the parking deck with half-dried tears on my cheeks and an ache in my heart. I jabbed at my iPod with a little too much force until I found what I wanted and unabashedly listened to "Take My Breath Away" on repeat.

Because I could, dammit.

I decided to go past Gran's house because I had no idea where Muriel lived, and my phone had been dead for hours now. I was surprised to see her car in the driveway when I pulled up, but I was happy she was there. I still had to at least somewhat catch her up on what happened, but at this point I was so exhausted I could barely keep my eyes open. I really hadn't slept all night and crying so much had the tendency to wear a person out.

Not to mention pole vaulting over rich people's hedges. Minus the pole.

Before I could knock, Gran had the door thrown open, squeezing me tight and ushering me inside. Tears welled in my eyes again as her sweet scent came over me.

Hugging her was the epitome of home, and I was crying again before I knew it.

She led me to the couch and sat down, gesturing for me to lie down with my head in her lap. Her soft fingers ran slowly through my hair, and she hummed gently to me until I made it through round three of my sob-fest.

"I've never felt so many conflicting emotions in my life, Gran."

"Oh, sweetheart," she groaned, picking up my hand and kissing it. "I hate to see you this way."

I sat up quickly and looked at her. "Hey, what are you doing home anyway?"

She suddenly turned white, like she'd seen a ghost pass right in front of her. "This morning Muriel and I were having coffee, watching the news when a breaking story interrupted. Unconfirmed shooting at the son of Senator Piedmont's home, it said. They were the only words on the screen; no other details were given because apparently they had none. When your phone went straight to voicemail, I immediately thought the worst. Since I couldn't get ahold of you, I wanted to make sure I was here in case you stopped by."

"Oh my God, Gran, I am so sorry!" I hugged her, feeling unbelievably terrible that I'd let my phone die amongst all the drama. It should have been priority number one to keep an open line of communication with my grandmother and Vivian when shit like this was going down. I'd never make that mistake again.

"It's all right, sweet pea. Thankfully I got ahold of Vivian right away, and even though I woke her up from a deep sleep, I couldn't bring myself to care because it meant my girls were safe." Gran started crying, and I just couldn't take it.

"I'm sorry. I'm so sorry." It was all I could really say, and nothing had ever been truer.

We held each other until we both calmed down, my head on her shoulder as we settled back into the couch. "It's been a long night, Gran."

"Can you tell me what happened?" she asked.

"V didn't tell you?"

She shook her head. "The poor dear sounded absolutely delirious from a lack of sleep. As soon as I knew you were both safe, I let her be."

"Well, in a nutshell… you know the guy we'd caught Lisa Piedmont with? Well, that was Angel. Angel was not a therapist, nor was he female. He was her lover, and a mobster from Bulgaria on a mission to take out Senator Piedmont."

"What?" Gran asked in disbelief.

"I know. He was using Lisa as his in to get closer to the senator. Anyway, Angel ended up killing Lisa in a fit of rage, and Angel got taken out by the police."

I'd left it at that. There was no reason for Gran to know we were there, or what part we had played in the entire situation. Hell, she didn't even know for sure that Vivian had been in the CIA, although I knew that's what she'd suspected.

Gran and I talked about the tragedy a little longer before the conversation switched to Carter. I obviously didn't elaborate on the majority of our evening together, but I did tell her that we were official and he'd dropped the L-bomb. Of course she was thrilled. "He's a keeper, sweetheart. I just know he is."

"I think so too, Gran. It's just, with everything that happened with the Piedmonts and then Carter going back to Cleveland, I have never felt so many different emotions at once and I'm just so tired."

She kissed my forehead and stood up, tucking a decorative pillow beneath my head and covering me with the afghan she pulled from the back of the couch. "I'm going to make you some chamomile tea, and then you are going to sleep until you can't sleep anymore."

I nodded, and before she could even put the kettle on the burner, I was out like a light.

I WOKE TO THE SOUND OF GRAN'S SWEET VOICE.

"Well, you need to talk to her about keeping her phone charged, honey. She gave me just as big of a scare when I tried getting ahold of her earlier."

I immediately knew she was talking to V.

"Tell her I'll call her later, or I'll be home in a little while. Or whatever..." I mumbled into the pillow, already falling back asleep as I wiped the half-dried drool off my face.

I was so damn charming sometimes.

BY THE TIME I GOT BACK TO THE APARTMENT, THE SUN WAS about to set.

Vivian stood to greet me, and I held up a hand. "Save your lecture about the phone, V. I need comfy pants and I need this bra off of my body immediately, okay?"

She narrowed her eyes at me but nodded, and I wrapped her up in a quick hug. "Find the most eightiesest movie in existence, and order the biggest pizza known to man, because lord knows we need it."

"I'm on it, P. And eightiesest isn't a word!" she called after me.

I didn't care. I needed relaxation, and I needed it fast.

Before doing anything else, I made quick work of plugging in my cell phone, three texts from Carter popping up as soon as it was powered on.

I made it home, so why does it feel so empty here?

You're not answering...should I be worried?

Okay, now I'm just acting like a creeper. Text me later, Park. Love you.

I typed out a quick response, letting him know that my phone had died and I passed out shortly after dropping him off. I reassured him that his home wouldn't feel empty once I was there to visit. That he shouldn't be worried, I was just majorly flaky that day. That I would never think he's a creeper, and I loved, loved, loooooooved him too. And that Vivian and I were having a movie night and I would call him tomorrow.

By the time I ditched my bra and panties in exchange for PJ pants and a tank top, *The Breakfast Club* was already on the TV. I plopped down next to Vivian and leaned against her, reaching into the bowl of popcorn on her lap.

I knew that we'd have to talk about everything that had happened, and soon. But for now, snuggling with the person I was closest to and losing myself in a classic movie was the best medicine I could take.

For just a little while, I needed to feel safe, and this was the only way I could achieve it.

17

VIVIAN

It was nine-thirty-two a.m., and I supposed I may as well face the fact that I wasn't going back to sleep.

I'd dozed a little after David left, but Gran called just after nine, in a state of barely controlled panic. It seemed that the media had caught wind of the events from the night before: an attack on a U.S. senator's family. Add that to the fact that a neighbor had shot some blurry cell-phone video of Jack being put into an ambulance, and later the medical examiner loading two body bags into their van... it was breaking news on CNN.

After I reassured Gran that Parker would probably be stopping by to see her at some point, she calmed down enough to urge me to drink some chamomile tea and go back to sleep. I was wide-awake now though, my mind on repeat, going over and over the events of the night before. Old habits died hard; I had to make sure that Parker and I hadn't left even the slightest clue that we'd been involved. I was sure with David's high-security clearance he would have known if the FBI was zeroing in on us, but then again, all the major agencies knew about David and me.

Work. Shower first, then work. That was exactly what I needed. Pistils was closed on Sundays, but I could go down there and do a little housecleaning. Shine the windows and dust the baseboards and scrub the floor with a toothbrush if I had to.

Forty-five minutes later found me sliding onto a stool behind the counter of our shop. I had a feeling that there might be an all-night chick-flick movie marathon in our future, so I idly clicked into the computer, checking to see how many orders had come in since closing yesterday. If Parker and I were going to be half-asleep at work the next morning, it wouldn't hurt to have some of the orders printed out and ready to fill.

A couple of birthday floral arrangements... a condolences bouquet... and a get well soon for...

Deliver To: *Jackson Piedmont, Mercy General, Room 3224*
From: *Vivian Carmichael*
Notes: *Get Well Soon*

I froze. I knew there was no way in hell that Parker or Gran would pull something like this as a prank. It would never even cross David's mind. So either I was hallucinating, or someone with a *very* sick sense of humor was messing with me or sending a message. Hell, they could be watching me that very second.

Moving slowly, I slipped into the back room where Parker and I kept my old Mossberg. A shotgun wasn't the most elegant of weapons, but it was more than enough to convince any would-be robbers that they'd picked the wrong store to mess with. A quick scroll through the contacts on my phone, and then ringing.

"Mercy General, how may I direct your call, please?"

"Hello, this is Pistils Flower Shop, calling to confirm on a patient before delivering an arrangement?" It was standard for us to call the hospitals in advance, just in case the recipient had been discharged or died before we could arrive with their Get Well Soon flowers.

"Of course, name and room number, please?"

"Room 3224, Piedmont."

Rapid typing on the other end. "Ahh, yes. That patient does require private security clearance. Your name, please?"

No surprise there. "Vivian Carmichael."

More tapping away on a keyboard. "You are on the list for clearance, but please make sure you bring a photo ID."

I thanked her and then disconnected the call, more confused than before. The security protocol wasn't surprising, but why had my name been added? And by whom? Well, as the old saying went: there was only one way to find out.

Parker and Gran kept one or two of the most popular arrangements fresh on hand, for people who came in at the last moment. I grabbed the smaller of the two Get Well Soon arrangements, changed into an extra Pistils polo, and locked my .45 in the safe we had in the back room. Guns weren't allowed at Mercy General, and if I was walking into a set-up, I didn't even want to take a chance on leaving it in the van.

As I tucked the flowers safely into the back and then climbed into the driver's seat, I tried calling Parker. Straight to voicemail. Gran was next, and she informed me that Parker was zonked out on her couch, dead cell phone at her side.

"Of all the times for her to forget..."

"Well, you need to talk to her about keeping her phone charged, honey. She gave me just as big of a scare when I tried getting ahold of her earlier."

I growled to myself. Well, so far I didn't appear to be in immediate danger, and Gran had gone through enough over the past twelve hours without me adding to it. "Tell her I'll be home later, okay? Love you, Gran!"

Absolutely nothing seemed unusual when I arrived at the

hospital, which only served to make me more uneasy. I found my way quickly to Jack's room, which was, as I'd suspected, guarded by a beefy dude in a dark suit. Private guard, of course, there was no way the senator was going to trust his son to hospital security. He gave me an impassive look as I approached.

"Hi, I'm Vivian Carmichael from Pistils Flower Shop. Delivery for Jack Piedmont."

He nodded slowly. "Can I see your ID, please? And I'll need to search the flowers."

"Search the... oh for God's sake," I sputtered. I fished out my ID as the guard yanked all the cheerful flowers out of the bowl, poking around inside to ensure I hadn't hidden a bomb in the flower foam. When he was satisfied, he handed the bowl and the flowers back to me separately before snatching my ID.

Jerk.

He finally grunted before holding out the small piece of plastic out to me, and I managed to grab it between two fingers. "You can go on in."

"Gee, thanks." I couldn't keep the sarcastic note from my voice as he opened the door for me and I walked in, water from the flowers dripping down over my shirt.

It was a private room, and Jack Piedmont was sitting up in bed, looking roughed-up but otherwise none the worse for wear. "Hey Vivian," he cleared his throat. "I thought you were a florist? Those flowers look like shit."

That was it, I had officially entered *The Twilight Zone*. "They'd look a lot better if that big goon hadn't torn the arrangement apart. We don't even deliver on Sundays, so I don't know why..." I stopped, and my eyes narrowed. "Did you order these?"

Jack lifted his smartphone and waved it slightly at me. "I like your app."

"You ordered yourself flowers. I think I've just about heard it all now." I plunked the bowl down on his bedside table, jamming the flowers back in, not even making an attempt to replicate the beautiful bouquet it had been just minutes before.

"Aren't you curious why?"

"What do you think?"

He shut his eyes and took a long, deep breath. "I wanted to talk to you."

"Jack, you're in the hospital. You still have a bandage on your head. I think whatever it is can..."

"Why were you there?" he interrupted, his eyes reopening slowly and focusing directly on mine. All the sand in the Sahara had nothing on my throat just then.

"Umm, what?"

"I saw you, there at the house." He shook his head. "I heard your voice, and just as I was waking up, I saw you."

Deny deny deny. "Jack, I honestly don't know what you're talking about."

"Vivian, I came home to find some strange man in my home, before he cracked me in the head. The next thing I know, that man and my wife are dead, and you're walking out the door. I don't know you very well, but something tells me you didn't kill either of them, so you want to explain?"

Shit. I took a deep breath and sat down in the chair next to his bed. "Where do you want me to start?"

"The beginning, obviously. Let me tell you what I know. I knew Lisa was cheating on me. My friend that I told you about, Rhiannon Simons, she was doing some undercover work to get proof, and she found it. I was going to file for divorce, but when I got home last night..." He winced, touching his fingertips to the bandage on his temple. "There she was with her boyfriend. Who apparently whacked me on the head, killed Lisa, and was going to kill me. She didn't..."

Jack stopped again for a long moment. "She didn't deserve that. No matter how bad our relationship had gotten, I would never have wished that on her. I would have done anything to have protected her from it."

"I know," I said softly, the memory of Lisa's bloody throat and shocked eyes still fresh in my mind. "No one deserves something like that."

"So where do you come in, Vivian? I've got plenty of time to listen, they're insisting on keeping me overnight for observation."

I made myself count to ten, organizing my thoughts, before I answered. "Pistils isn't just a florist shop. Parker and I also run our own private investigation business. Lisa hired *us* to get evidence that *you* were cheating."

His tired green eyes were disbelieving. "The flower shop is a *cover?*"

"Yes, well… no, it's a legitimate business. We just happen to have another, less well-known legitimate licensed business too, P&V, Inc."

"Ahh. This is starting to make a little more sense now. Lisa wanted to catch me cheating so she could get more money if we divorced, thanks to that little infidelity clause in our prenup. Problem is that I've never cheated on her. Did she want you to invent an imaginary girlfriend or something?"

"I don't know," I admitted honestly. "For a minute, we thought Rhiannon was your girlfriend."

Jack groaned, his hand going to his head again. "Hardly. Rhiannon and I are friends, just as I told you."

"Are you all right? Do you need a nurse?"

"No," he said faintly. "I just want the rest of the story. So I know that was Lisa's boyfriend, but how in the hell did the FBI just so happen to arrive in time to shoot him? At the same time you were there, no less."

I shrugged. "Parker and I were following you. Mr. FBI wouldn't tell us anything about the dead man, just that it was a government matter and that we were civilians and needed to get the hell out of there. I can only guess he must have been a really bad guy."

"What was his name?"

Keep it simple, stupid. "I don't know."

"I can't believe Rhiannon didn't catch on to you two tailing me."

I felt a ridiculous urge to defend my fellow private investigator, semi-inept though she might be. "Insurance fraud and the kind of work we do are two very different worlds, Jack. Rhiannon may have been in a bit over her head."

"I should have hired you two," he murmured, his eyelids beginning to droop again.

"Jack, I should really go, you need your rest."

"Pistils. I should have known. What kind of gun do you shoot, Vivian?"

"A .45 Bersa." No point in lying, I was registered and legal.

"Do you have it with you?"

"Jesus, no, not in a senator's son's hospital room. You want me to end up in jail?"

"No." He let out a long sigh. "God, this is like a nightmare I can't wake up from."

Just then, the door swung open, revealing the haggard faces of Senator Piedmont and his wife. I hopped to my feet immediately, feeling the need to get the hell out of there before I had to explain my presence to them as well.

"Jack, why aren't you resting?" His mother's voice was hoarse.

"I have been, Mom, don't worry so much. Vivian, I'll be calling you at some point this week. Thanks for the flowers."

I saw his mother eyeing the wrecked floral arrangement as I hurried out the door.

AS SOON AS THE FINAL SHOT OF JUDD NELSON FIST-PUMPING the air froze on our television screen, Parker yawned and shook the empty popcorn bowl. "You pick the next movie."

I'd thought about telling my best friend everything from the moment she walked in the door, but she had rolled in around sundown, looking like she'd cried a year's worth of tears in one day. So I kept my mouth shut, ordered some pizza, made some popcorn, and let her unwind from the past twenty-four hours. Now it was time to make the point I'd been putting off all evening, though.

"I pick *GI Jane*, enough of the eighties. I want me some Viggo Mortenson. But anyway, aren't you even going to ask what *I* did all day?"

Parker tugged her hair back up into a messy ponytail. "Ummm, I'm guessing David came over, and you rolled around in the sheets making sweet sweet monkey love for old time's sake?"

I rolled my eyes. "Just because you've had sex on the brain doesn't mean I do at the moment. Yes, David did stop by, but he's probably back in London by now. No, I delivered some flowers."

"Huh?" Parker tilted her head. "We don't do deliveries on Sundays. We aren't even *open* on Sundays."

"That's what I thought too! But then I happened to go by the shop, where I discovered that Jack Piedmont had ordered himself the *cutest* little bouquet of flowers and wrote the *sweetest* get-well note to himself, so who was I to deny the poor man? He's still in the hospital, after all." I added in a mournful sniffle for good measure, and Parker's jaw dropped.

"Did you get whacked on the head last night too? What the..."

"And he just wanted to touch base, since apparently he saw me as we made our hasty exit last night, and was curious as to why I was running around his house with two dead bodies in the living room. Now did you want popcorn, sweets?"

"Why didn't you call me?" Parker shrieked, just before smacking me hard with a pillow.

"I did! But I couldn't get through because oh, maybe because a certain someone *didn't charge her cell phone."*

"I... that is... you could have..." she sputtered.

"I *did* call Gran, and I seem to remember hearing someone mumbling faintly in the background about calling me later. What if Gran wasn't there, and I had another *jinx* situation?"

Parker scowled, looking as pissed as an adorable blonde with pink tips in her hair could. "Okay, okay, I get the picture, lesson learned. Cut me some slack, I've had a rough day."

"We both have," I pointed out. "But I'm going for tough love here. And I'm also buying you *another* charger and just leaving it at Gran's."

She blew out an exasperated breath. "Fine. Now tell me everything."

I did, and she shook her head. "Jack's a smarter cookie than we gave him credit for. So anyway... no hot monkey lovin'?"

"With Jack? Geez Parker, he was in a hospital bed!"

She swatted my arm. "With David!"

"Nope, not this time."

"Hot monkey love back in the day?"

I couldn't help but laugh at her pleading face. "Yes, back in the day."

"You never talk about *back in the day*." Her frustration with my answers appeared to melt away, and she settled back against the couch, throwing her feet up into my lap. "I only hear about it in little snippets, or see flashbacks of it second-hand. I feel like," she slowed, and a strange look came over her face. "I feel like there's this whole life you lived, and I know nothing about it. Which is weird, because otherwise we know each other better than anyone in the world. I don't know, I just wish you would talk to me about it sometimes. Especially since David showed up out of nowhere and it's because of some random Bulgarians from your past."

"Fair enough," I sighed. I'd told Gran and Parker little-to-nothing about my time in the CIA. Parker had known I was in, of course, being that I always listed her as my next of kin. I was allowed to e-mail her and tell her harmless things that any innocent American "businesswoman" would write to a family member. But when it came to details, especially anything having to do with my real assignments, and then the fallout after my last, I'd locked all that away and melted the key down to cold gray metal. She was right, though; I had lived an entire life away from her, and she deserved to know at least part of it. "What do you want to know?"

"Umm, why don't you begin with the dead Bulgarian guy?"

"Angelus Velichkov Atanasov," I started slowly. "His father, Velichko Atanasov, ran practically half of the organized crime in Sofia, Bulgaria. It's not like the Italian mob stereotype, though. These days, the Bulgarian families hide behind legitimate international businesses. It makes pinning anything on them extremely difficult. My first assignment was in Sofia, and that's how I met David for the first time. He was, and still is, considered something of an expert on a lot of the organized crime in that area. His knowledge and contacts were invaluable. It was considered unofficial protocol to check in with him if your assignment was possibly going to involve the crime families. He just so happened to be in London when I met him."

"Ohh," Parker guessed, and I grinned faintly.

"Yeah, 'ohh' for sure. No, I won't give you details about the hot monkey love yet, but I will tell you it started on my last night in London. For obvious reasons, our paths crossed more than once after that due to work, then we started planning to see each other when we could. We ended up with some downtime together, actually, and spent a couple of weeks at his family's place up near Edinburgh. After I was in Ukraine, remember?"

"I remember you e-mailed me that you'd be a little late coming back, yeah. So the CIA was okay with you two being in a relationship or whatever?"

I shrugged. "It was a little more delicate than if he had actually been CIA instead of MI6, so we kept it on the downlow. The agency doesn't really give a damn about the case officers' sex lives, as long as you aren't sleeping with the locals for information. If you're discreet and it doesn't interfere with your job, you could pretty much screw anyone you wanted to. Including your coworkers; it's like one big incestuous family."

Parker made a face. "Yuck."

"Yeah, but when they're the only people you can really talk to, relationships are formed. It's inevitable. David and I joked at first that we had the ultimate friends with benefits relationship, but..." My throat closed up a little. "We became a lot more than that to each other."

"I could tell," she replied softly. "Last night, the way you two worked together, the way he looked at you."

I chuckled roughly. "As opposed to how he was looking at the dead guy on the floor?" Before she could answer, I plowed ahead with the worst of it. "On my last assignment, back in Bulgaria, my partner was a guy named Randy. That was his cover name anyway, none of us actually knew each other's real names, for security reasons. David was the only one who knew my real name, and even out in public he called me by my cover name.

"Anyway, Randy and I had been gathering more intel non-stop for two years on the Atanasov family. We'd gotten enough information back so that... let's just say those who needed it had enough to take Velichko Atanasov down. I don't want to give you details because, as condescending as it sounds, it's honestly just safer for you not to know. David came in to help out so that we'd have everything tight for when the action started."

"So you guys actually took down a Bulgarian mobster?"

"Nope." I squeezed her feet, still in my lap. "Believe about a tenth of what you see and hear about the CIA. We train for it, sure, but day-to-day it's nothing like being a super-spy, or James Bond, or any of those crazy television shows. It's a lot of lying, a lot of conning or bribing people into giving you information, and a lot of paperwork. It's also very, very lonely. We provide the intel and then let special ops do the cleaning up. But it worked. Velichko Atanasov and a lot of his associates were arrested, tried, and went to prison. The rest of the family scattered after that, and our friend Angel apparently took off for Chechnya. But right after the take-down..." I stopped and took a deep breath.

"All the big fish were in jail, and there was no word of anything weird coming down the wire. David and I decided to get out of town for the weekend, just up into the mountains, to relax. My boss was fine with it, then I told Randy, and he promised to keep an ear to the ground. The next evening David and I got the news that the British ambassador's car had been bombed in Sofia. With his family in it."

Parker gasped. "Oh my God, I remember that! It was right before you..." Her voice trailed off.

"Right before I came back," I finished bitterly. "His wife and two little girls, incinerated. Randy didn't want to take the fall for what turned into an international incident, so he rolled on me, said that I hadn't been taking my job seriously enough, that I'd been out running around with David any time he was in town. The White House was screaming for answers, so the CIA rolled on me. They were on me before I even knew what was going on and brought me back to Langley. They didn't dare touch David since he was British Intelligence, of course. They made it clear that I was the sacrificial lamb, and that I would take full responsibility for shirking my duty and not providing adequate intel that could have prevented such a tragedy. I was told to be thankful that they were classifying my so-called involvement, and that my name wouldn't be made public. There was never any irrefutable proof found that Velichko Atanasov was responsible for the bombing, but it was generally accepted that it was retaliation and public blame fell on him. The bastards apparently didn't even care whose ambassador they targeted, as long as they sent a message."

Tears were rolling down Parker's face now, her hand reaching over to grab mine. "Why couldn't David tell them that it wasn't your fault?"

"I told them I had no personal relationship with MI6 officer David Coburn, and that any interactions I had had with him were for strictly professional reasons, including providing cover and sharing intel." My voice was as devoid of emotion as it had been that day, in the Director's office. "My career was over, there was no reason both of us should go down in flames."

Parker stared at me. "I can't believe he'd be okay with you doing that."

I took a moment before responding. "He wasn't. He feels guilty about it."

"*Guilty?* I would sure as hell hope so!"

"No, it's not like that. He blames himself for not doing more to protect me, in more ways than one. This morning he asked me to come back to London with him."

She yanked her feet off my lap and scooted over until she could wrap both arms around me. "Would it make you happier, if you were there with him?"

I leaned my head against her shoulder, the pain of reliving the past making my entire body ache. "I *can't*, P. The CIA didn't just blame me and fire me, they *burned* me. That means nobody will touch me with a ten-foot pole, here or overseas. I'm not allowed to ever hold a government job again. They wouldn't lift my cover, so I'm not allowed to tell anyone what I was doing for all those years. But everyone *knows* what I said about David, so I can't go back to him now. His career, his reputation, I'd be like napalm for it. In the entire time since it happened, I'd only spoken to him three times, with that call two weeks ago being the last. And he was calling to warn me, even if he didn't know the details. If Angelus had recognized me any of the times we were tailing them, I'd probably be dead right now."

"Oh Viv," Parker moaned. "Why didn't you tell me any of this? Why have you been carrying it all by yourself for so long?"

I swallowed hard. "Sometimes sharing things like that doesn't help, it only spreads the hurt around. It's not that I don't trust you, I just didn't want you to know how bad things got. Especially since they're better now. I'm happy here in Savannah with you and Gran. David and I will always have each other in one way or another."

"You really love him, don't you?" she asked wonderingly. No surprise, since I'd never told her the full extent of what David and I had between us. Even now it was difficult to put into words.

"Yes. We love each other very much, but I loved him enough to push him away, and he loved me enough to let me go. Our relationship wasn't conventional, but it was built foremost on mutual trust and respect. It's hard to explain. I may never see him again, or we may end up together one day. We're willing to wait and see."

I could see Parker turning that over in her mind; she knew me well, but my best friend was a true romantic at heart and would want me to be the happiest I could be. She'd never push me on it, but I knew she would never understand why David and I couldn't find a way to be together, if we loved each other as much as I'd said.

"So what about Angel?" she asked finally, pointedly changing the subject. "What the hell was he doing here, going after a senator?"

"I guess we'll never know the facts or actual plan, but we have a pretty good guess at it. The senator is in charge of a congressional committee that is investigating human rights violations in Chechnya. Angelus had lived there since his father went to prison, so it stands to reason that he fell in with the Chechen mob. Eliminating the head of the committee would send a powerful message, at least in their mind."

Parker squinted. "He came halfway across the world, seduced a woman he didn't know or care about, all to possibly get a shot at a senator who's on a committee investigating crime in his adopted country? Doesn't that seem like a stretch? Killing one senator wouldn't stop anything, it would probably make things worse for them."

"You have to understand how extremists think and work. Their logic and American logic are worlds apart."

We were both quiet for a long time before Parker spoke again. "This is heavy."

"Very. You shot a guy less than twenty-four hours ago, P.

Don't try and play it off like it was nothing, because it's never easy, no matter how much they deserved it. Cops will tell you the same thing. You and I may not have fired the killing shots, and it may have been necessary, but it's not something you can shake off right away."

She nodded slowly. "I was still running on adrenaline earlier, I get that now. I mean, he was a bad guy, and he was aiming a gun at us. It was automatic, like self-defense, you know?"

"I definitely know."

"It wasn't my shot that killed him. I know that. I think what's sticking in my head more was seeing the blood, and the bodies. One second Lisa was alive, the next second she was dead on the couch. And Jack, and all the blood..." She shuddered.

I spoke carefully. "As of tonight, I've shot four people, and three of them died because of me. It was self-defense, and it was necessary at the time, but I've never forgotten a single one, and I never will. That's part of being human. And if you ever want to talk about it, I'm here for you. Trust me, seeing Jack on the floor rattled me more than I like to admit."

"Okay. Hey Viv?"

"Yup?"

"I don't think I can handle *GI Jane* right now. Can we watch *Sixteen Candles* instead? I need something nice and normal tonight."

I gave her one more hug before grabbing the popcorn bowl from where it had fallen on the floor. "John Hughes, coming up."

Yup, just our kind of normal.

EPILOGUE

S *ix weeks later*

"HI, YOU'VE REACHED PISTILS FLOWER SHOP! WE'RE SORRY THAT *we're unable to take your call at the moment, but if you're calling between nine to six, Monday through Thursday, or ten to eight, Friday and Saturday, just hold on the line and one of us will be with you shortly! If you're calling during non-business hours, please leave us a message with your name and phone number, and one of us will be happy to return your call! You may also order from our website, or on your smartphone with our Pistils app! Thanks and have a wonderful day!"*

"AH, HELLO, MY NAME IS REGINA PIEDMONT, I'M JACK PIEDMONT'S *mother. I was just wondering if either Vivian or Parker could call me back? It's not an emergency, but there's something I think I need your help with..."*

A NOTE FROM THE AUTHORS

Thank you from the bottom of our hearts for purchasing *Pistils*, we sincerely hope you've enjoyed it!

If so, please know how much it will mean to us if you'll consider leaving a review. Thank you, this truly helps indie authors!

If you're interested in receiving updates, including book release information, sale announcements, giveaways, contests, and other fun stuff, you can easily sign up at Twin-typeBooks.com.

ABOUT THE AUTHORS

Kate McNeil and Britt Goodwin have been writing together since 2009, although *Pistils* was their first published novel. Living almost nine hours apart means a lot of texting and a lot of online chatting between the two...as well as a girls-only roadtrip each year!

You can reach them:
    On Instagram, @twintypebooks
    On Twitter, @twintypebooks
    At the blog, www.twintypebooks.com

ACKNOWLEDGMENTS

We would like to extend our deepest gratitude and appreciation to the following people for contributing their knowledge, their time, and most of all their unwavering belief that we could do this!

Thank you to Eleanor Crain and Krissy Halama for setting aside time in their very busy lives to pre-read *Pistils* for us, along with their honesty and friendship.

Thank you to J.S. Wallace for sharing his extensive gun knowledge and expertise, as well as paying for all the range time!

A very heartfelt thank you to our fanfic community friends who had faith in our ability to pull this off!

Additionally...

Britt: I'd like to thank my friends and family, from those who had no idea I was a writer to those who knew my secret passion and believed in me all along.

Mom, you and I have a special bond that no one else can really understand. You are my best friend, and I love you so incredibly much. Having your love and positive influence consistently throughout my life has been the greatest gift anyone has ever given me.

To my train boy... you are honestly the best thing that's ever happened to me. Thank you for standing by my side through thick and thin, for your constant support, and your never-wavering love for me and my neurotic little dog. I love love loooooove you!

And lastly... my twin, Kate. You know I don't believe in coincidences, and us meeting through our love of the written word is no exception. In you I've found one of my dearest friends and closest confidantes, and I will always be in debt to the universe for bringing us together.

Kate: Thank you to my family, both immediate and extended, for never once doubting that this would happen "someday," and for being the best cheering section ever!

A special thank you and I love you to my parents... I couldn't ask for or dream of a better mother and father than you are!

Thank you to every teacher, professor, and educator who taught me that "good enough" never is, while still making sure I had the skills and the drive to go after the goals I set.

Thank you to my twin and truly one of my best friends, Britt... you complete me!

And finally, my deepest gratitude and love to my wonderful ever-patient husband, who never stops believing in me, no matter what crazy thing I put my mind to doing... I'll back you up.

Pistils

by Kate McNeil and Britt Goodwin

Cover design by Kate McNeil

ISBN-13: 978-0615995281

ISBN-10: 0615995284

A SNEAK PEEK AT SUB ROSA,
PISTILS BOOK THREE

INTRODUCTION

For years, my past has hidden in the shadows, exactly where I wanted it to remain. But if you insist, I'll introduce you to the old me, CIA Case Officer Vivian Carmichael. You think being a spy is glamorous? Well then come follow in my footsteps...

...but don't forget to watch your back.

CHAPTER ONE

"Vivian, stay a moment after class, please."

My classmates were laughing and chattering as they gathered their books and final papers, already calling out goodbyes that would only last a few weeks. It was December, and almost every single one of them would be back in these familiar rooms in January, for the last semester of their college career. Only two of us were graduating early. This was it for me, and it was bittersweet.

The man who stood at the front of the room had been my favorite professor, mentor and greatest support in my time at MIT. Almost a father-figure, although I didn't believe in the whole father-by-proxy deal. I'd had, or maybe still did have, a father somewhere. Not that I considered him one.

He waited until the last student had jostled their way through the door, then turned to me with a smile and used his more familiar Russian nickname for me. "I suppose this is goodbye, Vivya, although I am selfish to be sad."

"I will miss all of this, so I suppose that makes me selfish as well," I replied in Russian, smiling. Any student foolish enough to speak English in the professor's classroom was just asking to be thrown out of the day's lecture at best, and perhaps a failing grade for the semester at worst. I wasn't willing to risk it, even if it was my last day.

He chuckled a little before coming over and settling his bulk into the seat next to mine with a slight grunt. "No regrets, eh?"

I hesitated slightly before answering. My high school years hadn't been miserable, but it was at MIT where I truly came alive, in the company of people like myself. People who either rarely spoke because their minds were working furiously instead, or people who spoke too much and too fast because what was in their minds spilled over their lips. MIT was a colony of geniuses and lunatics, and I'd finally found myself blossoming in their company. "I'll miss the campus life…and being here to get ready for the official graduation ceremony. But no, no regrets."

He nodded. "And your position with the United Nations?"

My smile was slightly more forced this time. Graduating early had its perks, but it meant that I'd have to wait months for the next Young Professionals Programme examination, a test that wouldn't be offered again until the summer. "I'm waiting to hear back about the internship at the New York Secretariat."

He grunted slightly. "You're too good for an internship, Vivya, even one with the UN."

"I don't have many options open to me at the moment," I disagreed. "I've had a few offers to teach English in Russia but…"

"*Nyet nyet nyet*," he barked. "Not for you. Come along now, I have things to discuss with you. Things better than an internship." He heaved himself up from the desk and waved his thick fingers at me, then smiled. "There is much more waiting for you, Vivya."

The mellow warmth of Professor Kuznetsov's office welcomed us and I sank gratefully into one of his guest chairs, having learned long ago that no invitation was needed. He huffed and shuffled through the bookcase behind him before finding a leather folio and tossing it onto the chaos of his desk. His ancient chair squealed beneath his weight as he heaved out an enormous sigh, shut his eyes, and templed his fingers over his considerable girth. His next words, though, made my eyebrows shoot up, one of the rare times I'd ever heard him speak anything other than Russian.

"Vivya, I will talk to you in English because I want there to be no confusion, no misunderstanding about what I am about to tell you, *da?*" He winced at his immediate slip, then continued. "You are one of the most brilliant students I have taught, and it is with pride that I send you away, knowing I had a part in your education. But the credit is yours. Do not let anyone tell you anything else."

"Thank you, *Gospodin,*" I said slowly, unsure exactly what he was getting at.

"I hope you will forgive me, Vivya, because I have been making inquiries on your behalf. Not because you need my help, but a letter of recommendation wasn't enough. I have thought for a long time about whether or not I should speak of this to you. But with your skills...you deserve a *challenge*, not plodding along through UN's programme, waiting for an opening."

I was too stunned to reply. The professor had congratulated and encouraged me every step of the way, his words now were a direct contradiction to everything he'd ever said before.

"When I said I'd made inquiries for you, it was because I had another career path in mind for you, one that is more suitable for your intellect and ambition. But there were certain complications that I was afraid might block your path. Now, though, I want you to consider it."

"Of course."

He leaned back in his protesting chair. "You know nothing of my background, *da?*"

I smothered a smile this time. Rumors about Professor Kuznetsov's background ranged from the fairly plausible to the outrageous amongst the Russian Studies students. "Nothing that you haven't told us."

He chuckled too, although the look on his face was anything but amused. "I know I do not have to warn you, Vivya, but it must not go beyond this room. Many years ago, before you were born, I worked with CIA, to go back to Russia." He shrugged slightly, a remarkably casual gesture. "*Shpion.*"

I was glad that I'd set down my books and bag when I'd sat down, because I surely would have dropped them when my entire body went numb with shock. "FSB?"

"They were KGB then, and I tried to avoid them whenever possible. No, Vivya, I worked for United States, after being recruited as a Soviet agent, because I could not stand seeing my home being ground under boots of Communism. It's a beautiful country, you know that."

I nodded automatically. I'd spent a semester outside of Moscow the year before as part of my degree, and it *was* a beautiful country, exotically enticing enough in its own way that I'd been seriously considering following a career path to work for the United States embassy there.

He leaned forward slowly. "Then you understand why I have thought of this for you. It is a career that will take you upward as far as you want to go."

"Is this as far up as you wanted to go?" It was a presumptuous question, I knew it the moment it left my lips, but not entirely unexpected considering my professor was telling me he'd turned on the Soviet Union for the United States government...probably anywhere from the Cold War all the way through Glasnost, no less.

He nodded, unperturbed. "I was a teacher, before. There are many things that sing to you, in your blood. Teaching was in mine. And I wondered ever since coming here to teach if there would be someone I could recommend to government, someone intelligent and loyal, and someone who craves adventure but keeps a steady head. You are first one in many years, Vivya, and I still have ears of many at CIA. They need people exactly like you."

I left the professor's office almost in a daze. He'd made a couple of phone calls after I'd hesitantly given my assent, and within minutes, I had an appointment booked at a hotel in Cambridge for the next day. I'd pressed him for more details but he'd declined, telling me that he'd already recommended and taught me as far as he could, and that the recruiting officers would give me more information.

"*Do svidaniya,* Vivya," he'd said firmly, putting his hands on my shoulders and kissing my cheeks in a traditional Russian goodbye.

Now I tried to appear confident as I strode across the lobby of the small boutique hotel and went straight to the room I'd been directed to. I had a fleeting last-minute wish that I'd been able to call and share the weird twist of events with Parker, but she was studying for her last few exams, and I hadn't wanted to bother her. Confidence, though. *Vivian, you have confidence in spades,* I could almost hear her telling me. Confidence that had too often been faked, though, to get me through situations when I was really scared shitless.

I knocked carefully on the door of the room number I'd been given, jumping slightly when it opened almost immediately. A hard-faced woman opened the door, looked me over, then nodded and stood aside. As I'd been instructed, I kept my mouth shut.

The door shut and locked behind me, then the woman swept past and gestured impatiently toward a miniature office area on the other end of the room. There was a telephone on the small round conference table, and a tired-looking man sat studying what looked suspiciously like the leather folio Kuznetsov had tossed onto his desk the day before. I stood awkwardly as the woman ignored me and the man finished the page he was reading. Finally, he looked up and a small smile cracked his face.

"Vivian Carmichael?"

"Yes, sir."

"Please, have a seat. Thank you for meeting with us. My name is Michael, and this is Lillian. I spoke with Kazimir yesterday, and then again earlier today. He has nothing but the highest praise for you. Higher than he's ever had for any of his students."

I set my purse on the floor, uncomfortable at the lack of their last names, also more sure than ever that the leather folio *was* the exact same one that the professor had had the day before. "That's kind of him."

Michael shook his head and smiled again. "*Kind* is not a word we use often around here. But being recommended by Kazimir Ivonovich Kuznetsov…that says a great deal more than you know."

I started a little at hearing the professor's full Russian name. "What did he say about me?"

"He didn't tell you much, did he?"

I shook my head slowly. "Barely anything, although I could figure out a little on my own. Are you with the CIA?"

"We work for one of the government intelligence divisions," Michael replied, tapping a finger on the folio. "There's normally a standard series of protocol, applications, and so forth, but it was recommended that we accelerate your vetting process. You'll still have to go through some of it, of course, but..."

"Wait a minute," I interrupted, noting when Lillian's eyebrows almost shot up off her forehead. "This isn't some crime television show, I haven't been told *anything* about why I'm here, or what I'm here for. Don't assume that I'm agreeing to anything."

Michael nodded. "Fair enough. But we're very interested in you, Vivian, and we're hoping that you'll choose a career path that includes us."

"Meaning?" A sense of claustrophobia was tightening around me; things were happening too fast.

Michael ignored Lillian's aggravated huff as he flipped open the leather folio in front of him. "Fluent in Russian, Ukrainian and Serbo-Croatian, shows remarkable aptitude for picking up other Slavic languages. Mensa-level intelligence scores across the board. Majored in Russian and Eurasian Studies from MIT, has expressed desire to work overseas, probably for the United Nations." Michael peered at me, lifting an eyebrow, before continuing to read. "Extremely proficient in the use of personal handguns as well as larger caliber weapons, more than capable in self-defense."

My throat went dry. "How do you know that?"

"Kazimir recommended we consider you over seven months ago," Michael replied slowly. "You understand we would have been investigating your background since then."

"*Spying* on me, you mean."

"What do you think we're talking to you about?" Lillian snapped. Michael raised his hand between us.

"Case officers have their backgrounds checked to the highest degree, surely you can understand that. Having a potential officer regularly visiting a gun range during her visits back to South Carolina would fall under that category, especially if it may indicate certain political or extremist leanings."

I swallowed hard, trying not to let the feeling of paranoia overwhelm me. "When I was younger, I had a friend of a friend whose father taught us how to shoot. None of our other friends had any interest, so he was thrilled when I did. Now it's a great way to blow off steam, nothing more. I'm not an extremist."

"But you are an excellent shot. That puts you well ahead of any other potentials in your class. Honestly Vivian, if you were a man, we'd have you in mind for SAD."

I stiffened in my seat. "I don't recall *asking* to be put in mind for the CIA, let alone SAD, whatever that is."

Michael grinned slightly. "It was a compliment. I was special ops myself for a while. So, should we get down to it?"

"Yes, please." The anger boiling up inside of me made even the *please* difficult to force out.

The grin on his face disappeared in a split second, as though it had never been there. "Bottom line, Vivian, you were recommended for recruitment by the National Clandestine Service division of the CIA. Fast-tracking isn't something we do. But when we have a need and someone talented to fill it…we can be flexible."

"Flexible enough to offer me a job this fast?"

Lillian was not amused, but Michael barked out an unexpected laugh. "No one is *that* necessary. We're not giving you a job today, we're offering you the chance to skip a lot of paperwork and waiting, since quite a bit of it has already been done. That's all. Although if you're interested in the job…take my word for it. You'd be a fool to turn this opportunity down."

The CIA. The little I knew about it was from watching television shows with lots of explosions and reading old Tom

Clancy novels. I wasn't quite sure why they would be interested enough in me to speed up the vetting process, but if Kuznetsov had recommended me for it, I would indeed be a fool to reject the opportunity out of hand. It wasn't as though my other job prospects were stellar at the moment anyway.

I sat up a little bit straighter in my chair and took a deep breath. "Okay. I'd like to hear more about it."

An hour later I left the hotel room, my mind buzzing, a folder full of paperwork clutched in my hand, and Lillian's words echoing in my ears. "This isn't an offer to *negotiate*, Ms. Carmichael. They'll want an answer at your next interview."

That interview had been helpfully scheduled by Michael for the very next day, just outside of Washington D.C. I was just opening my mouth to protest when he handed me a large envelope containing round-trip plane tickets that Lillian had printed out while Michael and I spoke. "You're already booked. Pack for a week. If there's anyone you need to notify of your absence, tell them you have a series of job interviews scheduled. Under no circumstances are you to mention the agency you are interviewing with, or what those interviews might entail. Get used to lying, Ms. Carmichael."

I drove back to my tiny apartment in a daze. Was there anyone I should notify of my absence from MIT, anyone who might notice, and worry?

Probably not.

To be on the safe side, though, I called Kuznetsov's office phone and left him a message that I'd be out of town for a week for a couple of out-of-state job interviews. I didn't bother leaving any other details; I had the feeling he knew more than I did at this point.

I packed a couple of casual outfits, the one professional suit I owned, and threw a few paperbacks into the bag as well...with my luck, I'd have one interview tomorrow and then not have another one until Friday. Rush hour was just starting to taper off as I called a cab and headed for Logan Airport.

"You're very lucky, do you know that?"

I smiled politely at my interviewer, a no-nonsense older man named Dean. It seemed as though CIA employees were big into first names only. "I do feel very lucky, and appreciative to have made it this far."

He shook his head. "Not just that, we have plenty of people who make it this far. Plenty who wash out too. I mean you're very lucky that someone pushed hard enough to boot you further along in the process...it can take a year or two to complete a background check, depending on the complexity. They started yours seven months ago."

The reminder still shook me to the core. "Seven months..."

"Yep. Speeds things up considerably. Of course that doesn't mean you're guaranteed anything." He flipped through the pile of paperwork I'd completed the evening before, in the hotel room. "So do you know what you're applying for?"

I'd done my Googling the night before as well, a long sleepless night pondering what I was getting myself into. "Yes sir, the Central Intelligence Agency."

He continued to page through my application. "And which division are you interested in?"

Confidence, Vivian. "The NCS, sir."

"No interest in an office job, huh?"

"No sir. I mean...I understand if I have to pay my dues, but..."

"And you will, but not for too long. On paper, you're a

model case officer. Like I said, though, the background checks. I've got a few things I want to go over with you."

I nodded obediently. My record was spotless, I didn't even have a speeding ticket, and I'd been too busy with coursework and a part-time job to get into any trouble during my time at MIT.

Dean pushed my application aside and put his hand over what appeared to be a lengthy typed report. "A lot of times when people come in here, they don't understand why we conduct such exhaustive background checks. They're used to the routine background checks for regular jobs. Maybe fingerprinting. We have to go far beyond that because we are employing people who literally have national security in their hands. We've had people that were ideal for the job, all except for one skeleton in their closet, and that one thing disqualified them. We can't risk it. So we don't just check you, we check your friends, family, roommates, employers, boyfriends, ex-boyfriends...everyone. Because anything that makes you vulnerable can make you a target, which obviously poses a problem for us. And sometimes it can be awkward or embarrassing. The best advice I can give you is not to lie to me, do you understand?"

"Yes, sir," I said quietly. I had a feeling I knew where this was going, but at least I could be honest about it.

"Good. The first thing I want to talk to you about are your parents. Are they both still living?"

I took a deep breath. He wanted honesty...at least the truth was simple. "I don't know about my father. He left when I was eight years old, and I haven't heard from or seen him since."

Dean's steel-gray eyes zeroed in on mine. "Why did he leave?"

"I don't know the details. He and my mother fought a lot,

and one day he came home, packed a bag and left. I asked my mom but she refused to talk about it."

"So you don't know of his whereabouts?"

"No sir."

"What about your mother?"

I forced myself to be calm. "She became an alcoholic after my father left. She wasn't much of a mother after that."

"And do you know her whereabouts?"

Tension was creeping up my neck and into my shoulders. "Not really. I left Charleston immediately after graduation. She may still live there, I don't know. I don't have any communication with her either."

"You've had absolutely no contact with either of your parents since the age of eighteen?"

"No sir."

"If your father left and your mother became an alcoholic when you were eight years old, how did you manage to survive, let alone keep it together enough to graduate at the head of your high school class, get into MIT, and graduate from there early?"

"I spent a great deal of time with my best friend's family."

"The Chase family?"

A horrible feeling of violation slithered through my stomach. "How..."

"Sarah and her mother Susan, after Sarah's husband Matthew was shot and killed sixteen years ago in an armed robbery. And Parker Chase, who I take to be the best friend you mentioned?"

"Yes sir," I managed.

"How close are you and Parker?"

"We're like sisters."

"Did you tell her about the interviews you have scheduled for this week?"

"No sir. I was told not to give anyone details. I left a

message for Professor Kuznetsov just telling him I'd be out of town for a week, in case anyone noticed I was gone. I figured he'd understand without any further explanation."

Dean finally cracked a small smile. "How is Kazimir?"

This was getting surreal. If there had been any doubts in my mind about the professor being in the CIA, they were evaporating rapidly. "He's doing well, sir. He's a wonderful professor, I feel lucky to have been taught by him."

"You should," Dean said bluntly, flicking the manila folder shut. "They were desperate to get him to teach at Langley, but he had his own agenda. He's the reason you and I are having this conversation…he's never recommended a student as highly as you. Ms. Carmichael, I'll be perfectly blunt with you. You are the absolute model, so far, of what we want in a case officer, should you choose to pursue the position. Your education is there, your familiarity with the area, language, and customs is there, and even your familiarity with firearms and rudimentary self-defense is there. You'd cruise through basic training with one hand tied behind your back.

"I'm not going to lie to you, though. You have two very weak spots, and those are your parents, and your relationship with the Chase family. You stiffened up like a board when I asked you about your mother, and you looked like you were going to puke when you realized how much I knew about your life. You're going to have to work on eliminating your tells, because any halfway decent interrogator would read you in a split second and have your weak spots like that." He snapped his fingers.

"But my parents…"

"They may not seem like a weak spot to you, but they're weak spots nevertheless. If someone got to your mother, don't you think she'd pick a bottle of booze over you again? If someone asked her where her daughter lives now, and who she works for, and waved a gallon of gin at her, don't you think she'd tell them all they need to know?

"And the Chase family…what would you do if Parker was in trouble? Wouldn't you abandon your job to come to her aid? That's what best friends are for, right?"

I was completely speechless in front of this stranger, stunned by a hurt that went deeper than I'd felt in a long time.

Dean leaned forward, and this time there was a flicker of sympathy in his eyes. "I'm sorry, Vivian, but that's just a tiny example of what you'll have to go through to become a case officer. An *excellent* case officer. Part of the process is a barrage of psychological exams, and regular polygraph tests for the rest of your career. We know your weak spots. We know Parker is taking her final exams at Duke this week, and," he paused for a moment, "We know where both your parents are. It's all right here, your life, in this one folder." He tapped it with his index finger.

"You know where my parents are?"

"We do. Do you want me to tell you where, what they're doing?"

I shut my eyes slowly. Remembered my mother drunkenly crashing the ninth birthday party that Parker, her mother and Gran had so thoughtfully organized for me, culminating with her falling into the pool. All the days I'd gone to school without lunch, until Sarah Chase starting sending an extra one along with Parker for me. The vacant stare when I told my mother I was leaving town right after my high school graduation ceremony.

The fact that I could barely even really remember what my father looked like, since my mother had destroyed all his pictures after he walked out.

The emptiness in my life where my parents *should* have been.

"No," I said softly, then repeated myself more strongly. "No, I don't want to know."

"I'm glad to hear that," he replied. "Because I would have recommended we not accept your application if you'd said yes. There are a few people who already feel it should be rejected because of your parents. Personally...I think you're making the right decision, as long as you understand what you're in for."

I nodded silently. Somehow, somewhere deep inside, I now knew I *was* making the right decision. Cutting my parents off, an amputation, wasn't just good common sense, it would mark a new beginning and a fresh start for me. One that had nothing to do with the lives they'd ruined and their failure to drag me down with them.

The rest of the week passed in an excruciating blur. I'd passed the drug tests and the physical exams, but the psychological tests and polygraphs left me feeling more beaten and exhausted than anything else. The examiners hammered at me about my parents, about how I felt about Parker's father's death, if I felt isolated, if I felt betrayed. I was asked repeatedly about what had sparked my interest in Russia and what motivated me to want to work there. Over and over I repeated the story about my maternal grandmother immigrating to the United States with her eight-year-old daughter, my mother, about the stories she would tell me, the tongue-twisting language I became determined to master.

Every night, I scoured the internet for information about the National Clandestine Service, the "spy" division of the CIA. The more I read, the more intrigued and determined I became. Although it hadn't been explicitly spelled out to me, I now knew that part of the reason Professor Kuznetsov had pushed so hard for my recruitment was my comfort with

Russia, its language and culture, while still being a patriotic American with no motivation to turn traitor.

And, when I forced myself to be completely honest, the idea of working as a spy...I had to admit, I was captivated by it. Traveling, immersing myself in cultures, languages and traditions of a world full of mystery and adventure sounded like a dream come true.

Just as the culture of campus life of MIT had once made me feel that I had found my niche, a place where I was welcome and useful, the lure of the NCS was calling to me. I wanted to get in, badly, even as they did their best to crack me into pieces and dissect me accordingly.

When Parker Skyped me to celebrate final exams being over, she assumed that I was still in Cambridge, and I didn't correct her.

"When are you coming home? And more importantly, what do you think of this color?" She wiggled her fingers in front of the laptop's camera.

"Very pink, and very you. I thought you didn't like glitter polish, though."

"It was pink, and it was on sale. I couldn't pass it up. So answer my other question, when are you coming home?"

Parker and I never lied to each, ever. It had never even been an issue between us. "Soon, hopefully. I have one more job interview coming up, but I should be able to come home for a visit at the very least."

"So you're not looking for a job in South Carolina?" The disappointment in her voice was obvious.

"I will, of course. There's just a lot of different opportunities I'm looking at right now. I'm still waiting to hear from the New York Secretariat too."

"About the U.N. internship?"

"Yeah. I don't know if I can afford an internship for six months, though. I did get an offer to teach English in Russia."

"Which you've already told me is last on your list," she pointed out.

"The money is decent."

"And you'd hate it. We both know it."

I sighed and rubbed the back of my neck; Parker knew me all too well. "I would, I'm no teacher. I don't know, there are a couple of other things I'm following up on. But enough about me, what's going on with you? How were your final exams?"

Her face brightened. "Aced them all, I know it. I got a job offer at the counseling place, but Shane really wants us both go back to Charleston at the same time. He's going to work for his dad, and he's already found us an apartment downtown."

I fought to keep my face neutral. The ugliest fight Parker and I had ever had was over her asshole boyfriend, and since that time, I'd sworn never to let that jerk come between us. "Oh yeah? That's nice."

"Uh-huh...I'm kinda bummed because I really liked the counseling center, but it wasn't much money, since I don't have my masters. Plus, I'm going to work in Gran's shop again...and she'll probably pay me more."

We both laughed. "How is Gran?"

"She and Mom are both doing good...although they want to know when you'll be back in town," she said pointedly.

"Okay, okay, I give up!" I raised my hands in surrender as Parker did a victorious fist-pump on my screen. "I'll be down as soon as I'm done with these interviews. I don't want to hear it if I can only stay a day or two, though."

"We'll take it. I miss you."

"I miss you too," I replied softly. Being away from my best friend and my second family had been rough, and after the week I'd gone through, spending some time with the Chase family was exactly what I needed. "I'll let you know as soon as I'm heading down."

On Friday, the last polygraph examiner shook my hand and wished me good luck. I checked in online for my flight back to Boston and then started packing. I could probably swing four or five days at home before I'd need to head back to Cambridge and make some final decisions. Everyone I'd talked to at the CIA had assured me it could be weeks or even months before I heard back from them, which meant a paying job teaching English in Russia was sounding more and more sensible. *Zhizn' prozhit' — ne pole pereyti*, as my grandmother used to say...life wasn't meant to be easy. Sometimes you were meant to be practical.

I'd just zipped my suit into its garment bag when my phone rang with an unfamiliar number. "Hello?"

"Vivian Carmichael?"

"Yes?"

"This is Dean Morris. It's my privilege to offer you a position with the CIA; you made it through. Congratulations."

CHAPTER TWO

Three years later, London.

Heathrow Airport was bustling as I cleared customs, resisting the urge to rub my dry eyes. It was approximately 7:30pm local time, I had a splitting headache, my stomach was fiercely protesting the lack of food and, in this sea of international humanity, I was somehow supposed to locate the case officer I was replacing.

After I'd corralled all my luggage, I looked around and prayed I didn't look as exhausted as I felt. I'd wrangled tougher things than this, I just needed a minute to collect myself and...

"Galina Iavlenskaia?"

It took me a moment to respond to my cover name, but I quickly smiled and held out a hand to the middle-aged man in front of me. "Please, call me Lina. You must be Henry Ricard?"

He gently shook my hand and smiled, but there were deep shadows under his eyes and his skin was sallow. All that I'd been told was that "Henry" was retiring due to health issues, but it was obvious the man before me was both exhausted and ill. "A pleasure to meet you, Lina. You are even lovelier in person than in the photo your uncle sent me. How is he?"

Ah, that explained how he had recognized me...or at least I hoped it was, and that I hadn't looked *too* lost. Langley had forwarded a picture along with my information.

"He's doing well, and sends his regards."

"How good to hear. May I help you with your bags?"

Everything inside of me screamed against allowing this ailing man to even carry the smallest of my bags, but I reminded myself that I would soon be in a country where a man would be expected to carry my bags even if he dropped dead while doing so. I should probably just get used to it...at least my largest suitcase was on wheels. "Thank you, Henry, you're very kind."

"Not at all. You must be very hungry after your flight, let's get you to your hotel, and then have dinner." He set off at a surprisingly brisk pace, and I concentrated on keeping up, trying my best not to whack any of the people slipping past us with my carry-on bag.

Henry effortlessly navigated his way through the crowd and quickly had us settled into a black cab that was soon dodging its way through the airport traffic. "It's not that far to your hotel. Have you visited London before?"

"No, I always flew through Paris." He nodded, although he had probably memorized at least the basics of my cover story: a twenty-four-year-old with dual Russian-American citizenship, having grown up and gone to school in America, now headed to set up a Bulgarian-based travel agency specifically aimed at younger travelers and ex-pats.

"A pity, London's a very nice city to visit, especially if you love history. So much to see and appreciate." We continued chatting lightly for the remainder of the ride, both of us careful not to mention my real travel plans. When we reached the hotel, I checked in and arranged for my bags to be delivered to my room.

"I thought about making reservations for us at the hotel's restaurant, but I know of a charming little place not far from here," Henry explained as we climbed into another cab. "Plus, as I'm sure you know, you'll recover far more quickly from jet lag if you try to stay up and match your body's rhythms to your current time zone."

In truth, I would have preferred the hotel's restaurant if it meant I could have showered, changed, and dragged myself into bed, but I knew he was right. Luckily I'd gotten used to dealing with sleep deprivation. "That was very thoughtful of you."

"I had originally arranged for a friend to join us, but he's been detained at work. We will meet up with him tomorrow if need be."

I mentally perked up at his words. The "friend" was a close-kept secret amongst case officers heading for eastern Europe with assignments like mine. As long as you hadn't pissed anyone off, as long as you showed true potential, someone might clue you in. I'd been lucky enough to have three different people pull me aside and tell me to make sure I checked in with this guy before I headed to Bulgaria...*if* he was in London. Apparently he was still extremely active in the field despite his high position within British Intelligence. God forbid the CIA officially acknowledge that their staff regularly swapped information with MI6, though...it was pride and bullshit within the agency at its best. Meeting him was strictly unofficial business.

Henry was still speaking. "This is a Georgian restaurant, the owners came to London over twenty years ago. The restaurant's name, *Supra*, means feast. If you have the opportunity to visit Georgia, I strongly suggest you take the opportunity. A beautiful country, and an incredibly rich history. Tbilisi, of course, but the smaller cities should be appreciated as well."

I nodded. "How long were you there?"

He gave me a quick look, which softened as he gave me a smile of approval. "I forget that my enthusiasm gives me away. Five years. Your uncle told me you were sharp, Lina, and I see for myself that he was right."

"I'd like to hear more about it, honestly." I would have to have been blind to miss how some of the tiredness fell away from his face as he spoke. "Unfortunately the only Georgia I've been to is in the U.S."

Henry nodded as the cab pulled up to a tiny café with a wooden sign beside the door, ornately carved with the word *Supra*. "The owners...they are friends of mine. Since before they came to London, in fact."

The meaning of his words clicked in my brain almost immediately. Henry had probably assisted the owners in leaving Georgia in exchange for something of value to the CIA. This was now my job too...extracting valuable information from foreign agents and rewarding them with things they wanted, or needed.

Bribery, sanctioned and funded by the United States government.

Henry extended a hand to help me out of the cab, and as he paid the driver, the door of restaurant opened and a small dark man hurried out, a wide smile of welcome on his face. "*Gamarjoba*, my friend! Henry! It is too long since I have seen you!" The two men embraced affectionately.

"*Gagimarjos*! Nikolaz Botkoveli, please allow me to introduce my very good friend, Galina Nikolayevna Iavlenskaia. She's like family to me."

The man turned to me and immediately reached out both hands in a gesture of hospitality. "Then you must consider me family as well, and my home is open to you. Please, please come inside. When I received your phone message, I closed early. Elene has been cooking for you, Henry, all of your favorites!"

"*Madloba*, my friend."

We were hustled into the tiny space, and Nikolaz closed and locked the door behind us. "Sit, my friends. I will get Elene, and *chacha* to toast to old friends as well as new ones."

He disappeared behind a curtain the back of the room, and as my eyes adjusted to the dim lighting, I saw that two tables had been pushed together in the middle of the room to seat six. The room could have probably only held twenty people at the most. The delicious smells coming from the back made a most unladylike growl erupt from my stomach.

Henry chuckled. "Remember I told you *Supra* means feast? They will have prepared enough for dozens, so don't be surprised."

"I feel like I could eat enough for dozens. What's *chacha*?"

"Have you had *samogon*?"

I winced. Moonshine. "Is it strong?"

"It is. If you'd prefer, just drink the first toast and tell him that traveling has worn you out. He won't take offense."

A slim dark-haired woman hurried from the back just then. "Henry!"

The greetings and introductions were repeated, Elene again urging us to sit. Food began appearing almost magically on the table immediately after that, and Nicolaz came back with several bottles and glasses. There was some ceremony regarding the pouring of the drinks, toasts spoken in the Botkovelis' native tongue, before the conversation switched back to English, "out of consideration for our new friend, Galina."

"You might consider that my Georgian is a bit rusty too," Henry said dryly, before turning to me. "I can personally guarantee that everything on this table is absolutely wonderful."

"Yes, please eat," Elene encouraged.

I managed to maintain my table manners as I dug into the piles of food that were urged on me. After the first toast, I politely declined any more of the *chacha*, and Henry poured me a glass of wine instead.

The conversation was almost non-stop as Henry caught up with his old friends, and they plied me with questions as well. I felt myself begin to relax for the first time since I'd boarded the plane in Washington D.C. hours earlier. I was feeling the effects of the jet lag, not to mention the enormous amount of food I'd just consumed, when Nicolaz put his hand on Henry's shoulder.

"My friend, Elene and I will go back to the kitchen and clean up now. Please, continue to eat and drink. We will give you privacy for as long as you need, only say goodbye before you leave us again."

"*Didi madloba*," Henry replied. Elene smiled at both of us before she and her husband quietly slipped behind the curtain in the back. Henry sighed and sat back in his chair. "I should always know better than to try and talk shop after one of their meals. But it's just too tempting, whenever I'm in London. Keep in mind this is a safe place for us to be honest, Lina."

"Did you help them come to London?"

"Yes, after the Soviet Union dissolved. The region they lived in became extremely dangerous, and Nicolaz had been a low-level government worker. I helped them come here and start the restaurant, which was something they had always wanted to do. He gave me quite a lot of surprisingly useful information in return." Henry ran his hand over his face, and for a moment, the look of exhaustion settled over his face again. "Sometimes it's hard to believe it was so long ago. But they are fiercely loyal to the United States, although they chose to live here. This is one of the few places in London where I feel safe to speak freely. Nicolaz is wise enough to play the part of the small restaurant owner and cook, but his eyes and ears are as sharp as they ever were. You can trust them both."

I nodded. "Thank you for telling me."

"Lina, I'm entrusting the lives and well-being of many people to you. Not all of them have left their homes. Some of them don't even live in Bulgaria. Many of them could lose as much as their lives for collaborating with the CIA. Don't ever forget that."

"I won't."

"I remember my first assignment. It was exciting, it was frightening, it was depressing, and sometimes it was even boring. To some extent, though, it will always be dangerous for you. Perhaps not as dangerous as it is for the agents you recruit, but you can't forget exactly what it is you're doing. Some officers get complacent, especially in locations that are relatively safe. Complacency isn't a luxury you can afford."

"At Langley, they gave me the impression that Bulgaria is safe."

Henry poured himself half a glass of wine, before offering to pour another for me. I shook my head. "It is one of the safest countries in that area, on the surface. And you're going in with a very solid cover. But you'll find that appearances are rarely as they appear. I'll brief you in more detail tomorrow, when we've both had a night's rest. When are you flying to Sofia?"

"Friday morning."

"And I'm leaving for the U.S. Thursday morning. That's good, though...I'll have a full day to brief you, and then David can fill you in on Thursday. It was pure luck that he was in town to talk to you…I've had to track him down in the mountains on foot before."

"David is our friend?"

"Of course." Henry took a sip of his wine. "The stuffed suit bureaucrats in their offices at Langley and here in London don't like to confess that their officers exchange information on a fairly regular basis. National pride and all. But of course we do…not unthinkingly though. We feel each other out and decide who we can trust, just as we do with our assets. David doesn't automatically share information with just anyone."

"Can you tell me about him?" I asked curiously. "He's half-myth, half-superhero, based on what people whisper about him."

Henry chuckled. "He'd get a kick out of that, if you told him. Lina, I'll tell you the basics, as they relate to you, but the rest is for him to tell. He's MI6, and pretty far up in the ranks across the board in British Intelligence, although I'm not sure exactly how high. High enough that he gets clearance to do just about anything he wants to, and he's usually right about anything he says or does. Consider any information he passes on to you actionable, but don't directly identify him in your cables back to Langley."

"What exactly is he an expert on?"

"Several things, but primarily organized crime in Eastern Europe and Western Asia. Did they brief you on exactly what kind of information we're looking for?"

"Yes, but I was told I'd be given more detail once I got here."

"I wish I had more time to spend here with you, Lina, but I've got a limited amount of time to get back home…medical appointments and procedures, as I'm sure you guessed." He held up his hand when I started to reply. "It's irrelevant to what's going on here, except that at this time, I'm no longer considered field-ready, which is why you're going in, in my place. Somewhat alone."

The kernel of confidence that had been building up inside of me suddenly disappeared. "Alone?"

"They aren't sending you into a war zone...or at least, it's not one yet. As I said before, Bulgaria is considered to be relatively safe, despite the government becoming increasingly unstable from within. The cracks aren't visible to the public, but the organized crime families waited for the perfect opportunity to cement the corruption that was already in place. *That* is what we need information on. You're going to find that the mob there is quite different from any of those Italian mafia stereotypes you may be familiar with. And David is the greatest asset you'll have to hit the ground running. If it wasn't for the mess going on in Ukraine and Russia, they'd have another one of our officers undercover with you, but I've been on my own in Sofia for two years."

I sat, speechless, staring at Henry. I was supposed to start tunneling my way into the Bulgarian mafia...alone? I'd been looking forward to starting my first real independent assignment, of course, but I'd assumed I'd have backup, or at least a partner. Instead, I was depending on my two-week crash course in the Bulgarian language and an unofficial British Intelligence friend who might or might not share critical information with me.

Oh hell.

Henry started to speak again when his cell phone vibrated on the table. "Perfect timing, that's David and... almost here. Meeting him might take some of that horrified look off your face, Lina. You look as though I told you that you'd be fighting a revolution with just a spoon for a sword."

"That's how it feels, to be perfectly honest," I said faintly.

"Don't worry, Langley wouldn't have picked you to do this unless they *knew* you were capable of it." He stood and crossed the floor in a few steps, unlocking the door and admitting a man who was soaking wet from head to toe, swathed in a heavy overcoat.

"David, glad you could make it." Henry slapped the man on the arm, and I stood up automatically.

"Would have been here sooner, but the bloody cab got a flat tire a few blocks away, and like an idiot I tried to outrun the rain. Oh thank God, there's some dinner left...and this must be my newest Yank friend?"

Piercing blue eyes met mine, blinking through the raindrops that clung thickly to his eyelashes. Dark brown hair was plastered to his head, and he gave me a teasing grin as he extended his right hand. "David Coburn, British Intelligence at your service, and your cover name would be...?"

"Don't act like an idiot, David, I think I've just scared her halfway back to Langley. I don't need you finishing the job."

"She doesn't look the type that would scare easily." The stranger, David, took the hand I finally remember to extend and gave it a firm shake.

"I'm not," I said quickly, tamping down a quick flash of irritation that they would discuss me as though I weren't even standing there. "Galina Iavlenskaia, but please call me Lina."

"Lina," David repeatedly slowly. "Did you pick your name, or was it given to you?"

This guy certainly hit the ground running. He had to know my name was a CIA cover, but he was also my unofficial cohort for the next few days. "Isn't everyone given their names?"

He ran a hand through his wet hair, making it stand up in short dark spikes. "Not always."

"David, I hate to interrupt, but quite frankly I'm overstuffed, exhausted, and had enough of Nicolaz's *chacha*," Henry interrupted. "If you can refrain from running off my replacement, I'll go say my goodbyes now. Lina, believe it or not, this reprobate is qualified to get you safely back to your hotel, is that all right?"

"Yes, of course," I said automatically.

"All right, give me a moment and I'll be back." Henry headed toward the back of the restaurant and David peeled off his soaked overcoat, revealing a dark business suit beneath.

"You don't mind if I eat, do you?" he inquired, his tone kinder than before. "Haven't eaten since breakfast, and I can't say no to Elene and Nicolaz's cooking."

"No, please, go ahead." I stood staring at him, wondering why he hadn't seated himself, when I realized he was waiting for me. "Oh, I'm sorry. I'm running on very little sleep and information overload."

"I've been there many times myself," he concurred, finally pulling out a chair as I plopped back down into my own. "Would a drink help?"

"No, I don't really drink," I murmured, watching as he filled a glass with the *chacha*. Henry returned from the kitchen, assured me that he'd be at my hotel at 8am sharp, and bid us both goodnight before slipping out the front entrance. I sat staring at my plate, half-asleep from the wine I'd had, as David took a sip from his glass. After a few moments of silence, he spoke again.

"Why is it that you don't really drink, *Galina Iavlenskaia*?" he said, putting heavy emphasis on the pronunciation, before switching to flawless Russian. "It will be hard to blend in if you're always dumping your vodka into potted plants."

"I practiced a lot," I replied. "The potted plants never complained."

He chuckled softly. "Your Russian is really very good. Do you speak Bulgarian?"

I shook my head slowly. "Just what two weeks could buy me. I've always been pretty good with languages, though."

"You'll be okay," he said, slipping back into English. At my surprised look, he nodded toward the kitchen. "Before Henry got them out, Nicolaz and Elene were living a nightmare at the hands of the Russians in power there, even hearing the language brings back memories. I don't want to remind them by speaking it when they might hear us. I'm surprised Henry didn't warn you not to slip by accident."

"I think he was in pain, it was probably the last thing on his mind."

"He's in a lot of pain," David replied bluntly. "Cancer. It's not good."

"When is it ever good?"

"You're right in that." He ate quickly, and after a moment I reached for the bottle of wine, pouring half a glassful. David watched me as I took a long swallow. "Who did cancer take from you?"

"How did you know?"

"I didn't get to where I am now by being oblivious."

I took a deep breath and pushed the glass away. "My grandmother. She was Russian, from just outside Perm. She moved to South Carolina with my mother after my grandfather died, using every last cent she could scrape together to get them there. *Baba* was the reason I became interested in Russia at such an early age, since my mom was determined to be as American as possible. Some of my earliest memories are of her sitting by my bed, telling me stories...it's how I first learned to speak Russian. Although I remember my parents hated it when she would tell me Russian fairy tales, because they were so much darker."

"They are that. So is that the truth, or is it part of your cover story?"

"It's the truth."

He looked at me thoughtfully for a long moment. "You can tell me the whole truth, you know. Off the record. You don't have to be afraid of me."

"I'm not," I said quickly.

"You're scared of this assignment though, aren't you?"

"I'm not scared, exactly. It's just bigger than I thought it would be. And I didn't know I'd be doing it alone."

"Will you be working out of Sofia?"

"Yes. Primarily."

"Any officers that come through might touch base with you, so you won't be as alone as you think. There's official staff based in Sofia that the Bulgarians acknowledge, but of course their government won't know about you. I've found myself in that area more often lately, though. And if anything big does blow up, they'll send in more officers. They're just not needed yet, because they've got you."

Although his words should have freaked me out even more, I found them strangely comforting. "Henry said they wouldn't have picked me if they didn't think I could handle it."

"Especially with only two weeks of Bulgarian," he agreed. He set down his fork and curled his hand around my wrist, his index and middle fingers directly over my pulse point. His fingers were shockingly warm against my chilled skin. "What's your real name?"

I wasn't too tired to react to the sudden heat that made my skin tingle. "Vivian Carmichael."

"Vivian," he said quietly, then nodded. "That name suits you. You aren't a *Lina*. But Vivian…it means *alive*."

I shook my head, suddenly unsure why I'd just technically broken cover and told this man my real name. His hand slid away from my skin, leaving goosebumps on my arm and a sudden clearness in my head. I sat up and rubbed my wrist defensively. "Why did you do that?"

250 | CHAPTER TWO

David didn't bother playing dumb, and I didn't have to clarify what I meant. He cocked his head, seeming to look straight into my mind with those bright blue eyes. "Because now you know you'll never be able to lie to me. Now let's go say goodbye to Nicolaz and Elene, so I can get you back to your hotel and you can sleep."